BOYAN S. B

ONE

rev. 01/1.1

PHABLE

2021

PHABLE

Original Artwork GEORGI MARINOV-HORHE
Cover LEWIZ HERIZ
Design and Format LUBA HALEVA
Developmental Editing MARINA LABOSSIER
Copy Editing RORY MILLER
Print ALLIANCE PRINT

This is a work of fiction.
Names, characters, places, andincidents either
are the product of the author's imagination or
are used fictitiously. Any resemblance to actual persons,
living or dead, events, or locales is entirely coincidental.

Revision O1/1.1

ISBN 978-0-9559442-1-5

Published in the United Kingdom by *Phable*

www.phable.org

ONE

The mountains come alive during an eclipse. Dry branches cracked beneath Ayla's tyres as she cycled up the amber-lit path. Sometimes it's important to let go. *Work can wait, nothing will explode – well, nothing should explode – if I take a few hours to myself.*

As the forest cleared, her path opened into a meadow. The light was beginning to fade. Tall grasses peppered with flowers mirrored Ayla's slender form and sharp blue eyes.

Only a few minutes left to reach the peak. She stood, pushing hard on the pedals, feeling the ground shudder through the handlebars and into her arms.

Back in the forest, branches curved and played on the shifting summer wind. The amber light faded, transitioning fleetingly through a pale emerald green. Nearly there.

Right on time. Almost. *If I pick up the pace, I'll catch it.* Sapphire shafts tore through the final few trees before the opening at the peak. Her path comprised no more than a few blue blots of light. Mount Rhoda was different to many other Hela mirrors scattered around the world.

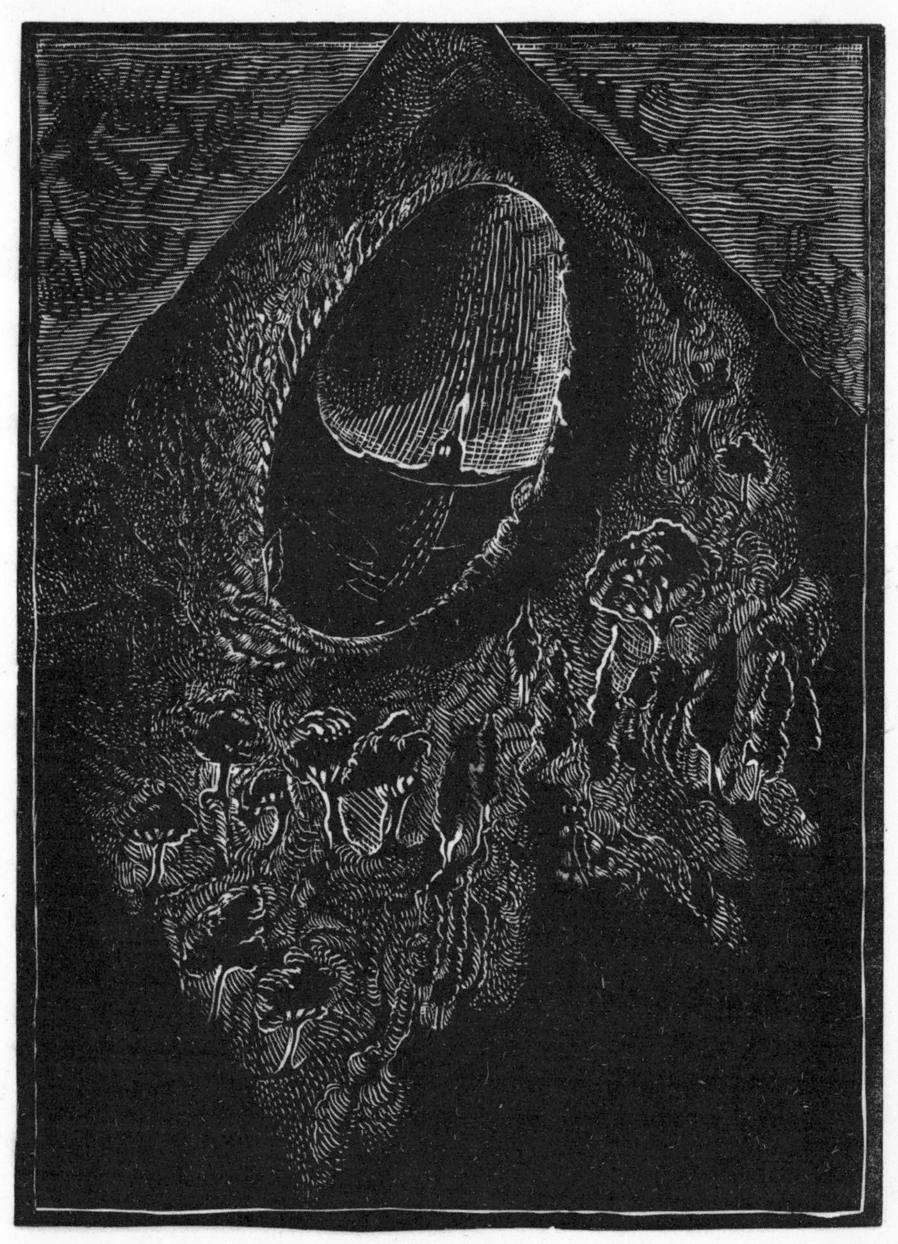

Mount Rhoda

As far as anyone could tell it served a purely aesthetic function. Yes, it announced an eclipse to the city of Flavia below, but the same could be achieved by simply looking up at the sky.

Right now, Ayla didn't particularly care. Seconds before the eclipse, she threw her bike to the side. She hopped a small fence and ran up to the base of the mirror, nestled in the peak.

Even in the near-darkness, Ayla could see the man-made crater, looming above her. The six-hundred-foot-wide stone dish had been meticulously carved into the mountainside by the most basic tools. Brushing away a thin layer of moss, she jumped up and sat on its ragged lip.

Then it hit. A thin crown of teal light surrounding the moon shone down. It was caught by the polished basalt of the monolithic concave mirror.

Ayla looked on as the reflection slowly came into focus down in the city below. From a feint blur, the ring quickly sharpened, fitting neatly into Flavia's inner-circular boulevard. The few imperfections she could make out were crowds gathered in the street to bathe in the shimmering light. The darkness was punctured by an iridescent circle placed neatly in the middle of the city.

She briefly thought about the engineering genius of the civilisations-old structure before the symmetry of the eclipse broke and the reflection disappeared.

*

As Ayla collected her forlorn bicycle from the base of Mount Rhoda, she couldn't help but wonder why she was the only person there.

Was everyone so caught up in their daily tasks that they couldn't even take a moment for a simple indulgence? Maybe it's for the best. Perhaps next time the view will be all mine again.

At twenty-seven, she had seen many eclipses from the peak but only a few by herself.

Careening down Mount Rhoda was surely the second best part about cycling up for an eclipse. With the sun exposed once more, its heat was free to soak the air. The calm of the eclipse was now only hinted at by the odd wisp of a cool wind. It blew caramel blonde flocks of hair around from under her helmet. Ayla sped down the steep track, overgrown branches slapping her arms along the way.

Passing through the forest at the mountain's base, the air suddenly became thicker. She rounded the manicured grounds bordering The Residence. No time to stop, she could see her destination in the distance.

Flavia spread out from the foothills of the Rhoda Mountains. The Residence was built on a naturally forming shelf jutting out from the rolling green hills.

The heart of the city, Flavia Park, started at the base of the path leading up to The Residence. No matter how many times Ayla went past, she couldn't help but take a second glance at the beauty of the city.

A mile long and nearly half as wide, Flavia Park was a lesson in green geometric design. At the centre stood the Hela fountain: a silver hemispherical pool reflecting the lawns and gardens of the park. Tooth-like outlines of tall stone buildings at the park's edge bit into the pool's curve.

Seven gravel paths radiated out from the fountain. At the fringe of the park they formed the start of seven tree-lined boulevards carving rays through the city.

Clinging on to her last remaining inertia from the descent, Ayla charged down the park's Grand Avenue towards the gleaming fountain. Fresh, ionised fountain spray dusted her salty skin. Banking left, she swept along Aria, the second path from the fountain.

Despite the onset of fatigue, Ayla couldn't help but race. It wasn't because she was running late for her coffee date – that wasn't too unusual.

Ayla felt like she was ten again, having just learned to cycle, zooming along Aria with her father at what then seemed close to light speed.

At that time, vehicles had only recently been removed from the streets. Now, the city felt like it had never had a single car, bus or tram running above ground along its avenues. The hum of their motors was a distant memory. What was held up as a paragon of revival now felt more than natural.

Most of Flavia's near-million inhabitants were involved in the sciences. The city was a seat of government for the Balkania Core and its two hundred connected states. It was also a global hub for engineering, experimentation and research.

Slightly late and slightly out of breath Ayla arrived at Merkum Market Square. Standing bolt upright on her pedals she tried to spot Tomias amongst the crowd.

Merkum Market Square was, shockingly, a former market that had been a popular gathering place for more than three millennia. Its four straight sides were bound by flush limestone walls punctured by five dozen arches. In the past, each arch was the nesting place of a trader from far away, selling his exotic wares.

Today, they were home to a different kind of trade. Every one of the two-hundred and forty stalls was now a café, teahouse or restaurant. The variety of food and drinks on offer would have made their former inhabitants proud. Countless tables spilled out of their cavernous mouths and across the square. One of the few remnants of Old Flavia, the market had successfully taken on a new life.

Thousands of people gathered in Merkum be it day or night to trade ideas, solve problems or just share gossip. Driven by caffeine and courage, conversations often grew heated.

Tables were often covered in doodles and scribbles, competing solutions or theories to the day's most pressing challenges. Not to mention the tapestry of crude caricatures born out of frustration when solutions were not so forthcoming.

There, she spotted him, nestled right in the middle of the gabble. Tall and neatly dressed in his standard white uniform, Tomias stood out with his prim posture and clean lines.

On the table to his left, a dominating, bearded fellow was shouting at three captive tablemates, grasping the small table with both hands. His flabby belly comfortingly supported by the table's edge.

To the right, unaffected by the forceful display, a willowy teen sat with her feet crossed, head tilted back, staring at the sky.

“You blend in so well,” Ayla smiled as Tomias got up to kiss her.

“I tried, and failed, to fit in,” he replied as they sat.

The square’s unceasing energy offered a strange kind of intimacy to each table.

Tomias nodded his head to the table at his left, “I pitched in with my thoughts, but they were rather unimpressed.”

“What are they talking about?” Ayla searched for a waiter before happily waving her espresso order.

“Scientists gathered on Merkum, what do you think they were talking about? They were arguing about food. The best way to prepare prawn ceviche.” Tomias scooped the coffee-soaked sugar from the bottom of his cup with his finger. “One said poach the prawns first, the other said use them raw. I suggested quickly searing but keeping them raw.”

“Such culinary wisdom from someone who doesn’t know how to use a spoon.” Speaking too soon, she dipped a finger in his cup.

Tomias swatted her hand away but Ayla caught it, pleating her fingers through his. Tomias smiled and nudged his chair over to put his arm around her. They sat there watching Merkum’s hubub - observers in the midst of the show.

“I could sit here for hours,” Ayla pushed into him.

"We could bunk the day off. Skip the lab. Let's stay here for a while, then get out of the city."

"That would be rather nice, but I think Sheng would have a meltdown."

Tomias kissed her cheek, "I'm sure it'll be fine. In any case, I have a role to play, too. The thruster isn't going to land itself."

"Well, that's actually exactly what it has to do, otherwise you'll have a rather hard touch-down." Her coffee arrived: a smooth ceramic eggcup with a neat tab protruding out at its base. The cup sat atop an oval silver tray with a thin lip along with a teardrop stirrer and three cubes of fine sugar. "The Abaryonic output isn't quite as stable as I would like. It is difficult to control at these higher power levels. If the timing is off by a fraction of a second the result is a surprising amount of fire," she plopped a cube of sugar into her cup.

"That makes me feel so safe." His own soggy sugar exhausted, Tomias now made an attempt at snagging Ayla's. She batted him away in an instant.

"I wouldn't worry," she patted him on the arm. "By the time you go up all you'll have to do is press a big red button labelled 'moon.'"

"Makes the years of training sound quite pointless, don't you think?"

"Explorers are there for the photo ops. Your job is to look nice in the suit and bring back a few sacks of topsoil. That's it. We could make a machine to do it, but it wouldn't be as photogenic, we need the public on our side."

“There’s nothing like a coffee together to boost my confidence,” he smiled. “So I’m a PR instrument for you?”

“Exactly... and a fragile one at that. Machines can take a lot more deceleration, you know?” She stood up from their table.

“I love you too, Ayla.”

The two laughed and embraced. They took in the blurred hum of dialogue around them in the mid-morning heat. The fresh mountain wind had morphed into a rolling breeze. It carried the smell of aromatic coffees from around the square.

Ayla touched a small, octagonal bronze token on the side of the table and they got up to leave. Both slim, toned and almost the same height, the couple were sometimes awkwardly confused for brother and sister.

They kissed again and said farewell for the day. Ayla headed on towards the laboratory.

*

The corners of Merkum held entrances to another world. Ayla could cycle to her office in a few minutes, but the Underground was so much more fun, she couldn’t resist.

Groups of people trickled out from the gloom below. Ayla weaved between them, down a mild gradient, bobbling over patterned tiles on the ground. Most would push their bike to the Underground, but she thought the odd quizzical look was a price worth paying for the ride.

Before her eyes had time to adjust, Ayla felt a cool gust of air rush out of the dark tunnel, accompanied by the feint echo of humming motors.

With vehicles removed from the streets, the Underground was by far the fastest way to move around Flavia. A large portion of the population used it on a daily basis to get from one corner of town to another. Flavia had recently limited buildings to four storeys so the city had started to spread out across the surrounding valley.

To the uninitiated, the underground might seem complex. Each station comprised a long saw-toothed platform. Every tooth contained several bays. Ayla walked up to a monitor next to a vacant bay. An angular city map was dotted with a hundred lit coloured dots showing all possible destinations.

She pressed a green spot several intersections away. The monitor responded with a satisfying click. No small part of the fun was pushing the buttons.

A few seconds later a pill-shaped pod floated into the bay. It stood motionless, hovering a couple of feet above the ground. The pod had a smooth metallic shell with covered with pearlescent white paint. Following its contours, three of its sides were lined with tall windows.

A broad oval door slid open. Ayla stepped in, placed her bike against a parapet beneath a window opposite and grabbed a central handrail above her.

An equally satisfying 'ping-ping' and the capsule reversed out of the bay and quickly gained momentum. It joined a snaking procession of identical pods speeding above a central magnetic rail.

The string of pearls ran beneath Aria at great speed. Ayla always stood, pretending to ride the rail as if it were a tidal bore pushing her along.

Finding the way to its destination, the pod twice changed rails. Each shift was preceded by a soft warning 'ping' and the flash of a warm orange light in the ceiling.

All in all, the ride took no more than a couple of minutes, hauling Ayla from the city centre to the periphery where the Balkania Institute of Space Exploration was located.

Halting with a prolonged 'piing' Ayla jumped on her bike and sped straight out of the station.

Flavia had no shortage of greenery. When remodelling the city, the focus was on creating open spaces and filling them with an abundance of vegetation.

BISE was a sprawling complex of buildings and brains. From a small research institute only two decades ago, the site was now home to more than thirty thousand scientists. They came from every corner of the world.

The mission had united them.

Entering the BISE grounds, her second home, Alya took a deep breath and smiled. Low brick buildings with even grass roofs were dispersed throughout the grounds. Crystal blue ponds potted green spaces. The odd grassy knoll breaking the eye line. The visual calm masked the pressure felt by all those who worked there.

Ayla walked the final straight to her office, leaving her bicycle outside. In her mind she paced through the order of tasks for today's experiment.

*

Sheng was an outwardly stern man slightly softened by his bushy brows and curly grey hair. Today he marched through the halls of BISE with a hurried, heavy step.

The first manned mission to the moon had seen the world come together. In hope and expectation alike. The mission had been more than twenty years in the making... To be fair, it had been in the making throughout all of human history, but the world's resolve had finally been pushed to unite, aiming to make the age old dream a reality.

No one element of the task was guaranteed to succeed, yet too much was at stake for it to fail. There was already speculation amongst some Core States that failure could challenge the still fledgling social order, bringing a return to instability.

Sheng tried to push such thoughts out of his head and focus on that which he could control. After all, at his disposal were thousands of the world's most prominent minds.

One of those bright minds, Deputy Director to the mission, stumbled through the heavy wooden doors ahead of him.

"Ayla, I do hope the eclipse was worth it." Sheng's dry voice echoed through the corridor.

"I haven't missed a single one yet. If you ever came up, you'd see why," Ayla composed herself, walking closer.

She stopped in front of Sheng, his podgy, bearish frame loomed above her. The soft lines of her face stood in contrast to his craggy furrows. A firm handshake and the two headed towards the fabrication halls.

"The Council has sent a delegation of observers for this test. It seems some of our partners are becoming anxious to see results."

"You know that's a terrible idea," Ayla broke pace. "We've made a lot of progress but there are still so many unknowns. Every solution we create opens up new uncertainties."

Sheng continued walking, "At some point we have to decide. Go or don't go?" he looked square into Ayla's eyes. "Uncertainty is in the very nature of a mission that has never been attempted before."

They entered the cavernous fabrication halls. Every conceivable element of the moon mission was brought to life within this hangar.

Ayla paused, "Lives are at stake."

"Jonah and Tomias are well aware of the risks involved. They will write history," Sheng replied.

"... Yes, Sheng, and it's our job to make sure that history involves no accidents."

They approached the engineering team as they assembled the last few test components.

Strewn around them, the halls were filled with equipment and rigging. Cranes, wires, lathes, welders, rolls of aluminium as well as countless other presumably vital components. Order was known only to those working there; bits scattered and stored in every conceivable nook across the spider web of ladders and walkways.

The team for today's test was huddled around a ribbed metal cylinder the size of a stool. A rounded tip was fitted to the end of a stumpy tube. Smooth rivets connected both parts. The whole assembly was bolted to a sled.

Chief Engineer Petra emerged from the group as they stared at the connection between cone and cylinder. She placed a crystal cube into her lab coat pocket, brushing her cinnamon curls out of the way.

"Ready to go!"

"Bring it outside, place it on the rail and I'll get the gawkers," ordered Sheng.

"Have you had any noteworthy issues?" Ayla asked as she ran a hand over the engine's smooth outer shell.

"I'm confident that we have finally solved the overpower issue, however, I'm still apprehensive about its stability." Petra mimed her hand landing hard on an invisible surface.

"This topic has been exhausted," Sheng barked. "We have five buildings full of mathematicians and physicists who have calculated timing, forces and stresses on every nut and bolt of the system. There has never been a more intensely scrutinised pile of metal."

"Hopefully it won't end up a pile of metal on the moon," Ayla retorted, "Considering my partner's inside. If we focus on improving Advanced AB, it will be able to handle the landing."

"We don't have time for this argument, Ayla. Your technology is little more than a prototype. A mission of this scale can't rest on a fanciful idea."

"I need to prepare for the test," Ayla walked away from the group. The rest of the team began moving the rig outside.

*

With regular live tests of all kinds, BISE had an on-site facility capable of powering a scale model Spinlaunch system and launch craft. After a few early mishaps above ground, an improved facility had been burrowed underground.

A wide circular shaft sank through the soil. Sticking out of the hole was a thick steel rail. Surrounding the hole was a raised earthen mound covered in trimmed grass.

Mounted to the rail was the day's experiment: a tenth scale run of the descent and landing engine. It was fixed in place above the chasm using a heavy pin connected to a wire.

Power control had been a significant issue. Massless propulsion was in its early days. Delivering a steady landing curve was one of the largest hurdles facing the team. The difference between a soft landing and a ... faster arrival to the moon's surface was a matter of nanoseconds of throttle.

Competing solutions from other Cores had been shelved in favour of an AB impulse system aided by a passive suppressant. It resonates a series of massive and massless particles at an exact height above the moon's surface, ensuring a smooth landing on a cushion of baryonic matter. While this gave control, the short distance and constant phase control left little room for error.

Due to the risks involved, such tests were usually closed to the outside public. Today, six months before launch, a dozen onlookers gathered in a safety cage, some distance behind the raised earth lip of the test shaft. The group consisted of observers from the six other Cores. Between them, they represented thousands of city states, over two billion citizens.

With afternoon turning to dusk, only the rail's tip could be seen poking out of the hole. Its edge shone, lit by the waning sun.

Cameras projected the interior of the shaft to monitors clustered ahead of the assembled group. Thick blast shields were placed in front and above them. The countdown was already in motion.

Five minutes.

The observers stood in silence. Ayla flicked through a set of final checklists with the engineering team.

Three minutes.

Industrial fans inside the shaft kicked in, preparing to remove any dust brought about by the experiment.

"Will this test incorporate our Contained dynamo as the suppressant module?" asked Frey, the representative from the Continental Core.

"No," replied Sheng. "It was deemed not ready."

Emotionless, Frey took note and stayed focused on the monitors.

One minute.

Ayla hopped from one corner of the cage to another. She caught an engineer by his coat sleeve and repeatedly tapped a line item on the list.

"Tomorrow we move to full scale tests." Sheng told Ayla.

Ayla scarcely looked at him, instead she turned her attention on the counter and monitors.

Five. Four. Three. Two. One.

Sheng gave the order: "Release."

A metallic flick echoed in the shaft as the wire snapped tight. It removed the restraining pin with force. The first second seemed to go by in slow motion. The group huddled around the monitors as, driven solely by gravity, the sled picked up speed. The odd squeak and squeal of metal scraping on metal rang out.

The silence was forcefully shattered as the thruster kicked in. The shaft was illuminated by a soft blue-purple light. A fine ring of glowing white dust escaped out of the hole. It mixed with the rays of the sun setting above the site.

The observers watched as the rig could be seen hurtling towards the bottom, bathed in light. The base of the thruster glowed with an uneven, orange, red and white light.

Suddenly, one of the cameras went dark.

Immediately the group trained their eyes to the remaining monitors. It was clear something was wrong. Badly wrong. The cone could no longer be seen. Instead, a blinding white fire shot out around the model in all directions.

A moment later a violent explosion shook the ground. Every monitor went dark. It hardly mattered. All attention was focused on the eruption of fire and smoke spewing out of the shaft.

Alarms sounded throughout the campus as burning debris rained down. Nearby lawns were littered with mangled metal.

A few silent seconds passed. Just as it appeared as if calm had descended, a metallic bang rang out from the blast shield above their heads. A deformed rivet from the engine bounced off of the safety cage and on to the lawn in front.

Stunned, the group stared motionless and mute. Frey looked above his spectacles.

"Next time, use our dyno as the suppressant."

TWO

Dharma was nestled in the soft hills of the lower Himavan. Long before the Core System, the town had been a seat of learning. Scholars would come to the region and establish a school, each with a different focus. The temperate climate created a relaxed atmosphere for learning.

Over time, the schools slowly joined, forming a community which then drew even more scholars to the area, establishing Dharma as the foremost seat of learning in the world.

Headquartered in Dharma, the Kap had been established as a global school and college. Every child on Earth between the ages of six and twenty could spend time at the Kap. The school had a campus on every continent. Students would move between several campuses during their education.

Classes were made up of twenty to thirty students of mixed ages from twelve to twenty. They all called The Kap their home from Monday to Thursday. Most headed home over the weekends.

“There’s something curious about our world,” Adroa cast an imposing figure. As head of the Kap, Adroa steered the education of a quarter-billion students.

"To be fair, there are many curious things about our world." Tall and defined, she paced across a stage, under the matted shade of the cedar trees. "For hundreds of thousands of years, early humans lived a primitive existence. Hunting, gathering, hunting some more."

Adroa wore a blue shoulder-length blue linen tunic with a matching sarong and simple woven sandals – the uniform of a teacher in the Kap.

"They left few clues of their experience of the world," Sirem joined in, "Apart from some gnawed-on gazelle bones and Hela statues." She sat at the side of a limestone amphitheatre focused on Adroa. Short with finely carved lines, Sirem's emerald green eyes pierced through long black hair. Her uniform was identical in all but colour – the linen a plain white, marking her out as a senior student of the Kap.

"The bones are rather clear," Noake, a stout young man from an island in Oceania, added. "Ambush a herd, lob off a leg and get to chewing." Sat two rows in at the opposite side of the amphitheatre, he mimed slashes and bites.

The class of twenty-something students laughed. They fanned out over four rising arcs of benches.

After a brief pause, Sirem continued, "The figures are more interesting. They resemble a rough sphere of rock with five bobbly mounds. Two for legs at the bottom. One on each side for arms and a wider lump representing a head."

"Why do you single out the Hela statues?" Adroa asked.

"Why wouldn't you, they're sexy!" Polim, a sinewy teen, shouted from the back row.

"Hilarious, Polim," Sirem barely turned. "The Hela figurine is a defining symbol of early humanity. Hundreds of these curious statuettes have been found scattered in caves, forest clearings and even riverbeds throughout The Great Continent. Our best guess is that Hela was the moon in anthropomorphic form."

"Why do you think they chose a feminine form?" Adroa signalled to Noake.

"I believe it's a representation of a mother figure," Noake leant forward. "I agree with the idea that early humans saw our origin, our birth from the moon. It's a small step to represent that concept in the figure of a woman, a mother."

"Do you think so?" Adroa questioned him, "In hindsight, does it not seem like a rather small step? You're talking about abstract expression. The ability to represent an idea, a connection."

Some students took notes, but most listened on.

"As far as we know, humans are the only species able to create such abstract associations. I like the idea that this ability is what allowed us to manifest abstract notions in real life," He leaned back.

The student's seats were hewn from soft limestone, worn with the grooves of the generations who had sat there before. The Kap in Dharma was built on the site of an old Indus college dating back some two thousand years.

The curve of the amphitheatre cut into the side of a hill so that the last row was cushioned by a grassy lip - perfect as a soft backrest.

"Exactly," Sirem took the baton. "Curiously, around 150,000 years ago the figurines start to become smaller. We know, our archaeologists have measuring tape. Over a few thousand years Hela halves in size. The quality of carvings also decreases, as if the figurines were done in haste. Some even had their spherical form squashed into more of a rugby ball.

"From 140,000 years ago Hela statues started popping up all over the place. The statues, along with the smelly humans who crafted them, explode out of the Continent. Up through Arabia, Balkania, the Indus and all throughout Oceania. Within the space of ten thousand years homo sapiens dominated a good chunk of the Earth."

"Ten thousand years is an entire age!" Polim slouched into his seat.

"Ten thousand years might sound like a long time, but it really is an instant." Adroa cut in. "Think about it. How did they get there? How did they know there was a there to get to? Land links exist in some places but there are several key crossings which require a rather large leap of faith over the horizon. And yet, leap they did."

"If I agree, can we skip the homework I feel coming?" Polim sat up.

Adroa stepped over, "We'll let Sirem and Noake decide - at least in your case."

The class giggled.

"It is a fascinating topic though. Think how brave those early explorers had to be."

"Or scared," Noake darted. "Perhaps they acted out of necessity and not choice. A clue on the question of how humans spread so far, so fast can be found with the Akyristan people of central Sibir. Their origin story is a legend about gods finding their homeland, vast woodland full of animals, navigating the world with their sky map. They arrived, it is said, by following the moon. It is possible that early humanity believed the moon was a map of the earth. Emboldened, they set out to explore, always sure of their destination."

He part-raised from his resting state.

"That story is connected with another curiosity of our world – the round shoulder tattoos found almost universally in early civilisations. It was a longstanding belief that the tattoos were dedications to a moon god, Hela herself."

"You're saying this isn't true?" Asked Adroa, leaning against the first row of desks.

"Perhaps," Noake made a wry smile. "A recent find, in an old cave, potentially upends the view. A long mural portrays a group of six; four men and two women collectively pushing a raft into water. The artwork is primitive. Then again, my own art skills are questionable, at best. Especially if I were working down in a cave lit by animal fat."

The class laughed again.

The sun broke through the early-morning clouds, gently warming the limestone rings. The heat was partially dappled by the surrounding cedars.

"Artistic merit aside, the most interesting aspect of the drawing is what's depicted on their shoulders: an apricot-sized tattoo. Drawn in an ochre pigment, each one is criss-crossed by an identical set of lines etched in feint green pigment. Assuming the artist was aiming for blue, it seems like the tattoo could have been a map, scribed permanently on the skin of our forefathers." Noake rolled up the sleeve of his tunic and pointed to his shoulder, "In this explanation, over time, as navigation improved, the lines were lost, leaving a symbolic circle. This process repeated across the world leading to a mark uniting humanity across seas and oceans."

"That interpretation raises some sad conclusions," Sirem sat forward. "Archaeologists are impressed by early people's knowledge of what lay beyond the horizon. But the map theory suggests plenty would-be explorers launched their primitive boats, together with their families and all they had, carried out to nowhere by the strong tides and currents. It's hard enough to navigate the oceans today."

"Knowledge is permeable, malleable," replied Noake. "All those who made it still *knew* their maps were correct. Their knowledge held true. It took many generations to realise the costly mistake which led to our even spread around the world."

"For our understanding to change, we must have an understanding to begin with. Society is built on knowledge passed down through generations." Adroa walked over and sat on the front row.

Noake took the cue, hoisting out of his seat, "Exactly." He bounced down towards the stage like a fresh jelly, "For example, the city of Pacha sits almost exactly on the other side of the world from us here in Dharma. Three thousand years ago, Pacha was one of the few coastal kingdoms in the world. Endowed with unique topography, it sat perched like an eagle's nest on a sharp volcanic shelf. In front lay the endless Southern Ocean. Behind it, the mighty Andes pierced the clouds. Pacha was one of the few places on the Patagonian coastline capable of docking ships."

"It must have seemed like a fantasy," Adroa scanned across the class.

"It was," he replied. "In ancient times Pacha was a near-mythical realm. Tales of its lighthouse were known by every sailor. With rather large variations in the details, mind you. It was said to have the power to turn night into day. The lighthouse beckoned ships to the city as soon as they crested the horizon. At first, it appeared as a faint star at eye level, slowly rising out of the ocean. The light became stronger with every mile."

Noake confidently paced from one end of the broad stage to the other. "Fifteen miles out it formed a triangular path of feint golden light, the elongated point converging right on the city's deep port. Every night for two thousand years the enchanting light guided countless ships to safety. Nearly every night, that is. The lighthouse was 'in maintenance' on cloudy nights – which, I'd say, is the more likely time a ship needs guidance. But that's being unfair."

"Why would you build a lighthouse which only worked on clear nights?" Sirem asked.

"The lighthouse above Pacha was as much a symbol of control as it was a functional instrument. We still don't know how many legions of stonemasons worked to carve out the mountain above the city. The result, a perfectly polished nine-hundred-foot Hela mirror. Its smooth curves were completely at odds with the jagged rocks surrounding it. Today, the best way to describe it is like a giant radio dish tilted between the ocean and moon. It sat flush with the mountainside. Many years ago, scientists discovered the secret to its shine. Remnants of a thin silver coating were discovered in distinct layers, plastered on top of the polished basalt."

"It is hard to believe how such a feat of engineering would be achieved only for functional reasons," Sirem thought out loud. "I've seen that place a few times and it is amazing – in size and scale. It seems like they would have had far easier, and more effective, options to build a lighthouse if that's what they wanted to do."

Noake turned towards her, "I agree. Not only did the people of Pacha dig a nine-hundred-foot crater out of the Andes but they went and coated it in reflective silver. What's more, the layers suggest they did this over and over again to maintain the surface. The whole thing acted like an enormous concave mirror, smoothed to give a linear focal point along the water."

"Perhaps the mirror was lit in some other way when the moon was covered by clouds," Adroa added.

"It's possible." Noake replied. "Many ancient drawings of the lighthouse survive to this day. Most of them show the light from the moon shining down and then out from the mirror. A few show a ball of light closer to the mirror. Some believe fires could have been lit at a second focal point in front of the mirror."

"I don't think navigation was their priority!" Polim concluded.

"It was mainly two things – a tribute to Hela and a statement of power. Pacha is not alone. Ancient cultures around the world made similar creations. Some functional, some symbolic; all dedicated to the moon. Take Flavia. There seems to be no functional reason for the mirror's creation. Only to glorify Hela at the time of an eclipse by focusing the light on to the city below."

"Why do you think humanity took this radical shift away from neat statues to grand building projects?" Adroa asked.

"With organised society came the need to unify around an idea. We traded small, intimate Hela statues for large public symbols," she replied. "I feel like these statements of power were as important to the citizens of Pacha as they were to the sailors and travellers coming in from outside."

"Feels like they were trying too hard."

"Sometimes you have to try hard, Polim. Doing the bare minimum only gets you so far," Sirem turned towards the back row and winked.

The class laughed.

"They had to create a shared identity. That takes effort," she added.

"It does. They created a shared identity, but they also showed who's boss," Noake clasped his hands.

"If we can coordinate so many people to dig out a mountain, just think what else we can do," Sirem laughed.

"Exactly," Noake continued. "Along with the desire to build, coordinate and control, came a desire to understand. The Hela mirrors were a spark to mathematics and science."

"They couldn't take it easy and enjoy their creation, could they?" Polim was almost laying down on the now hot limestone bench.

"Curiosity is a difficult trait to stop." Sirem smiled.

"True, the knowledge they generated was precious," Noake added. "Kings and their courts would covet their charts and tables, locked up behind palace doors. Predictions were used to demonstrate a connection with the seas, with the seasons and with the moon, Hela. There's a story about Pacha.

The leaders had a law. Every ship that docked in its port had to surrender any book, pamphlet or manuscript it was carrying. While the crews went about their business, an army of scribes would copy the works. Over the years it led to Pacha amassing the greatest wealth in history: more than a million texts from every corner of the earth. The Pacha library would become a place of pilgrimage for scholars and the curious alike.

He walked to sit near Sirem, facing towards the rest of the class.

"However, at the time, the city's rulers had no desire to open their doors to foreign scholars. They had no desire to open their doors to anyone for that matter, not even their own citizens. Amassing such a wealth of knowledge would guarantee their grip on power for generations to come. Or so it was thought."

"I see this story turning," Polim raised from his slumber.

"We all see it turning," Adroa smiled.

"Indeed." Noake continued, "Their iron grip on knowledge led more to resentment than awe. The people of Pacha knew they had a right to share the contents of the library. Unrelenting, the rulers kept the doors bolted, only opening them for deliveries of new texts, freshly copied. Tensions built until they reached boiling point. An armed mob, torches in toe, marched towards the palace demanding access to Pacha's wealth. On its own this would be a rather run of the mill, unremarkable revolt."

"As you do," Polim leaned forward, resting on his hands as a light wind blew through the trees.

Noake paid him no attention. "However, the palace, which was hiding the king and his information-greedy court, happened to share a closed piazza with the library. The nobility would sit in the piazza and discuss their secret texts in peace and privacy.

"As the mob started pounding at the gates, the court scattered throughout the compound. Some hid in, around, under and through the palace while others sought sanctuary in the library. Two hundred scribes were working by candlelight within the library's basement.

"Hearing the commotion, they ventured upstairs. The scribes begged and pleaded with the nobility. Leave this place! The nobility refused outright.

"Beside themselves with fear, not for their lives, but for the million precious parchments, the scribes stood in unison behind the piazza gate.

"Whipped up into a frenzy, the mob broke through the dense wooden gate. The crowd tore apart the first rows, undeterred by the defenceless guardians. They knew the elite lay beyond.

"The initial charge turned into a massacre. The scholars offered their own bodies as a shield. Halfway through, barely standing on a pile of fallen scribes, the pack slowed. The anger in their eyes gradually spiralled into a look of horror.

"Some fled, others froze and collapsed, paralysed by the scene around them. A few begged anyone who'd listen for forgiveness.

"Pacha's Library, along with the collective knowledge of humanity, was saved at the cost of a hundred lives. Dismayed, the rulers emerged from their hiding places.

"It is said that as a show of respect to the fallen, they opened up the library to the public. I would rather imagine they didn't want another mob knocking on their door in the middle of the night."

"What's the moral of the story? Don't hoard?" Polim leaned back against the grassy lip.

"Kind of," Noake agreed. "It's a bloody story but one worth remembering. Knowledge must be shared. When it's hoarded by the few at the expense of the many, division and resentment build."

THREE

"Every part of this mission is about more than getting to the moon," Petra stared through a wall of windows looking out from her office onto the BISE campus. "If we're successful, each system, every nut and bolt will be *the* nut and bolt which first reached the moon."

"It makes our task that extra bit harder." Ayla scanned a long blackboard strewn with equations and formulas. The entire wall was covered with calculations and insect-like diagrams of particle interactions under a title reading 'shadow'.

"The world is watching us, waiting to see the result." Petra circled a wooden table running the length of her office. On top was a partially assembled maze of clamps, mirrors and reflectors. They all focused on a central area which was currently empty.

"I've lost a lot of sleep wondering what that result will be," Petra looked towards the blackboard.

"Wondering if we're going to be successful should keep you up at night. Especially with Tomias riding this thing," Ayla turned around from the board and came to the other side of the table. She picked up a cracked crystal cube placed at one corner of the table.

Petra smiled and tidied discarded clamps and mounts from the large rig. "I'm not so worried about that."

"True, there are other Explorers after all," Ayla returned the smoky crystal cube back on the table.

"Don't be silly. I'm confident the boys will be safe. We've been working on their safety for years." Petra took the cube and placed it under her desk, "Not to mention Rassi and her training schedule."

"I always assumed that was secretly an excuse to go and party without me," Ayla smiled. "What's your worry then?"

"My career has gone into this mission."

Petra walked over to a scale model craft in the corner of her office. A rounded cone was fastened to a waffled silver cylinder.

"It's an opportunity to change humanity's path. I want to send a message."

"What message do you want to send?" Ayla came over to look at the model. She ran a hand over the crimpled chrome cylinder.

"Perspective. I want to show a new perspective," Petra paused. "There is more than one way to look at things. Sometimes it is difficult to shift our perspective. The mission gives us an amazing opportunity to do that and I want to make the most of it."

"Rarely poetic."

"It's something I believe in rather strongly. The way we get there matters, too. Our Advanced AB can work. We have to push for it."

"Three billion people have their beady eyes trained on us, waiting to see someone finally step on the moon. The Spinlaunch at Kamrun can take us to Hela. I wish Advanced could help us land."

"What if it could?" Petra looked up from the model, "I think Advanced can generate enough steady push to slow the landing module and make a safe landing all by itself."

"I would love to see Advanced work in real life. It's little more than a prototype," Ayla glanced back at a corner of the blackboard filled with wave equations. "The technology will probably take years to work properly. We have three months before launch."

"This whole mission is a symbol." Petra placed her hands on the model between them. "It isn't about where humanity is now. It's where we see ourselves in the future. We have to push harder. You might be surprised how far we've taken it."

"What is this model?"

"This is Advanced version one," Petra headed for the door, "let me show you version five."

Sheng looked through a large window beyond his desk, surveying a flurry of activity in the fabrication halls below. Today, the typically cluttered aisles were cleared. A team of engineers choreographed the movements of a section of fuselage towards a cleanroom.

An oblate metallic spheroid, they'd likely call it. More like half a mango, cut lengthways. The thirty-foot mass hovered a few inches from the ground. A light wind blew at the engineer's trousers as it drifted through the aisle. Polished to a mirror finish, the hull contorted reflections of the team as they swarmed around. The faintest purple glow reflected off of the smooth concrete floor.

A square ivory envelope lay in the middle of Sheng's desk. It was placed face-down, showing only a deep red wax seal. The seal had the head of a kob antelope, dipped down, twisted horns pointing forward, ready to attack.

Sheng broke the seal and opened the envelope. Inside were two thick pieces of card. The first had only two words printed in thick caps at its centre: 'landing curve'.

The second had a table of hexadecimal bounds printed on one side and a diagram showing a steep curve with waypoints touching a semicircle at the bottom of the page.

Tearing up the envelope, Sheng placed the pages in his jacket pocket and stood from his desk.

He made his way out of the office and down several flights of stairs to the fabrication halls. Having completed their manoeuvre, the team he previously observed were back at their workstations.

Sheng signalled to the senior engineer.

"Did you stabilise the wobble in the Spinlaunch inner coil?"

"Yes, sir, we have it to well within normal bounds."

"Follow me," Sheng led the engineer away from the group.

The two marched past rows of storage shelves almost touching the towering ceiling. They entered a small room with an unmarked door.

"I need you to revisit plans for the suppressant."

"But I thought we took a final decision to omit the module?"

The room was practically empty aside from a single desk placed against the far wall and a monitor mounted above it. Sheng activated the monitor and brought up a set of diagrams.

"The architecture allows it to be incorporated at any time. I want you to make sure we can add it at any point."

"When will you decide whether it will be included?"

"Whenever I decide. This is a direct order."

"I understand."

Sheng removed the second square piece of card from his jacket pocket and gave it to the engineer.

"To anticipate its inclusion, I want you to create a standby landing curve profile according to these parameters."

The engineer reviewed the data, "Are Ayla and Petra aware of this?"

"I don't want to repeat myself. Create the profile and maintain the current architecture. Is that clear?"

"Yes, sir."

"Speaking of, have you seen Ayla?"

"I think I saw her heading down towards the basement with Petra a little while ago."

Sheng turned and briskly left. The engineer stood in the middle of the empty room holding the card. His gaze alternated between its rows of parameters and the monitor in front.

***

Ayla and Tomias shared a spacious top-floor apartment at the edge of Flavia Park. The tall, timbre-framed block had a vibrant living facade. A local moss peppered with wildflowers created a patchwork punctuated by angular terraces. Large square windows looked like ponds dotted vertically up the building's six floors.

Their apartment was bathed in light pouring in from three glass-faced walls. The front opened out on a terrace which overlooked the entire length of the long park. Mount Rhoda towered above Flavia's neatly trimmed skyline.

Tomias was out on the terrace, reclining on a simple ottoman. He read through a series of lander instructions in the captain's manual.

A morning talk show played on a large wall-mounted monitor inside the flat. Through the open terrace door, Tomias could hear the host excitedly speculating on the mission.

He placed the manual on a low table made of thin copper lengths. A spherical model of the moon slowly rotated above the table next to a cold cup of coffee.

The terrace floor was made of square blocks of cream limestone. He stood, picking up the coffee on the way. The soft stone warmed his bare feet as he walked over to the chrome parapet. Leaning over, he stared up, past the mountain peak. It was a perfectly clear day; he could see the moon suspended in the sky.

Soon, he thought.

"Tomias." A stern voice came from inside.

He bolted upright, nearly dropping his coffee on the street below.

"One second!" Tucking and tightening his pale linen gown, Tomias paced inside. The marble floor was freezing. "Yes, Colonel Rassi."

The monitor showed the Colonel sitting straight at her desk in full uniform. "Captain. I have received a new set of instructions for the lander." Rassi was a veteran of several active conflicts in the past. Repeatedly showing great calm under pressure, she was the obvious choice to be placed in charge of the strict training regime for the mission.

"Any significant changes?" Tomias stood in the centre of the open living space. A large, framed image of Ayla and Tomias embraced in front of a tropical lake hung next to the monitor.

"There's a small update to the release sequence and some minor timing amendments," Rassi's curt grey hair was combed to one side. "But, as you know, the details make all the difference."

"I'll be sure to read up on them."

"Appreciated. We will go through them next week in BISE."

"Thank you, Colonel, see you then." The monitor changed back to the morning show. They had moved on to a cooking segment.

The basement floor of BISE was a honeycomb of laboratories and experimental chambers. A windowless world: thick ventilation pipes snaked through every corridor; heavy metal doors controlled by long levers which kept the rooms sealed.

Two generations ago, the laboratories had yielded humanity's most important scientific discoveries.

Petra hurried ahead, speaking without turning, "My work forces me to challenge my perspective every day."

First was the detection of the Phion family of massless, Abaryonic, particles. Scientists discovered that, alongside the matter-based universe we know and understand, there exists an equally rich, equally abundant universe made up of massless particles. This went far beyond the Photon - one of the few known AB particles.

"Having Sheng constantly breathing down your neck forces you to question yourself." Ayla kept pace behind her as they weaved through the corridors.

The Phion detection upturned the standard model of physics and led to a subsequent wave of discoveries enabling breakthroughs such as the AB Drive.

"I get so absorbed with my work, I barely notice Sheng," Petra stopped in front of a closed door at the end of a bare concrete corridor.

The door was secured by a set of four bolts plunged into the wall. They were connected by a flat Z-shaped lever with a diagonal handle at the centre.

"Working with this technology is almost like an exercise in meditation." She lowered the lever with a dull thud and the bolts retracted. "We assume that the universe is a book, waiting to be read. A truth understandable by our senses." The door creaked open revealing a tall, near-empty room. "But there's no reason why that should be the case. It's even a little arrogant to assume everything is created with our perspective in mind."

A thick wire hung in the middle of the room.

Ayla peered into the chamber.

The wire was attached to a slim metal cylinder, no taller than a trash can. It was held in place by a release pin. The pipe had finger-thick grooves running evenly along its length tapering to a smooth oval tip. The grooves, like the model on her desk, were darker than the main skin of the cylinder.

"I suppose my first question is what the hell is this?" Ayla asked.

"Our Gliders work by momentarily resonating massless particles with run of the mill baryonic matter. The craft literally glide through the fermionic field."

The world was still limited by its early understanding of this technology. Near to the ground, or in space itself, it could achieve astonishing feats of levitation and high-speed movement. The technology still lacked the energy density to escape Earth's gravity well. Nor Hela's, for that matter.

Petra toggled a switch at the side of the room, a string of fans whirred into life. "After the explosion I thought there might be an opportunity to try a different approach," Petra went to the stand. "When toying with the technology in the past, Phion resonance can be focused and shaped."

Ayla edged several steps toward the rig.

"But it's hard to keep it focused for long enough to provide reliable launch or landing power." Petra continued. For launch, I do still think we have a way to go. We can however make a successful landing using Advanced"

"And this is your solution?" Ayla looked at the rig.

"It's a step in the right direction. I have found a way to control the baryonic/abaryonic horizon. With some tweaking, the approach can act like a pillow, cushioning the fall."

"That's a lot of fancy words. Are they enough to bring it to a stop?"

A panel was mounted on the wall next to the door. Petra flipped a switch. It triggered a low buzz in the wire connected to the top of the model. "With a bit of tweaking, it should do, yes. The system takes a bit of time to power up."

Ayla reached to touch the model in front of her.

Petra pushed two buttons side-by-side. No immediate effect.

"Instead of trying to emulate old propulsion methods, why not create a whole new approach."

"What's the result?"

"Push the button on the bottom-left and stand back. You'll see."

Ayla pushed it firmly. She jumped as three sharp horn bursts echoed throughout the empty room.

As soon as the horns silenced, the model came to life. A low-pitch vibration started at its base. It was followed by a rush of cool wind streaming out across the concrete floor. Ayla felt the wind rush over her feet. The gust rose up the wall behind and traced a path around her neck.

The release pin holding the cylinder clicked open. In a fraction of a second, the rush of air disappeared. The model dropped like a rock. A few inches from the ground, it slowed its descent. Ayla felt a shiver run down her back.

A wave of piercing diamond light glistened across the cylinder's surface from base to tip. Cutting through the frame, it cast sharp shadows on the ceiling. Deceleration turned into a rapid acceleration - straight towards the ground.

The model drove hard into the solid floor.

Ayla attempted to keep balance as the room shook and filled with dust. Wall-mounted fans kicked into action from their passive state, clearing the grey haze.

The model vibrated around its newly created crater for several more seconds before gradually reducing power. It finally stopped and keeled over, having burrowed a melon-sized dent in the concrete. The smell of charged cement filled the room.

"Wow!" Ayla smiled. "What just happened?"

"Well," Petra slowly walked towards the experiment, "It wasn't quite meant to do that."

"Pretty impressive though," Ayla joined her.

"You can say that again. That was less than 10 kilowatts on a five pound model. The wave formed as it should, but it must have lost stability a little before touching down."

"Hence why it buried itself in the floor?" Ayla studied the depression as the last of the dust cleared. "If we don't use it as a rocket, it could always be tuned as a drill!"

Petra laughed.

The door slammed open, hitting the wall and causing Ayla to jump at the peak of her elation.

Sheng stormed into the room.

"What… is going on? There are alarms going off across the entire floor."

Ayla and Petra spun around toward Sheng. Glancing at each other on the way, they each noticed something strange. Both looked as if they had stood under a fine sieve, waiting patiently as a bucket full of charcoal was carefully sprinkled on top of them.

Ayla nearly let out a laugh. She flicked back her hair, letting out a cloud of dust as she did.

"Petra has made a breakthrough on Advanced," she barely managed to finish her sentence before descending into a cough.

"Right… as the world is watching, as we move from one failure to another on our main flight systems, our Deputy Director and Chief Engineer are wasting time and resources on this stupid prototype?"

He pushed past the two women to examine the now still experiment. At its base, the ribbed cylinder was lightly scratched. The rest of the model was pristine apart from the odd scatter of dark powder clinging to some of the grooves.

"I... I believe it is a good idea to explore Advanced for future missions. Stability issues are nearly solved, and the benefits of its implementation are huge." Petra gained some conviction in her voice. "We still have many unanswered questions about what the moon will be like. Let's be honest, our missions so far have yielded less information than we would have liked."

"Future missions?" Sheng turned towards Petra. "We've yet to make one successful journey and you're talking about future missions?"

"This is the start of a long journey, Sheng." Ayla interrupted. "Yes, we still have challenges to solve but we also have a responsibility to the people of this planet. The example we set will be followed and built upon for centuries to come."

"I won't be here centuries from now. I'm here now and I want to see us put an Explorer on Hela three months from now. That's all that matters." Sheng pushed the rig, "Every step, every action which doesn't directly contribute to that goal undermines it. Understood?"

"...Understood." Petra replied, enthusiasm drained from her face.

"I completely disagree," Ayla's feet dug into the concrete. "You're being short-sighted and weak in what will be one of humanity's defining moments."

Sheng glowed red. He opened his mouth, but no words came out. The two stood no more than a couple of feet apart, staring straight into one another's eyes. Neither moved.

The silence continued until Sheng relaxed his posture. He took a hidden breath to compose himself, "Frey is still pushing us to use their power suppressant."

Ayla wondered whether to allow a change of subject. "Why? It isn't necessary. Even with the current technology we can glide down to the surface."

"Nussa have been refining their design. He believes it will make the landing safer and increase the prospects for success."

"Decrease," Petra muttered.

"We don't know how this suppressant would connect with our systems." Ayla spoke before Sheng's attention could swing towards Petra. "The argument for using it is no stronger than using Advanced."

"The argument is made up of a thousand states and half a billion people." Sheng answered like a teacher bored of explaining himself.

"If Frey wants it then Kala wants it."

FOUR

A teardrop Glider raced along Lacka Canyon. It passed tunnels piercing a series of sheer granite rock faces. The chrome capsule cut silently through the air, almost grazing the ground below.

Inside, Ashok was staring out, trying to fix his gaze on any single detail as it zipped past. The five hundred-mile journey from Flavia to Dvor took no more than an hour; slow, due to the mountainous terrain. Still, travelling at normal speed in the narrow canyon would have reduced the view to little more than a brown-green blur.

Only the sky blue waters of the Lacka River remained constant as the Glider followed its path through the valley.

Ashok had asked that his team travel separately. An hour alone was an opportunity not to be missed. The staff had prepared a light lunch. It was presented on electrum plates placed on top of a fine white cloth draped over a low cherry table at the capsule's tip.

Sitting in a soft chair facing the panorama ahead, he enjoyed a curious combination of sashimi accompanied by a lightly garnished fresh tomato salad. Next to the plates was a round porcelain bowl covered by a silver lid.

Travelling a few feet above the ground, at half the speed of sound, eating fine sashimi is a rather special experience. Thirty years into his self-created position Ashok still appreciated such moments.

"Sir, we'll be arriving in fifteen minutes," a voice from the monitor interrupted his musings.

"Thank you, Mito how far back are you?"

"We're twenty miles behind you. Do you have any requests?"

"Now that you ask, yes." Ashok relaxed into the cosy chair. "Everything seems set up for the meeting. We're even running ahead of schedule. Could you go ahead of me? Go over to the castle and sort out any last minute issues. I'd like to take a walk through the city."

"Of course," replied Mito. "You're going to want to go alone, aren't you? Little point in asking if you want anyone with you?"

"So little it's not worth mentioning," he laughed. "I'll do a quick circle of the old town and come over."

"Of course, we'll have everything prepared when you arrive. The meeting starts at three o'clock. You will have two hours to yourself."

"Thank you, I'll wave as you pass."

Ashok tilted his left wrist. His thick linen cuff sprang back to reveal a polished masterpiece of engineering. The carefully restored chronograph had cogs, springs and even a fuse.

A double-rattrapante, it could lap times to within a tenth of a second. Not bad for a century-old mechanism. He looked at the clean grey dial in its smooth electrum case and smiled.

Sashimi and salad vanquished, he turned his attention to the covered bowl, teasing off its loose lid with his little finger. To his delight underneath lay a freshly prepared panna cotta topped with two wild raspberries, surrounded by a swirl of raspberry sauce.

A bright flicker hit his eye right as he was about to mercilessly dig into the dessert. The second Glider passed in-front of him, reflecting the sun as it briefly drew level before streaming out ahead.

Ashok could barely make out the silhouettes of his team, waving through the Glider's front window.

Still holding his spoon, he waved back.

Dvor was a picture-postcard city, carrying its difficult history with a sense of pride. Straddling the banks of the Lacka River, Dvor had been the heart of arts and culture since before The Collapse. The Old Town, Dvor's heart, was neatly divided in two halves by the boisterous mountain river.

The bazaar sat on one side with its warren of stone alleyway, craft shops, and coffee and tea houses. Across the river, rising up along the steep hillside were broader cobbled streets lined with houses and official buildings. Each of the two and three storey houses was painted, or at least highlighted, in a different pastel colour.

Above the houses, looking over the city, was Dvor Castle. It was constructed from imposing stone blocks. High turreted walls were pierced by narrow archer slits.

More than thirty years on, the castle still bore scars from Dvor's more recent history. 'Flowers', as locals called them, artillery pockmarked the outer walls. Railgun shots fired during the city's time as centrestage of someone else's war.

Virtually all other remnants of those times were removed. The flowers were left purposely as a reminder to locals and visitors alike. Unavoidable warning signs, pointing to the lows humanity is capable of reaching.

The city was warm and vibrant despite being known for its harsh winters. At the height of its cold spells, the Lacka would freeze over so hard that children would spill out on the river, skating and skimming stones.

Today, the city's proximity to Flavia as well as its rich cultural and social scene made it a destination of choice for gatherings of leaders, artists, and fun-seekers in the Balkania Core. In early Spring, the cold was only a recent memory. Nevertheless, a crisp morning breeze ran along the river.

Ashok's capsule eased to a halt on the bazaar side of Lacka. He could see his team already ascending a boulevard leading up to Dvor Castle on the other side.

Content he had successfully ditched his entourage, Ashok disembarked the Glider and wandered into the market. Citizens of Flavia were by now accustomed to his walks around the city, but the residents of Dvor were always a little puzzled, to say the least.

Ashok strode through the streets. He wore a white hemp tunic, crumpled linen trousers and tan brown sandals. People stopped in their tracks, looked over, then pretended to go about their day whilst keeping one eye squared on the peculiar visitor.

"Emperor," an old fruit seller waved from her stall, "welcome to Dvor."

"In Flavia it's illegal to use that term." Sensing the lady didn't catch his joke, he continued, "Ashok is fine, as is pretty much anything beginning with A."

"My apologies, sir, but this isn't Flavia." The lady smiled and shook his hand.

"You're very right. Could you please fill a basket with some strawberries?"

The lady picked out several large handfuls of ruby-red fruit and placed them in a woven basket.

His quota of clumsy social interaction concluded for the day, Ashok tapped a token at the side of the lady's stall before she had a chance to protest. Thanking her he walked deeper into the bazaar.

Ashok hadn't visited the city in a few months. Like a guide dog, he followed the crooked streets to his destination: a small coffee shop tucked away on the side of a dead-end passage. The café's open facade was exactly wide enough for two people to pass each other. A decorated wool rug was thrown between inside and outside, shop and street. Together with the smell of freshly roasted beans it was a strong sign that the place was open for business.

Upon noticing Ashok, a large man with a peppered grey beard emerged from the shop. Sweaty from the roaster's heat he dusted off his plump hands in a thick woven apron. Without saying a word, the man grabbed Ashok, embracing him.

"As soon as I heard silence in the bazaar, I suspected you might be to blame," his voice boomed, still not letting go. "Last time, half the town came to interrogate me after you left."

"I think you'll find I've been more than subtle." Ashok emerged from the hold. Placing the strawberries on the rug, they sat and reclined to one side.

"Very subtle. Did you come in that oversized disco ball again?"

"I'll have you know the Glider has revolutionised travel around the world, Sabil."

"It has, I know. It doesn't mean you look like less of a prick parking it in the middle of town." Sabil laughed like a child at his own witticism. He disappeared inside.

Ashok looked around at locals and tourists rambling through the old streets. He felt at home here, merging into the echoes of the busy market.

Sabil emerged embalmed in a fresh layer of coffee scent. He carried two metal cups and a small plate.

"Strawberries are great, but I think we both prefer some lokum."

Ashok paid a passing thought to the dessert he had consumed a little while back. He grabbed at the gummy cubes, powdered with icing sugar.

"What brings you here this time?" asked Sabil as he leaned next to Ashok against the rug.

"The usual retinue of people and topics."

"You remade an entire city over in Flavia, but you can't seem to keep away from here, can you?"

"What can I say, I have a thing for lokum." Ashok reached for the plate again.

"We have a lot more here than the lokum..."

****

Full of more sugar than fruit Ashok climbed the hill leading to Dvor Castle. Smiling and full of energy, Ashok was ready to tackle the afternoon's main event.

Flanking each side of the boulevard, long before the castle entrance were two companies of ceremonial soldiers, rail-rifles by their side.

The men and women stood to attention in full parade uniform: oak brown woollen trousers with a thick wool jacket in eggshell white. Electrum piping along the edges matched domed buttons inlaid with the Dvor eagle. Round pressed wool hats topped with an ostrich feather completed the outfit.

Not the best year-round attire Ashok thought.

As soon as he passed by the first soldiers, they raised their cumbersome rifles in salute. A choreographed wave rippled out to the castle gates.

Ashok strode through the rigid columns. They stood like cypress trees flanking a country road. Saluting the troops, he smiled and made his way to the castle entrance.

Feeling inspired, ten men before the end he stopped. Facing down the assembled lines he raised his voice. "What a beautiful welcome to your beautiful city!"

Starting from the gate, the soldiers lowered their guns... A wave ran back down the columns in salute.

"May I ask why you're haranguing my soldiers, Ashok?" A stern voice came from the entrance gate.

"Aren't they my soldiers too?"

"If you continue teaching them to drop discipline, they might end up no one's soldiers."

"It's great to see you too, Irnes." Ashok smiled, "I do sometimes wonder why we still have soldiers."

Tall and composed, Irnes looked on at Ashok. She wore a floor-length indigo peacoat matching her piercing eyes. "We'll have time for ponderings later. This will be a difficult meeting. Let's go inside and get started."

****

The meeting room was compact, almost cosy. A heavy oak table sat in the middle. Nine plush red chairs were placed, equally spaced, around it. Boxing the room were four flush stone walls adorned with a mix of old and modern canvases. It was an attempt to convey the city's history as well as its current cultural standing.

Ashok and Irnes walked in. A group of six stood around the circular table, talking in small groups. Ashok walked around, greeting them individually, a handshake for some, an embrace for others. When he finally made it back to his seat, he nodded at Irnes.

"Thank you for being here today, let's take our seats." Irnes pointed to the red chairs.

The group sat. A crystal chandelier illuminated the room in a golden glow.

Gathered around the table were the leaders of Seven Cores. Together they represented nine thousand individual city states. As mayor of Dvor, Irnes was hosting the day's meeting. She looked over at an empty seat, "As per protocol, a seat was reserved for the head of the Kap, however, she is not in attendance today."

In front of each guest was a crystal jug coupled with a tall tumbler. Irnes slowly poured herself a glass of water and continued.

"Ashok, of course, from Balkania,

Arun from the Indus,

Ra-bia from the Western Steppe,

Khin from Oceania,

Matias from Patagonia,

Yana from Sibir and Kala from the Continental Core."

"We have a long agenda today, but two topics dominate." Irnes first looked toward Ashok. "An update on the mission," and then to Kala, "and the advance of Contained AB."

Irnes looked to Ashok. "Please update us on mission preparations."

"Hi everyone, after our setback several months ago-"

"Catastrophic failure, you mean?" Kala interrupted.

"Following normal setbacks three months ago, we have conducted a long list of tests to make sure all systems are ready for launch, sticking to the three-month launch." Ashok looked towards Kala who cast a commanding figure even when sat in a plush red chair. "The mission is ready. All that remains now is to prepare the world for a show."

"I fear exactly what kind of show that will be," Kala cut in again.

"Achieving a goal which has been within our dreams but beyond our grasp since the dawn of humanity," Ra-bia added in a light melodic voice.

"After leaving the facility at Kamrun, the craft, Orus 5, will travel through space for sixteen hours before approaching Hela at a little over a mile per second," Ashok visualised every step, "the landing thruster will activate, slowing Orus from this great speed, touching down softly on the moon near the Tethys Ocean.

"The surface mission will then commence. It will last for seven days and eighteen hours. During that time, the Explorer will conduct over two hundred experiments.

"Research items have been submitted by states in all of your Cores throughout the preceding years. The list of desired operations was considered in its entirety by BISE and a prioritised checklist was drawn up in alignment with the main mission objective."

"After so long simply getting there feels like more than enough of a mission objective," Ra-bia smirked.

"It feels that way at times, but the mission will take us to a new level of unity and understanding."

"Do we know if the explorer will be able to breathe on the surface for the entirety of the mission?" Asked Khin.

"We're almost entirely sure he can."

Kala laughed, "Well, there's nothing more reassuring than that answer, Ashok."

"Probes sent to date have confirmed an atmosphere very similar to ours. They have shown a consistent, stable environment, able to sustain human life without breathing apparatus or pressure gear. The Nuwa probe is still in constant orbit around Hela."

"And the anomalies?"

"We have sent a total of three probes, two in orbit and one on the surface. Several years ago, Nuwa saw several rapid spikes of methane, spaced a few minutes and miles apart. Those spikes have never been seen again. Hence almost entirely sure. In any case, there will be enough air on the lander as a backup. Is that a better answer, Kala?"

"Our safety concerns for the mission as a whole have been relayed to BISE. We want the Contained dyno included in the mission."

Ashok poured himself a glass, offering water to Matias and Ra-bia, sat on either side of him. "My feeling is that safety isn't your top concern with that request."

"It achieves two goals at the same time, if that's what you mean. The Contained dyno makes the mission safer and demonstrates to a global public that the technology is also safe and stable."

"What's the function of this dyno again?" Matias asked.

"As they are, the landing modules are difficult to control. If the timing between pulses is off by just a little there will either be too much or too little thrust." Kala raised his empty glass above the table. "We have designed an alternative suppressant module based on our Contained technology to smooth out the pulses." He slowly lowered it towards the surface. "Think of it like the torus in the old fusion reactors... It can either constrain the reaction or add thrust at will." He placed the glass gently on the table.

"Perhaps we should stick to the order of topics," Irnes tapped her agenda.

"The two go hand in hand," Kala pushed ahead. "Thirty years ago, we made a commitment to the Core System. We laid the groundwork for this mission. We did it in the belief that it will unify our brittle new world. As time has gone on, we have drifted further and further into hegemony."

His gaze circled the table. "AB promises to transform our world in the same way our ancestors first harnessed the power of the sun. We must do this in a way which benefits everyone. It should be open and accessible for all, not squirreled away in some BISE lab. If we fail to go down a collective path, the world could descend into chaos once more. Everything we've dedicated our lives to will be lost."

"Are you done?" Ashok asked, slouching in his chair. "It feels like your argument is ever so slightly hollow, given Nussa's desire to push Contained. We want the same things, Kala, but it isn't there yet. It's not safe for widespread use. We would be putting lives at risk."

"Your attitude is almost insolent to the system *you* designed, Ashok. You have to see what's at stake here. This goes beyond energy or control. Our whole system is at risk. The abundance we've become so used to requires an ever-increasing demand for energy. AB can solve that. We need to propagate the technology out through the Cores, to the people."

"I see it perfectly clearly, Kala." Ashok raised from his slumber. "We need to act. But this isn't our solution. The few experiments done have shown Contained to be an inferior, unstable energy source. Our current approach is sound. The technology has been proven in the Gliders. Orus will be the next step. With a little more work it will easily provide all of the energy we need. Then we will roll it out in every community in the world."

"Currently it is little more than a toy, a showpiece." Kala leaned back in his chair, "There are no indications you are capable of scaling to provide sustained energy. Sure, it's an impressive showpiece but we don't even know exactly how it works yet."

"Exactly why your Contained push is so ridiculous!"

"No, Ashok! I want the people to see it, to improve it, wherever they are, be it in a Core Capital or a dinky village. We can all understand how devastating a fall back into chaos would be. I cannot risk that. A thousand states have placed their safety in my hands."

"What risk? The world is safer than ever"

"You're blinded by your Hubris." Kala looked to the other leaders. "We see our people, we feel their concerns. A pressure is building below the surface. We cannot ignore it."

"I receive citizens from all of Oceania who say they've heard rumours." Khin spoke up. "Many of them fear the future. For the first time since the start of peace we have uncertainty. The mission binds us together, our constant need for energy abundance threatens to tear us apart." Khin looked over to Ashok. "Abundance is great, as long as it can be sustained. People have started taking it for granted."

"I don't undervalue the risks," Ashok took a sip of water. "Too little time has passed to rely on stability and peace. I believe we can provide an alternate solution: one which doesn't involve risking lives to cut corners. There are researchers, engineers, chemists, you name it, working hard in laboratories throughout our Cores. They will provide a lasting, sustainable solution."

"Too late, Ashok, all too late." Kala leaned on his hefty hands, spreading them out on the table. "We need a solution now. Something we can touch and show to the people. Not a maybe jotted on the chalkboard of some institute, something tangible and real to give them confidence in the future. Give the Contained dyno a chance. Include that small module in the mission. If the scientists devise an alternative solution, we will never mention it again."

"Why is this module so important, Kala? I understand its function, but what does it matter, really?" Yana looked towards Kala.

"We need to start from somewhere. All of you know that change takes time. The mission will stay in people's minds for a long time. Stories will be passed down to those too young, or yet to be born – 'yes, I was there, I saw'. It is an opportunity to spark change in people's minds, in their imagination."

"You know I'm firmly against it," Ashok pushed his glass to one side. "Our current path is solid. The mission will show that. As soon as AB is ready to scale it will be rolled out across the world.

****

The Council leaders stood to say their goodbyes. A round of handshakes later, Ashok looked at his chrono. Eight o'clock. Time for a drink.

Emerging from the room, the group walked through the castle's imposing corridors, their steps muted by a heavy red carpet.

Ashok nudged through the crowd, "Kala, let's grab a drink."

"Can we do it another time? My team is waiting to leave."

"I'm sure they'll want to have a drink somewhere, too. The Glider literally pilots itself. Come."

Outside the main gate, the leaders gathered with their teams for a brief press session and group photo before another round of handshakes.

As the clustered groups walked down the hill, Ashok and Kala headed back towards the castle. Passing through the main gate, they soon took a turn down a sparsely lit passage.

Ashok's chief of staff, Mito, and Kala's chief of staff, Frey, insisted two guards follow at some distance as they meandered through Dvor castle's inner walls.

"Are you abducting me, Ashok, trying to force submission? We already took the vote. It seems a little pointless."

"When was the last time we did this? Must be at least five years. Come, a bit further down we'll get through the walls and into the old town. There's a funky place around the corner."

A few steps later they reached a heavy wooden door. It filled the corridor. Pushing the door open, the men found themselves on a dark cobbled street. It hugged the walls of Dvor Castle on one side and was lined with high stone buildings on the other. Walking on, they left two confused guards who had been stationed on the outside of the door.

Two minutes down the street, they came to an unassuming stone portal cut into the rocks which formed the castle's foundations. A distant flicker of candles illuminated a tunnel ahead. Kala looked unimpressed.

"Come on, through here." Ashok ordered his guards not to follow them and, begrudgingly, Kala asked his to comply.

Entering the tunnel, Kala ducked to fit through the entrance. Inside was a thin path kindly borrowed from the rock. It was like a passageway to another world. Odd irregular steps raised and lowered their trail.

After a hundred feet through the rock, they emerged to a surprising sight.

A rocky outcrop projected out from the base of the castle; A ledge no more than thirty feet wide and at least two hundred long. It had been adopted as a natural terrace overlooking the city.

People gathered in small groups on thatched mats, enjoying a drink as the hot day was dissolved by a cool evening breeze.

They sat on a mat by the end of the ledge. Heat absorbed by the rock from the day's sun still emanated through the rough covering.

An unassuming waiter came beside them, "Welcome, what can I get you?"

"Two whiskies, please. Sinmi Quarter Casks."

The waiter disappeared.

The men looked across the flickering lights. It was a clear night.

The moon's feint blue glow covered the city.

"All over the world, we used to know the best hidden bars." Ashok let out a childish smile.

Kala turned, "You're right. We did. It feels like another life."

"Do you think it was simpler then?" Ashok focused on his watch. The moon reflected off of the crystal. He polished it gently with his sleeve.

"Quite the opposite. We didn't realise quite how big of a world it is."

"Maybe because we kept sneaking off to bars."

"The planet had just emerged from a century of conflict, we were emboldened, young and determined to build. Your daughter wasn't even born."

The waiter returned with their drinks on a shabby tray. The silver plating had worn through to a patchwork of dull tin. Two thick crystal tumblers balanced in the middle.

"Cheers, Kala." Ashok raised his glass. "We might not be as young as we once were, but I don't think we've lost any of our edge."

"Perhaps not. Time has changed our outlook though. I still believe we share a common vision. We differ in the path to it."

"Maybe. At least we don't differ in our whiskey."

FIVE

"What is life?" Adroa sat under the shade of a centuries-old oak tree on a slight hill, overlooking Dharma. "What do you believe life is? Have you ever stopped to ponder? Many have. It is perhaps one of the oldest still unanswered questions."

"There is no single right way to answer it. The answer is in itself, a reflection of our beliefs." Sirem spoke out. She sat within a small circle surrounding Adroa.

"That's true," continued Adroa. "If life is the phenomena of being alive, then perhaps the old priests of Saphan will have a suitable answer for you. Their scriptures, written out by hand one generation to the next, describe our souls descending into our bodies from the heavenly moon along a diamond path."

"However, if life is about context then the Continental prophet and poet Simar might appeal. Living in the forested town of Kasai near the Great Trade Road, she described life as a single page within a thick book. Simar asked her followers to consider their actions because she believed everything we do leaves a mark."

"All of these stories have always seemed a little too flowery, for me." Noake turned to look down the hill towards Dharma, bustling in the distance.

"Our beliefs change with time, Noake." Adroa stole his gaze. "At least, they evolve. What's your favourite story?"

"As the sciences became central to our lives, it has had an impact on our beliefs, too. Personally, I side with the mathematician Aaron. He lived in the mountain city of Giro on the West-Adriatic coast. Less than a century ago he simply stated that 'life is a multidimensional object passing through four-dimensional space, experienced by the rest of us in three dimensions."

Adroa looked across the small class. "Mathematicians have a knack for simple explanations, don't they? Even the most emotive topics."

The students laughed.

"What's your favourite explanation of life?" Sirem asked.

"I could go on for hours and the day is getting late," Adroa smiled. "I believe that the truth contains a dash of each story. Most of all, I believe that for us to understand what life is, we need to be prepared to completely change our definition of life itself."

"In what way?"

"All of our current definitions focus on our physical senses, our human interpretation. I believe we have to abstract ourselves from these senses in order to even ask the question." Adroa continued. "The story of the Saphic priests is, however, interesting because it is not unique. All early religions placed the moon in a godly role."

"It's not difficult to see why," Sirem interjected. "Looking up during a clear night, without the need for any magnification, the intricate details of our celestial neighbour are easy to see."

"True," answered Adroa. "Oceans, rivers, forests, clouds and even rainstorms. Rhodinia, the moon's largest landmass, can be seen plainly. Rhodinia is blanketed by rich, green vegetation. Some of the other landmasses even end in faintly perceptible whiskers of golden beaches. Rivers run through the lands and into the main body of water, The Tethys Ocean. A snowy oval covers the south pole."

Noake joined, "I guess humanity, in the dawn of our existence, can be excused for believing the moon was a reflection of earth. Every time early people looked up they would see a familiar sight."

He drew two circles next to each other in the soil. One was larger than the other. A dotted line connected them. "After so many millennia of wondering, sometime soon we will finally find out whether those early civilizations were right in their belief that life started on the moon and came down to earth."

"It will definitely take some of the romance away though." Sirem looked up towards the sky.

"What romance? This is one of the most important questions we've ever asked."

"I can see what she means, Noake." Adroa jumped in. "As our world has developed, we have definitely lost some of the mystery and wonder. It's one of the reasons I like to keep the stories from our ancestors alive. As science has evolved, some of those myths have turned out to be rooted in a grain of truth." Adroa touched the soil around Noake's drawing. "Perhaps others are yet to be explored. Some other civilizations believed the moon was a reflection of the earth in the sky. This explains why early navigators used Hela as a map. Ill-chosen, as you've said in the past Noake, but effective."

"As the years have gone by, our understanding has improved." Noake doubled down. He drew a slanted line through the smaller circle. "The moon spins on an axis slightly tilted away from Earth. The synchronous spin between the Earth and Hela means that a day on the moon is exactly as long as a day down here. We know a lot about Hela."

"And so much we have no idea about." Sirem smiled. "How the moon's atmosphere formed as well as how it manages to hold on to it are questions still left unanswered."

"Hela has been a guide to humanity for all of history," Adroa stood. "She holds mysteries we're not even aware of. As we answer one, three new ones will emerge."

"Sounds like our classes won't be ending any time soon," Noake dusted himself off and the class walked down the hill towards the town.

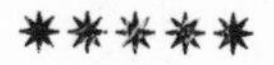

THE KAP OVER DHARMA

purely symbolic shrine anywhere on this planet. Everything has to have a purpose."

She continued forward as they left the centre of Dharma, nearing The Kap campus. "The Morel Temple, outside modern Nussa is an interesting example. Built two millennia ago, its walls are angled to line up with key moments in the complex dance performed by the Earth and moon around the sun."

"Today it looks like an ancient attempt at art deco." Polim, walking at the back of the group, chuckled. Another student gave him a nudge.

"More importantly, it is still accurate," Sirem glanced back through the class.

The group walked through the sculpted marble gates of the Kap. The gardens were filled with small clusters of students and their teachers discussing all manner of subjects in the rising heat.

Adroa took them to a carefully cut lawn next to a square pond. The group sought shade under the umbrella of a willow tree.

"But it was more than a temple." Noake watched over to the pond in the hope of spotting a carp. "Morel was a hub, a link in a long chain of communication and collaboration."

"It wasn't all happy families," Polim lay on his back, propping up on his elbows. "They enjoyed their fair share of conflict."

"They did," Adoa looked on at the other groups of students. "But that focus on communication kick-started our reliance on the rest of the world."

The group walked through the streets of Dharma. While the town was tightly packed, its mountainside perch meant that every shop, every teahouse was bathed in sunlight.

"The mission forms a natural step forward in our species-old craving to understand the moon."

"It's a large step forward, admittedly. Ever since we lay down on the great Steppes of the Continent and stared up at her, we wanted to know *more*. Soon this drive for knowledge took astronomy and, by happy extension, math as its tools. From antiquity these two fields were as important to early kingdoms as the size of their armies."

"Sometimes more so. The ability to predict became an instrument as well as a symbol of power." Sirem was originally from Meda, a valley city ringed by hills on a high mountain plateau a thousand miles north of Pacha.

"The tradition of Shoba arose East of the Indus around 2500 years ago before spreading around the world." She continued as the group weaved through the hubbub towards the Kap campus. "When two kings had a quarrel – say one was quite fond of a certain valley and the other was less than keen to relinquish it – they pitched their army of astronomers in combat instead of their soldiers."

"In Shoba, they would agree on some celestial phenomena, say an eclipse, and then 'battle' to predict exactly when it will occur."

"Predictions were made. The winner got their way," Noake jumped in. "Gives a nice predictability to conflict, doesn't it?"

Adroa turned towards the young students. "Pragmatism is a strong trait of ours. You would be hard pressed to find a

"It is impressive, when you think about it." Sirem glanced over at the pond to see what Noake was so interested in. "Archaeology has shown that our long, high tides made it difficult for coastal civilisations to form. The few that did learnt to harness Hela's power well before we knew how she moved the seas and oceans."

"This early exchange of information enabled those civilizations which did develop to thrive." Noake had yet to see a carp. "Sunk into the shallow water, paddles the size of canoes pushed and pulled on pistons connected to gears and belts which in turn powered millstones on the land."

"The wheat they ground into flour came from other communities, often far inland." Adroa covered her head with a linen scarf from her shoulders. "Complex networks were established between kingdoms of the interior and those on the coasts along the Great Trade Roads."

Sirem also felt the heat. She went over to the pond to splash a handful of water over her arms. "Over time, many kingdoms specialised by trade. Some grew crops, some processed them, and others supplied tools. Those in-between either aided transport or provided rudimentary financial services to keep the system moving along."

Sirem reached her hands in, as soon as she disturbed the water, a speckled orange and white carp darted away.

"There he was!" Noake pointed and Sirem shot him an apologetic smile.

"... So, they had half-wars?" Polim turned on his side to face the pond.

"Disputes would arise, but it seems they had to be settled quickly. No one kingdom could survive on its own and they knew it." Adroa looked on as an emerald and white hummingbird perched on a branch above her. "It is said that a message from the court of Saphan could reach Nussa, deep in The Great Continent, in half a day: a distance of twelve hundred miles."

Noake took the word. "Communication and trade also led to travel and exchange. The constant movement of humanity meant that then, as now, no one race dominated a given region of the world. Tribes, if such can be defined, identified along creeds. Farmers would worship a god of the land, fishermen and millworkers a god of the seas, and blacksmiths a god of fire. Many modern states still reference these deities in their crests and flags."

"It would be fair to say that a direct result of this history is us sat here, under this tree." Adroa observed the bird. It sat as if wanting to join the class. "Above all of these local deities stood Hela. Under many guises and names from continent to continent, the world shared one god. I would like to take a tangent and tell a story from my childhood..."

The god, Orus, ruled over the earth. Every inch of this planet belonged to him. He spent his days wandering the lands, seas and deserts, marvelling at his dominion.

Respected by his people, Orus brought rains whenever the land became dry. His long, regular tides drove mill wheels and brought ships safely back to shore.

The earth was a peaceful and prosperous place. The people thought Orus was content, the ground often rumbled like a dog rolling over in the afternoon sun.

But Orus was sad. His people were happy, but he had no one to share his kingdom with. For far too long, he'd wandered the earth alone.

One day, as morning broke, he lay atop a snow-covered mountain. He stared up at the sky as the sun rose. As it burnt through the clouds, the moon appeared above the Western horizon.

In the crisp morning light, he gazed at the distant snaking rivers. Their glistening lapis veins flowed into the moon's seas and oceans. Her lands were green and lush. Only a silk wisp of clouds stretched across the surface.

Then he saw her, standing by a shore, all those thousands of miles away. Hela, he called her, goddess of the moon. In that moment he became obsessed.

Though he was a god, he was merely the god of Earth. Try as he might, Orus couldn't leave and reach her. Each morning, he could see her there, in the distance.

His patience depleted, Orus became angry. He picked up a stone and threw it into the sky. The stone turned out to be a gem. It stuck in the sky. He could jump barely high enough to touch it.

If he couldn't jump from the earth to Hela, he could build a bridge to her.

The next hundred years he scoured the planet for every gemstone he could find. Nothing else mattered, he had to get to her.

Orus gathered his gems, first in a small pile, then a mound. Finally, a tall mountain made of glistening stones.

His people rarely saw him. They had been abandoned. Crops failed when the rains didn't come. Ships were lost as the tides became uneven. Orus didn't notice.

He had finally collected all of the gems in the world. Picking up the mountain of stones in one go, Orus took a step back and, like a fisherman casting his net, he threw them into the sky.

The stones scattered across the heavens, laying a shimmering path straight to the moon. Finall,y she would be his.

Two days went past until he saw her coming, gliding along the diamond bridge. They met in a valley, green with spring grass, dotted with pine trees, infused with the smell of flowers.

Orus struggled to find the right words to say. Before he had a chance to open his mouth, Hela spoke.

"I've been watching you for a hundred years. Why would you harm the most beautiful thing in the sky?"

Orus was confused, "Harm how? All I have done is try to reach you."

"All you have done is cause hardship to your people and pain to the planet. The fields are dry, the seas are violent. Every day I look towards the earth and cry."

Hela turned and left, drifting back along the sapphire bridge, leaving Orus alone again.

SIX

"A very good morning to all of our viewers. We have a special guest with us today. Responsible for taking us to Hela, Ayla, Deputy Mission Director at BISE!"

"Thank you, Laaro, it's a pleasure to be here."

A row of bright lights pointed straight at her as she shuffled in her seat. The studio was cavernous and cold. *Television*, Ayla thought, *is a curious experience*. On the monitors at home, people see an intimate exchange.

The reality is far from intimate. Two-dozen crew hurried about a cavernous room. Some positioning set pieces for upcoming interviews, others prepping guests and edited scripts.

Yet, in amongst this frantic activity, it was somehow still two people having a conversation.

"Ayla, my dear. It's been a few months since we last had a chance to chat."

"Nearly six months, that's right." Ayla wore a loose cotton blouse tucked into her favourite blue cotton trousers. She assumed they wouldn't be caught on camera but wanted to wear them regardless.

A morning show, the set resembled a rural country kitchen and living room. Plastic vines crept along stucco walls punctured by portico windows. Laaro could wake the drowsiest viewer.

"Our last conversation wasn't exactly positive," Laaro dipped his head. He wore a white silk shirt with an oversized rose-piped collar. His head perched neatly atop the folds. It was topped by a mushroom of chestnut hair. Regardless of tone or topic, Laaro always carried an infectious cheeky smile. It was that smile which brought millions of viewers every day.

"Problems inevitably arise when – "

"But today is different. Today we have good news, exciting news!"

"Indeed. The mission is ready. We only have some final preparations to make before the launch next week."

Ayla wondered whether she should drink the coffee placed on a wicker table between her and her host. No one said whether it is a prop or it is real. Caution to the wind. Picking it up, she sipped. Yep. It was as real as lukewarm TV coffee can be.

"Isn't our coffee delightful?" Laaro exclaimed. "Tell us what we can expect."

"The best," Ayla quickly placed the cup back on its saucer, nearly knocking it over. "The mission will last a week and a half. After leaving earth, the Orus 5 will reach the moon in sixteen hours."

"Not eighteen, not fourteen?" Laaro taunted.

"Sixteen. We want to make it easy for you to plan broadcasts along the way."

"Love it! We'll be watching every step of the way."

"Once there, Orus will separate into two parts. A module called the Nest will stay in orbit while a lander will descend. Then the Explorer will take his first step on to Hela's surface. After setting up a base, over the following week he will run hundreds of experiments. As well as the tasks set by institutes from all seven Cores there are more than thirty experiments chosen by the public."

"Now," Laaro clasped his hands. He brought his index fingers to a point. "You have some news for us, don't you?" A flop of hair fell out of place. He blew it back without flinching.

"Do I?"

"Don't toy with me. The world is waiting. Who will be the first person to step on Hela?" He moved to the edge of his seat, pinching his trouser legs. The matching rose silk flowed through his fingers.

"There are plenty of cameras on board, wait a week and you'll see when he steps out."

"Don't you dare, Ayla, tell me, tell us, right now! Will it be Tomias? Will you watch as your partner walks on lunar soil, cannonballs into a lunar lake, swings from a lunar tree?"

"Glad it's clear we're going to the moon." Ayla raised her cup again as Laaro edged closer. "The Council have selected ... Jonah to lead the mission." She could hear gasps and murmurs from the studio crew. She was briefly reminded of her surroundings.

"Wow! Jonah! How exciting! A native son of Nussa!"

"Jonah is an exemplary commander. He'll make us all proud."

"To remind our viewers, Captain Jonah was born and raised in Nussa before studying aeronautics and biomechanics at The Kap in Saphan. It is there that he met Captain Tomias. The two later moved to Flavia, becoming BISE's lead Explorers-in-training."

"You have no idea how much training they've been put through."

"I am sure you haven't been easy on them, Ayla. Are you disappointed that it won't be Tomias taking those first steps?"

"We've been working on this mission for so long. The world has been working toward this dream for so long. Those first steps will be taken by every man, woman and child on this planet."

"How poetic. You're very right. Jonah. Exciting. We have to get him here."

"He's all yours. After the mission," she winked.

"What? Noooo, I want him here nooow!" Laaro stomped. "Fine. One last question for you. Especially as you're sending our boy up there. There have been a lot of technical problems with the mission. Have they been fixed? Is he safe?"

"All systems have been checked and re-checked. We have back-up systems and back-up systems for the back-up systems," Ayla looked straight into the camera. "At the same time, we're launching a craft into the unknown using new technology. As much as we prepare, there's only one way to see if we've done our homework."

"You're a tough one, Ayla. That's why we've entrusted so much to you. Thank you for coming on the show today and sharing the thrilling news."

******

Nussa was an old capital. It formed naturally over many millennia. Much of its layers were still preserved.

The Central Broadcast Building was right in the city's centre. Unlike the grand surrounding architecture, it consisted of nothing more than a faceless concrete cube with an equally uninspired office tower affixed on top. The building's exterior was in stark contrast to the colourful world held within.

As she left, Ayla decided to take a quick walk around, stopping to pick up a bottle of wine for the evening. The Flavia Core Residence had insisted on sending a Glider. This gave her two extra hours not sat in a Tube.

Nussa was hot. Even in autumn it was a lot to take. The sprawling city was saved by its greenery. Each and every street had a row of perky shrubs. A tree here, a bush there or even a desert flower placed perhaps deliberately by town planners, perhaps randomly by hot winds from the interior.

Many of the streets were partially surfaced. Pavements were all patterned with traditional local mosaics. They formed long, intersecting geometric waves. Many of the streets themselves, especially side-streets, were covered in a sturdy grass found only in that region.

City blocks looked like islands, surrounded by ribbons of light green connecting to parks like canals flowing into the seas.

Despite its informal cosiness, Nussa was an imperial capital. Public buildings were grand, visible along designated lines of sight which defined everything from street directions to rooftop height.

Even prior to the Core system, Nussa was the capital of the largest nation in the world. It was a regional seat of power for the better part of two millennia.

The city, and its people, had quickly adapted to their new role as the hub of an entire continent.

While Flavia focused on the sciences, Nussa specialised in manufacture and engineering. Ayla spent four years as a student in the city. The Kap campus was another island of stone, surrounded by green, and lapped by the bustle of a thousand cafes, bars, sounds and conversations.

She walked along one of the city's green arteries. A couple, ten or twenty paces ahead, walked barefoot through the emerald turf.

Turning a corner, she smiled. There it was. The little wine shop hadn't changed a bit. No sign hung above its entrance. None was necessary. The shop stood at the end of an acute intersection of two side streets, tucked in from the city's main boulevard.

A homage to its contents, the teak door followed the corner's curve. It bulged at its centre like a barrel. Inside, three thick limestone walls were covered in teak posts. Drilled at an angle with a bottleneck lodged in each hole.

Ayla ducked in from the mid-morning heat.

"Princess, it has been some time!" A gentle giant loomed next to a small wooden counter.

"Ha. Hello, Hallough, how have you been?"

"Same old, I can't complain. We have lovely wines, as always, and we have lovely people coming in to take them, sometimes." His chubby cheeks were peppered with dimples.

"Smooth, as always."

His eyes lit up, "Let me show you something interesting."

Mildly hunched and somehow wearing a wool cardigan in the heat, Hallough had the appealing spark of a career salesman in love with his product.

"A few years back a friend of mine, Tisa, bought a crumbling caravansary not far from the desert's edge. Turned out its wells were still full. A thick underground aquifer. Mad as a cat, she decided to make a winery around the old inn." He stepped behind his counter, resting on it with one hand while bending down to a cardboard box. "The Verbesh Winery. This is their first harvest."

Ayla peered into the box, "I'll take the case!"

"If only it were that simple," Hallough smiled. "She gave me strict instructions. At most, I am to sell two bottles to each of my favourite customers. He said, 'if they want more, they'll have to go to Verbesh."

"So, as well as being one of your favourite customers I also happen to be one of the luckiest."

Hallough placed two bottles in a woven bag as Ayla tapped a token on the side of his counter.

"How are people here, Hallough?"

"Well, Ayla, happy as always. The sun is out, people are happy. Everyone is looking forward to the launch."

"And below the happy surface?

"Always curious." He winked, "People are well. It seems like we have been waiting for this mission for so long, sometimes we forget why so much focus is on it and not on other troubles before us."

"What kind of troubles?" Ayla took the bag from the counter.

"Tisa, for example, yes, she had a dream to make a winery, but she could have done that anywhere. She chose to because there's a village, Nyore, near the caravansary. The people there don't want for food or water, but they are afflicted."

"How?"

"They have no hopes or dreams, no vision or desire for the future. Nyore was a village right on the frontier, a harsh place between life and death. Now they are like satiated cattle, lurching from one day to the next. Any spark they once had is gone." Hallough leaned over the counter, "Having everything isn't enough. People need a spark; we need a reason to dream."

"Poetic, Hallough," Ayla explored the wines on display as she spoke, "but I find it hard to believe. There are so many challenges, so much mystery, so many problems to solve."

"For you, perhaps. We all live in our own little bubbles. Sometimes it's hard to see. Properly see our neighbours." Hallough raised himself and followed her to the door. "It was so nice to see you. Do come again when you're next in town."

"Thank you, Hallough, I'll see you soon."

"And good luck, Ayla. Good luck."

******

"Did you see the interview?" Frey asked.

"Ayla has grown. More every time I see her," Kala looked ahead.

"What do you think?"

"They're putting on a good show, I hope they're ready to deliver on it."

They stood on a wide terrace. It opened onto the lush grounds of Nussa's Core Imperial Residence. The wide two-storey ochre brick building framed a row of arched windows. Each window was surrounded by a thin white wooden frame, doubling as a door to the encircling terrace.

Few Core leaders used the term 'empire'. It was seen as clumsy and out-dated, an inaccurate representation of the post-Collapse system. Kala was an exception.

Possibly referencing Nussa's pre-existing status as an Imperial Capital, he never dropped the title.

The city had been the centre of an empire covering the best part of a huge continent. While it was an empire built by coercion and force, it still carried meaning for its citizens.

"A number of our state heads are voicing concerns." Frey wandered along the terrace, his wiry physique dwarfed by Kala.

"I understand their concerns." Kala flexed his wrist and leant on the window frame. "We must show patience. What results are coming out of the experiment?"

"Contained is even more stable, Sir. Once we have perfected it, it will provide readily available, simple to harness, inexhaustible energy. It will be more flexible yet more powerful than Flavia's AB. We need to expand the team."

"Ever more stable doesn't sound entirely reassuring?" Kala turned toward him.

"Progress is being made every day. We have also been aided by Sheng and his efforts to add the dyno to the lander."

"Just how far have you intervened with Sheng?" Kala stared at Frey.

"Only as far as to ensure we use the mission to test our technology. There is a mutual benefit. The dyno is key to Contained."

"Make sure you maintain the integrity of the Hela mission. We've made a commitment and I want to stick to it."

"Of course, sir. My sole belief is that it is wise to secure a direct benefit for Nussa from the mission."

"Wise is hardly a perfect word. A successful mission will reap benefits for everyone," Kala looked past Frey into the Residence's mature gardens. The palace was set almost exactly in the centre of Nussa. While the grounds were expansive, the feint city hum could always be heard in the background.

"Further research on Contained will take time. Development will take time. We don't have time, sir. We're putting the future of so many at risk."

"Expand your team but do not meddle in BISE's work. I want to see results before we push Ashok any further."

"Of course, sir," Frey withdrew with a satisfied smile.

SEVEN

"How much further?" Frigid river water seeped through Jonah's suit. Every stroke through the rapids was a chore.

"Why do you expect me to know?" Tomias swam ahead. His arms crashed into the water. Arcs of spray flew into the air, reflecting off of the sun like diamonds.

"It looks... it looks like you've done this before." Jonah struggled to get the words out as his thick cotton landing suit weighed down. Physical training was a regular, and arduous, part of the training. The men had to be prepared for any eventuality upon reaching Hela.

"Sooner if you shut up and swim."

Today was a mild eight mile course in the forests behind Mount Rhoda. After several heavy strokes they reached the opposite shore. Tomias raised himself out and turned to give Jonah a hand. A shower of murky water fell to the ground as he stepped on the riverbank. Tired and worn, Jonah still cut a striking figure. The sun accented his muscular body.

"What's the aim of this exercise?"

"Beyond the joys of swimming in a cold river?" Tomias took a deep breath, "Water landing training."

Both of them sat hunched over by the shore.

"Far simpler," Jonah leant back on his hands, "learn to steer the lander so it doesn't fall in the Ocean."

They let out a lax laugh.

"What next?"

"You have the exact same brief as me, look at it... you're the one who should be taking the lead." Tomias straightened his back.

"Do I sense a little jealousy? Feeling like The Council made the wrong choice?" Jonah slipped a wry smile.

"Very funny. I'm sure they went through a rigorous process of flipping the shiniest token they could find."

Jonah opened his mouth in mock shock, "So you are jealous! Don't worry, I'll name some shitty hill after you."

They stood up and started moving. Burdened by their wetsuits they slipped on the riverbank's fine gravel.

"Do make sure it's a big hill."

"I can't guarantee that. On the mission maps I noticed a scraggly mound to the side of a forest similar to this one. Seems about right."

"Good stuff. So generous of you." Tomias waded through thick grass as they made their way towards a tall forest.

"Make sure you pack bars of chocolate in that suit." Tomias pointed to the tallest oak in the forest, "I assume you'll crash into a tree. It's okay, by the time you hoick yourself down, I'll come to the rescue. Try and collect some wood for a fire, I'll bring beer."

"That's a good point, Tom, with all this training they haven't taught us how to brew up there. I should take some hops with me."

"I'm not sure the hopes and dreams of planet Earth will be satisfied watching you brew on the moon."

"You say that, but what if the water is contaminated. It's a tried and tested method of water purification."

"Right, and the hops?"

"Well, they'll make it nice and crisp. Might as well have a good taste."

They dusted off grass and pollen which had stuck to their wet suits and made their way into the forest.

"Focus up, alchy, three miles through this and we're back to base. Haul ass or we'll be late for dinner... Ayla will be harder to handle than this trek."

****

Colonel Rassi waited at the entrance to a partially concealed hut. Seeing the men emerge from the forest, she shouted, "Hurry up, we have work to do."

Training was tough. BISE believed they could never be too prepared. Despite a decade of probes and research, there were far too many unknowns. The only solution was training. To help prepare the Explorers, the institute had recruited a host of former military heroes as trainers.

Rassi stood firm in the face of a series of lingering ailments from distant struggles. She patiently waited for the trainees to take their final steps.

The hut was an easy base for training. It was set in forests and grasslands behind Mount Rhoda. It aimed to simulate the moon terrain as accurately as possible.

In-front of Rassi lay a table covered in a matt black cloth.

"You prepared a picnic for the end of training, thank you so much, Colonel."

"Is your suit dry, Jonah?"

"No, Colonel Rassi."

"Would you like to sprint a mile in your not dry suit, Jonah?"

"No, Colonel Rassi."

"Listen up then. We have one last task for the day," she looked towards the table.

The cloth was stretched flat apart from a lump outlining an unknown object.

"We're confident there are no large mammals on Hela," Rassi trained her gaze on the men. "Though it should be noted that The Natural Sciences Observatory outside Manau has been struggling to explain intermittent noise and gas emission patterns picked up by the surface probe."

"Encouraging," Tomias glanced towards Jonah.

"The noises most likely come from any number of weather sources or geological events."

"What are you building up to?" Jonah grew curious.

"We want you to be prepared, that's all" Rassi removed the cloth, revealing the object below, an elongated silver pebble.

"We're going hunting!" Jonah shouted.

"Jonah!" Rassi turned red. "This is an adapted taser based on a military design you should both be familiar with. Keep it on you at all times."

"I apologise Colonel, I understand. But, but... moon-hunting!" he laughed again.

"For the sake of this mission, Jonah, take it seriously. The world is watching you." Rassi was less than amused.

Rassi waited for him to calm down before continuing, "The last thing we want is for the world to watch as you are killed by some unforeseen danger. The weapon can fire focused pulses or a broader field."

"What is its range?" Jonah examined the cold device.

"The single pulse can reach three hundred feet." Rassi took the taser from his hand. "It is being issued to you in confidence. There should be no mention of its existence during the public mission feed. The consensus is that encounters requiring its use are highly unlikely but you need to be ready for any eventuality. That's why we train. That's why we prepare."

She reached underneath the table and brought out two folders, "The NSO have prepared their requests in this text. Read it. Understand it. They are an important stakeholder in the mission. We will go over the materials next week. Dismissed."

The boys saluted and hurried off, hoping to be on time for their dinner.

Rassi covered the table and headed inside the hut. The old bunker had an intentionally deceptive facade. Its roof consisted of a thick layer of branches, covered in moss and leaves.

The contrasting interior was only given away by a foot-thick concrete door frame cutting into the otherwise natural pile of forest debris.

Inside, the hut was rather sparse. A series of cabinets lined two of the bare concrete walls and a simple wooden desk was placed in the centre. It pointed towards a monitor mounted opposite.

Rassi sat at the desk and activated the monitor.

"Are they prepared? Is Jonah ready?"

"Jonah is still fighting the excitement of being chosen."

"He will calm down."

Rassi opened a copy of the files she had handed to Jonah and Tomias. "There is a section in here about a potential new landing sequence. It doesn't follow our typical approach."

"It is a reserve scenario. Did you hand them the information?"

"I did. I made it clear that it is important."

"Good. It is important that they adhere to them," The wiry silhouette disappeared from the monitor.

****

Jonah lived in a stylish maisonette in Flavia's fashionable Patagonia district. Before joining the mission to Hela, he had been a senior military construction engineer. His move to BISE opened a new chapter away from Nussa.

While Flavia's role as a global centre of science didn't exactly make it a home of design, it was still a global hub. That brought with it a diversity and variety which Nussa lacked.

Jonah's home was clean, organised and planned to the very last detail. Just not by him. Even so, it was the first space he could define as his.

BISE made sure to take care of its Explorers. In their absence, cleaners had polished the apartment and caterers had carefully arranged several platters of food about the home.

Jonah and Tomias stumbled through the door. Jonah headed straight for his shower. On the way he peeled off his damp, grassy uniform and threw it in a corner. Tomias unzipped a hemp duffle bag, spilling the contents onto the floor. He picked up some crumpled clothes and headed to a guest shower.

After some time and a good amount of steam, the two emerged dressed in near-matching baggy white linen shirts and coarse grey linen trousers. Creased from head to toe.

A selection of bites was placed on the balcony dining table. A large cream candle in the middle. Its lit wick was mostly invisible from the still-setting sun.

They headed over to a U-shaped sofa. Plates of exotic fruits had been placed on a low, square table at the centre of the sofa.

As they were about to sit down, the door opened again. Ayla walked through in a hurry, "Am I late?"

"Not even close, TV-star." Tomias walked over and kissed her as she placed her small rucksack on the floor.

She looked at the scruffy figures, their pile of clothes by the door. At least they'd had time to change. In their minds they'd made an effort. "Didn't come across an iron, did you?"

"You don't understand fashion, Ayla. This is the latest trend." Jonah teased holding his arms out so she could get a better look at the whole outfit. "After the mission, you should co-host that show with Laaro," Jonah winked. Ayla walked over and hugged him.

Jonah led them over to the balcony.

"Yes, yes, very funny. We'll get to that." Ayla reached into her bag. "More interestingly… I brought wine!"

Whilst it might not be a capital of fashion, Flavia was definitely a food capital. The city's location at the cross-roads of four or five continents, depending on how you count, brought with it tastes from around the world. Locals experimented with flavours, creating rich and unexpected experiences.

Jonah sat at the end of the dining table with Ayla to his left. Tomias sat next to Ayla so the three could watch the fading sun.

"So, how has the news gone down?" Tomias asked, his eyes fixed on the city.

"About Jonah?" Ayla reached for a spiced oyster as Tomias opened and poured the wine. "Well, overall. It was expected. Nussa provides balance to the weight Flavia holds in the mission. It was the right way to go."

"And because I'm an overall better candidate, obviously!"

Ayla placed a hand on Jonah's thigh and gave him a light pat.

"What about your father, how's he feeling?" Tomias continued after finishing his first glass of wine.

"The same as all of us, he wants to see a craft heading to the moon as soon as possible. On the other hand, Sheng has been very difficult," she continued. "I understand all of the considerations we have to make but I can't help but feel we could have been smarter about our approach."

"He's risk averse, Ayla. It isn't unfathomable to understand his position." Jonah placed a spoonful of ceviche on a crispy tostada.

"We all decide where to strike the balance. He's focused on operational concerns without being able to see the big picture." Ayla took the bowl of ceviche, trying some for herself.

"I've said it before and I'll say it again. It would be so much easier to fake the whole thing and film it in a jungle around Manau or something." Jonah poured another glass of wine for everyone.

"We'd still have to do all of the training, Jonah."

"They wouldn't let us get away without it, yeah."

"And it might be a tough sell to the public if they can see the video but there's no lander up there." Ayla reached for an oyster. She swallowed another sip of the complex desert wine. "This mission feels surreal enough as it is. We could easily fill more than a single novel."

Tomias raised his glass towards Jonah. "A few days and we'll all be watching you."

"Cheers to that!"

They relaxed after a heavy day. The setting sun left a mild orange glow above the horizon. Still hot, a hint of cool air brushed across their skin.

"How was your day, boys?" Ayla focused on a seasoned avocado slice while waiting for an answer.

"Turns out we have a bit of surprise weapons training," Jonah lit up with delight.

"Yes, I thought that might entertain you. Pretty sure we should open the other bottle before you carry on." Ayla reached for the unopened wine. On the way, her hand strayed, undoing a button on Jonah's shirt.

"It looks like Jonah will be not only the first person to walk on the moon but also, the first person to hunt on the moon," Tomias relaxed into his chair.

"Tommy, don't you mock." Ayla waved her finger, tapping Tomias on his nose. With a light swing in the opposite direction, she undid another button on Jonah's shirt.

Tomias pulled her hand to pull her back towards him and gave her a quick kiss.

"It's been a long day. Do you both mind if I take a quick shower?"

Tomias smiled, "Just don't take too long."

Ayla stood and went inside.

They both watched her leave. Tomias broke the spell by raising his glass. "Take care up there, Jonah, you have a lot to come back to."

They sat facing the city.

"Ayla is right you know, we've been so focused on training and prep, I rarely get a chance to think about it."

"What do you mean?" Tomias tried the ceviche on a slice of soft avocado.

"We're carrying a lot of responsibility up there."

"Well yes, the whole world has literally been waiting for this moment since people could tilt their head back and see Hela, alive, green and verdant."

"Thanks. That really takes the pressure off."

"Well, at least I'd imagine you'll get the odd statue or tree named after you."

"Yeah. And a massive parade!" Jonah toasted again.

Ayla soon returned. She stepped barefoot along the polished stone floor. A soft white towel was wrapped around her. Passing the two boys, she went to lean on an opaque glass railing, looking up at the moon as its pastel shades slowly came into view.

"Nice shower?" asked Jonah.

"Why yes, thank you for your concern," She arched further over the railing.

"Do watch out that your towel doesn't fall." Tomias raised in his chair.

Ayla turned back and smiled. Her hand wandered to her chest, unravelling a fold in her towel.

The towel dropped to the ground. Ayla remained still, resting on the railing, looking out over the city.

"Don't forget Flavia, now, Jonah," she turned. Her skin was still wet, radiating heat.

She walked across the terrace and stood between the boys, gesturing to Jonah to make space. He edged his chair out and sat straight. Ayla placed herself on his lap, running her hand across his collar, pulling him in for a long kiss. She felt him tense below her.

Tomias placed his hand on her shoulder and she turned to kiss him.

Jonah slipped a finger between Ayla's lips before gliding it through a light tuft of hair between her legs.

Reaching over, Ayla undid the buttons on Tomias' trousers and stroked.

With his free hand, Jonah moved for his glass. He missed, hitting its side, nearly knocking it over.

"Come on Jonah, promise you'll focus harder during the mission." Ayla rubbed against his fingers before standing up.

She walked inside. The boys followed. Ayla sat upright on a slender chrome chair with her hands perched on her knees. Tomias came over and knelt, pulling her into his tongue with his hands squeezing her back. Jonah went over to the sofa and took some cherimoya fruit.

A clear night, the moon shone above them now in full view. Continents and oceans dabbed its surface.

Ayla stood, took Jonah's hand and led him to the other arm of the sofa. She glanced and stepped over to Jonah. He undressed and sat on the opposite arm. Looming above him, she turned to face Tomias and sat down, absorbing Jonah.

Tomias undressed, watched and ate a piece of honey mango.

Outside the detached city hum crept through the terrace doors.

Ayla raised herself again, stepped along the sofa and crossed over to Tomias.

EIGHT

Fifteen feet wide and perfectly round, the fountain was hewn from a single boulder of lapis lazuli. Placed in the centre of Flavia Park, it symbolised the unity of the world.

Throughout most of the year, the fountain functioned as a large reflective pool, its waters kept still. The breeze was kept from disturbing the water by a thick flat rim of speckled blue stone. Masons had selected the rock in such a way as to separate the rim from the bowl. Veins of gold shot up from the base. They ended right below the speckled lip.

Today, a jet threw water high into the air. It sprayed down, neatly within the confines of the fountain. The inside was carved to a smooth reflective finish. It tilted towards the Hela mirror on Mount Rhoda. The mountain rose out immediately behind the park. As the spray fell it caused a shimmer of lapis to dance over the surface.

Adroa hugged Petra with a light kiss to the cheek. "I'm so happy to see you again."

Petra kept a hand on Adroa's hip, "Thank you for making the time."

The two met by the side of the fountain, veils of mist drifted over them.

"Are you all set? How have the last few weeks been?" Adroa wore a formal white tunic with electrum piping above a matching ankle-length skirt. She leaned against the fountain's edge.

"It hasn't been easy. Safety and efficiency, time and pressure from all sides. It's hard to balance," Petra leaned next to her.

"So many interests, bound up in a single journey. My students look on with wonder."

"What do they wonder about?"

"Most of the conversations I have with them are either on understanding why the mission is important or on what happens after. There's a big debate between those who think everything will change forever and those who expect us to forget rather quickly." Adroa took a few steps around the fountain.

Petra wore a white cotton uniform, the jacket fastened by a dark sapphire belt. It denoted her senior rank within BISE. "I often wake up with the thought that whatever happens, it cannot justify the weight of expectations everyone has."

"That would be impossible, everyone has their own."

They walked down one of the rays leading off from the fountain, towards Mount Rhoda and the Residence.

"I do hope that at least some are met. How much do you tell them about our work?"

"Here and there. Never directly. Did you manage to include the experiment?"

"Unfortunately, no. There was no way to add it without being noticed. The official description as a 'refracting interferometer' was deemed of lower importance than other experiments."

The geometry of Flavia Park was in contrast to the greenery it contained. The grass flanking the gravel paths was wild, like a mountain meadow, flowers sprang up wherever the wind blew their seeds.

"Who took the ultimate decision?"

"Sheng. Even though she didn't know what it was, Ayla was supportive because she knew it was important to me. Sheng barely informed me of the decision."

Reaching the edge of the park, the path led to a broad limestone staircase which led up to the Residence.

"That is a shame. It will set us back some time."

****

The Residence perched above Flavia, nuzzled by Mount Rhoda's dense forests. It was Ashok's official home and the seat of government for the city as well as the Balkania Core.

Entry to the Residence was through the Gate of Nations. Rock-cut carvings stood fifty feet high. A lion prowling on the left flanked an eagle about to take flight on the right. The gate opened on to a corridor carved with scenes from ancient mythology.

The scenes reflected stories from a city state within the Balkania Core. The fishermen and the stork from Giro, the hunters and the frog from Dvor, as well as several colossal depictions of Hela.

Every carving was flavoured by the mix of cultures comprising Balkania.

The corridor finished at an imposing hypostyle court. A wide square bound on either side by two rows of fifty-foot stone pillars. Each pillar was uniquely shaped into the abstract form of a tree trunk. Flavia could be seen spreading out across the valley through the gaps in the gigantic columns.

Ashok talked with a small group gathered near the entrance to the court. He welcomed guests as they came. He wore a clean ivory linen jacket reaching down to the knees. Polished buttons ran on a light diagonal down the left side. Over the collar he wore an electrum torc. The fine ring came together at the front with the heads of two animals, a lion and an eagle squaring off at each other with their gaze.

"Welcome, everyone." He waved as guests arrived. "We'll start soon, grab a drink."

Staff carried thin, perfectly flat silver trays with smooth oval crystal wine glasses. Other trays carried oeuvres, each from one of the seven Cores. The guests were a similar mix. They came from every corner of the world.

"Hello, Irnes, nice to see you here for once," Ashok greeted her with a kiss.

"It's a special occasion, after all." Irnes held him by the shoulder. "To be honest, I rather miss this place. It tidies up nicely."

"And so do you."

"Was that a compliment?"

"Difficult to say, it definitely wasn't a negative comment," Ashok smiled.

Irnes turned and walked towards the centre of the court, the folds on her olive silk gown almost touched the polished granite ground.

The sun had already fallen behind Mount Rhoda. Through the court's columns, a wave of honeydew light could be seen receding back across the city.

Ayla walked into the gathering group. She wore a simple white dress with light electrum piping. Around her neck was a thin, delicate torc ending with the same lion and eagle as Ashok.

Upon seeing Ashok, Ayla immediately went over and embraced him. "My my, Dad. You tidy up well."

"It seems like that's the phrase of the day," Ashok smiled. "You look fantastic, Ayla."

Ayla took a long flute of flamingo pink wine from a passing waiter. A rare sort found only along the steep sandy hillsides around Saphan.

Mito walked up to the group, seeking Ashok's attention, "We're running on time. Two minutes and we'll start."

As dusk settled, the edges of the grand hypostyle court were illuminated by a golden glow. The lights had been placed between the inner and outer ring of columns in such a way as to project the pillars' shadows on the ground. Their straight lines interweaved to create a perfect circle in the centre of the court.

Guests instinctively cleared the stage made of light. A small orchestra emerged out on to it. A violinist was joined by a cello and flute. The violin started while the guests were still murmuring in the background. Its flutter brought the court to silence.

The flute added a floral dance, followed by the cello's weighty tones. The trio played out a colourful melody, reflecting the warmth of the early summer's day. The sounds drifted through the court and down into Flavia.

As the music faded, a deep gong resonated throughout the space.

The reception hall was grand, for sure, but not opulent. During the day it functioned as a public space for discussion and debate, much like a formalised version of the cafes in Merkum.

Ashok raised his glass and the hall echoed with the sound of clinking crystal.

"Tonight, we raise a toast to everyone who has had a hand in this historic moment. In the coming days we will finally realise the eternal human dream, standing proudly on the shoulders of all who have looked up in wonder, imagining their first steps on Hela, their first breaths of her air."

The floor mirrored the pattern of shade out in the court, the shadows echoed by snowflake obsidian. The room was oriented towards its two long walls.

Along the South wall, a row of floor-to-ceiling windows opened onto Flavia. The city unfurled below. Along the North wall, the same windows opened towards an inner garden with flower beds and hedges. The gardens were hemmed in by Mount Rhoda's rising slope behind.

"It has been our pleasure to support this endeavour." Kala sat next to Ashok on one of a dozen circular tables arranged around the hall. "The world came together, and we have achieved a feat indeed only dreamt about until our lifetimes. We all await to see the discoveries awaiting us on Hela. My toast is to the team at BISE, who have brought a world of talent together. Also, to Jonah and Tomias, our sons, currently in final preparations at the launch site in Kamrun."

The room echoed again.

Staff arrived carrying dishes to the tables. In step with tradition before an important occasion, the food was simple but beautifully presented.

The focus was on fresh, grilled vegetables accompanied by cheeses and oils from the region. In contrast, the wines were far from simple.

The centre of each table held a dozen crystal carafes. Each was filled with a different wine from every corner of the world.

"Thank you, Kala." Sheng stood from a neighbouring table. "Getting here has been a difficult journey with countless hurdles along the way. I'm humbled by the responsibility entrusted in me and my team to deliver on this mission. We hope to make you all proud." Sheng took a seat next to Ayla and Petra.

Speeches over, a bustle of chatter slowly rose throughout the hall, accompanied by the clang of cutlery on china. As was custom for official events in Flavia, the serving staff ate on tables alongside the official guests.

The musical trio from the court appeared at the end of the hall and provided a light melody to accompany the dinner.

“Petra, we still have a lot of work to get through on the ground,” Sheng reached for a carafe of rich red wine from Manau.

“We do. I am meeting with Rassi in the morning. We are going over the final training tasks.”

“Good. We still have a long way to go before the men are back here safely.”

Petra poured Alama olive oil from Giro. The oil had a unique dark yellow, almost marmalade hue. “How are Tomias and Jonah? I haven’t spoken to them today.”

“They are well. Going through the final few checks. Practising with the new dynamo.”

“What new dynamo?” Ayla overheard their conversation from the side.

“The modified landing system,” Sheng answered.

“Modified how?”

“With the Contained AB module from Nussa. Set to kick in on final approach.”

“Why don’t I know about this?”

“Let’s not do this now, everything is prepped for launch.” Sheng leant over to get a carafe of sweet white wine from Nussa.

"I find it unfathomable that such a decision would be made without my knowledge. You obviously intentionally didn't tell me," Ayla raised her voice in tandem with the clatter of dishes as the staff came by once again to clear the empty plates and bring out the dessert.

While tradition stipulated a simple vegetarian main meal, it said very little about the dessert. Ashok was never one to miss the opportunity to delight his guests, as well as himself, with dessert.

Square wooden trays emerged, one after the other. They fizzed and banged. The staff placed them on the tables to reveal a cast iron plate with a high rim dug into the centre. The plate contained a rich chocolate brownie topped with ice-cream, all covered in a simmering gold sauce.

"You know the pressure we've been under, I had little choice," Sheng stared forward.

"And now, what? We bolt on some unit to the lander and hope for the best? Is that how we work? Has it been tested? Do we know anything about it?"

"The engineering team in Nussa have put the module through its paces and we have had time to perform tests, too."

"This is insane, Sheng, you're risking the mission. Worse, you're risking Jonah's life."

Not noticing the wooden dessert tray, Ayla knocked her glass into the iron plate, smashing the stem of her glass. Petra quickly took it from her and cleaned up before an attendant came. Ashok, Kala and several guests from neighbouring tables looked over.

"We have had many differences, Sheng, but I never once believed you would place politics before lives."

"As usual, you're being unreasonably dramatic. No one wants the mission to succeed more than me."

"It's a farce, Sheng, ridiculous. You should be ashamed of yourself," Ayla shouted as she screeched her chair back, stood and headed out.

"You're completely out of order!"

After she left, the silent guests refocused their gaze on Ashok. He made a weary smile and continued with his brownie. The bustle and clatter quickly filled the hall again.

****

With the dinner concluded, guests diffused out of the reception hall and across the Residence grounds.

"My apologies, Emperor, I didn't expect such an outburst," Sheng bowed.

"It's not the first." Kala walked behind the columns at the edge of the hypostyle hall.

"It was a little unnecessary," Frey paced two steps behind Kala. "Importantly, we have everything in place."

"Yes," Sheng walked alongside him. "Everything is in place and we are looking forward to the launch."

"Ayla can't do anything to mess up the plans?" Asked Frey.

"Of course not. She has had no oversight on this part of the mission."

"It's important that we have no issues these coming days. A lot of people are relying on this," Kala paused at a column. It was carved in the form of a jackfruit tree, native to Nussa.

"I got word from the launch-site that they are running on schedule and that the equipment is stable."

"Good," Frey snapped.

"What happens after the mission, Sheng?" Kala placed a hand on the column.

"Upon his return, Jonah will be a hero. I imagine you will want to take him home."

"We have a tour planned across all of the Cores. We want to make sure everyone sees his success," Kala turned to face Sheng. "I'm glad you accommodated our requests for the mission. They are extremely important to us. Following the celebrations, we will discuss your future."

"A pleasure, sir."

They neared the corridor leading towards the Gate of Nations. The last of the evening's guests had left. Light security regiments remained, scattered around the large open space.

The group stopped short of the corridor. Kala looked back towards the Residence and then across towards the gate. "You know, I remember Ashok making the plans for this place. A flavour from every part of the world, he said."

"The centre of the world," Frey added.

"Indeed. I hope he hasn't bought too much into his own vision," Kala walked on towards the corridor with Frey. "Good luck tomorrow. It's the start of a new era."

"We'll make you proud, Emperor."

****

"She's not getting any calmer, is she?" Ashok leaned by a window.

"I can't say it's entirely surprising." Adroa stood next to him, looking out over Flavia.

"Maybe it was me, but I thought getting through her teens was going to be the hardest." Ashok sat next to Adroa on a plush velvet couch.

Separate from all of the formal spaces of the palace, through a series of corridors, lay Ashok's private rooms. They were arranged perpendicular to the layout of the main building. Like a terraced house cutting through its entire width.

To the front, a curved stone balcony stood proud over the city. Behind it, a series of living and working spaces and, at the back, the most private place within the entire estate – a perfectly ordered garden directly opening out onto the slope of Mount Rhoda.

"I would still rather her be the way she is instead of a quiet little mouse."

"Ha! Can you imagine?" Ashok laughed as he poured two small glasses of whiskey. The night was quiet and still. "It's actually a lot more entertaining this way. Did you see Sheng's face? He went so red. It was hard not to laugh."

"It's not kind to say, I know, but that man has a stick so far up his arse I feel bad for him," Adroa raised her glass.

"Strong words, coming from a headmistress."

The sound of their glasses coming together startled a peregrine who had been sat oblivious on the roof above. As he descended down into the city towards Flavia Park, the bird's wings were lit by the palace lights.

"It's going to be a bad night for some poor little mouse," Adroa stated without a hint of remorse for said mouse.

"Peregrines are people too, they deserve to eat a nice meal."

"Are you sure you finished school, Ashok, perhaps you want to come to Dhrama and take some refresher classes?"

Ashok laughed. "How is the Kap? It's been a long time since I've been to a campus."

"It has turned into a magical institution. Twenty years and it's already produced so many amazing leaders. Remember the start?"

"Seems like an age ago," he swirled his glass.

"Come to Dharma, come see the school."

"You know I will. And there's no way I can get you to stay here a little longer?" He tucked a loose strand of hair behind her ear.

"I love Flavia and I'm so proud of everything you've done every time I come. But my home isn't here, it's with the students. It's amazing to see them grow. I'd much rather you come to Dharma once you step down."

"Don't remind me." Ashok leaned on the carved stone balcony, it was still warm from the sun. "This isn't the easiest job in the world but it's all I know." He turned and sat on the parapet facing Adroa. A sheer drop fell behind him.

"Sooner or later, it has to come to an end." Adroa stepped over and embraced him, "At the end of the day, it's how you designed it."

"I know, I know, very good. But there's so much left to do."

"There's always going to be a lot left to do. At some point you have no choice but to let go. Look at Ayla, she has found her own path. All we did was give her a start."

"Yes, I have no worries about her."

"It's still pretty warm. Weren't you going to show me the garden?"

"Was I?" Ashok smirked.

Adroa turned and walked inside. She slid out of her skirt leaving it, as well as her shoes, in the middle of the drawing room floor. Ashok pushed off from the parapet and followed her. Moving through the bedroom, she threw off her tunic. Adroa waited for Ashok, slipping aside his jacket and unbuttoning his trousers as soon as he came.

Two large sliding doors led to the inner garden. They were made of thin lengths of oak, bracketing a lattice of bevelled glass. Ashok slid them open and the two walked out onto the wild grass, barefoot and naked.

"Our favourite part of the palace." Adroa ran her toes through the grass.

"By far. Remember how hard it was to design?"

"Yes, we took our sweet time."

On two of its sides the garden was enclosed by sliding doors. The third was a stone wall carved with a stylised map of the world. The fourth was Mount Rhoda's steep slope rising up.

The garden mixed fruit trees with flowers. It had borders made of berry bushes. A square pool with mirror-calm water stood in the middle.

Ashok embraced and kissed her.

"Come on!" Adroa pushed away, skipped across the grass and jumped into the still pool. Her plunge drove a splash of water towards Ashok.

NINE

"Welcome everyone, welcome indeed." Cameras framed Laaro in a close portrait shot. "The day is finally upon us. You will always remember where you were today." Only the tips of a gold silk collar prodded up into the frame.

The camera stepped back, opening a view onto Laaro's white epoxy desk. The studio was blurred in the background.

"I hope the smile on my face reflects how we all feel today," he continued. "It is hard to describe the honour of being here with you to share this moment… I'll try anyway.

"When I was a little boy, my father would set me off to sleep with stories of adventure. As we lay in my bed, we would look out to the moon. He would tell me of serpents, monsters and heroes. Their dramatic battles filled my dreams."

Laaro took out a small wooden Hela statue and placed it on his desk.

"When I was ten, my father carved this statue for me. The previous night a large branch had broken off of a tree in our garden. It had startled me."

He ran his fingers over the smooth grain.

"The statue still sits on my nightstand. As ferocious as those battles were, the statue was a reminder that Hela was always there. A constant force. Whatever human, or not so human, dramas played out, there was a higher force, a higher meaning."

He turned the small statue towards him and cupped it with his hand.

"Today, those adventures become real. Jonah and Tomias, the heroes of our story, will go up there and fight our battle. In this story, this very real story, the battle will be for knowledge. Answering questions carried through the ages. Did life on Earth come from Hela? If not, what is the life we see up there and how did it arise?"

Laaro stood and took a few short steps out from his desk, carrying the statue with him. The camera panned to show the edges of his usual studio set, the rustic living room.

"That's what we know, what we expect. Personally, I believe we will discover so much more. So much we can't yet imagine."

A large monitor came into view as he continued to move through the studio. It was placed between the two halves of his set and displayed the station's logo.

"I will be here with you for the whole day, from prep to launch. Throughout, we will talk to a number of special guests. Kicking off the day, I'm joined by May."

His guest appeared on the monitor. May sat on a small blue sofa with her back arched. Her bowl cut hair touched a garnet satin blouse. Laaro came into the frame and perched on a tall chrome stool. A fine porcelain cup rested on a pedestal next to him.

"May, welcome." He slid a cotton coaster out from under the cup and placed the wooden statue on it.

"It's a pleasure to be here." May sat forward on the sofa.

"May is a senior engineer from the Kap here in Nussa currently stationed at BISE. She will guide us through what we can expect today."

"Yep, I hope so." BISE had carefully positioned her makeshift studio however, every so often, a hurried technician would zip past in the background.

The monitor changed to show a close-up of the launch facility. It focused on a razor-straight track, resting diagonally up the foothills of the Lurish Mountains. The track looked like a giant bobsled path cutting right through the rocky slopes.

"Right," Laaro raised his cup. "Take it away, May. What's in store for us today?"

"On the monitor, you are currently looking at the launch ramp outside of Kamrun. It is difficult to get a sense of scale in this image, but the magnetic track is nearly six miles long. In less than an hour we will see Orus 5 shoot across the mountains at fourteen times the speed of sound." May shuffled in her soft seat.

The scenes changed. They showed a small crowd gathered on a bare metal platform surrounded by desert.

"Now we can see the Core leaders standing several miles from the launch site itself."

"Why are they not watching from mission control?"

"Everyone wanted to see the launch in person, Laaro. Wouldn't you?"

"Absolutely. What I wouldn't give to be out there!"

"We're all excited but celebration is still some way away..." May paused "Oh, here you can see Ashok standing by his daughter, deputy head of BISE, Ayla."

"It must be a mixed day for her. So much hope and preparation. Now she's waiting for her partner to be fired into the sky."

"Indeed," The monitor turned back to May. "While it might be easy to expect at least a dash of envy from Tomias, I can assure you that there has been nothing but an extreme sense of camaraderie between the two Explorers."

"Can the same be said for Ashok and Kala?"

May straightened her skirt. "You know I'm not in a position to comment. There have been well-known rifts between the two in the past. However, the mere fact we are here, watching these scenes shows that they have reached an agreement."

"So, tell us what to expect from the launch?"

"Launching a craft into space is a daunting task. Abaryonic Drive is not yet quite powerful enough to fully overcome Earth's gravity. The challenge is how to get Orus up to the right velocity. The Spinlaunch Inner Coil will accelerate the craft along a vacuum-sealed closed loop. Upon reaching the correct speed, the Inner Coil will open, releasing Jonah and Tomias into the Outer Ring. They will cover the four mile distance in four fifths of a second. Finally, Orus will emerge out of Spinlaunch and onto the final ramp running up the Lurish Mountains."

"Once the boys exit the Outer Ring, we will lock on to them, tracking Orus as it zooms off into the sky." Laaro zoomed his closed palm diagonally across the shot. His flowing silk sleeves looked like a trail following the improvised craft.

"Yep. After launch, the vessel will clear Earth's lower atmosphere in no more than ten seconds. Once in space, AB Drive will steer them the rest of the way."

"And the new tech will take them all the way to Hela?"

"That's right, they will essentially glide over to the moon. Halfway through the journey, approximately nine hours in, the craft will invert Drive and begin the process of slowing down."

"And then orbit!" Laaro glanced over to his side, focusing on the small statue.

"Yes. After successfully slowing down, Orus will reach Hela's orbit tomorrow afternoon. Captain Jonah will then ask Tomias to begin the landing sequence. First, Tomias will then inspect the terrain and confirm the primary target landing site. Orus will then separate into two parts. Tomias will stay back in the vessel's body. Jonah will descend down to Hela in the craft's nose."

"The Nest and The Egg," Laaro smiled. "So, by tomorrow evening we should have the first shots of Jonah stepping foot on the moon's surface. Incredible!" He paused and the camera centred on him. "Join us again after a short break to continue our coverage."

"Two minutes." A hard voice rang out on the studio monitors.

"You have a long couple of days yourself, Laaro."

"I'm so full of adrenaline, I think it will wiz past."

"It's a big day for Nussa, I'm looking forward to coming back for the celebration."

"Too true" Laaro clapped. "So many bright young minds from Nussa hand a hand in the mission. As soon as you come back, we'll have to have you here in person."

"It will be a pleasure. We've given everything for the mission."

****

While the ability to harness Abaryonic propulsion had recently given birth to Gliders as a rapid form of transport, they were still only able to carry relatively light loads. Heavy cargo was shipped by Tube while bulky items were had to go by sea.

The clear, flat deserts outside Saphan had been home to BISE's space launch programme since its very start. Flavia was unsuitable due to its hilly terrain and the lack of a nearby port.

Research and development was carried out on the BISE campus in Flavia but practically all launches happened between Saphan and the port city of Kamrun.

The port, not far from Saphan, offered the perfect delivery site for craft of all sizes. The deep, hook-shaped natural harbour provided relatively easy access even during low tide. Its shape buffeted the huge open ocean waves.

The port's walls were formidable. Kamrun had been a defensive outpost since antiquity. Protecting the rare resource, ruler after ruler had bolstered its shores with immense rocks.

Thirty miles inland from the city stood the main launch facility, fittingly named Gateway to Hela. The giant white Spinlaunch coil was like an island in the desert. Its final launch ramp cut out from the coil, across the flat plains and into the mountains. Inside coil's centre sat Orus 5, the craft which would launch Jonah and Tomias to Hela.

At two-hundred feet long, Orus 5 was an awesome wonder of engineering. The silver teardrop rested on its side within the darkness of the coil, like a bullet in the chamber, ready to fire. Thirty feet wide, the ship was made as large as Spinlaunch could fit.

Jonah and Tomias were already safely on-board. Boarding complete, they calmly ran through a series of final checklists. The only hint of impending violence was a thin strip of red lights illuminating the gently curved tunnel ahead.

Far away from Spinlaunch, a small crowd huddled together on their own desert island. Ashok, Kala and the rest of the leaders had gathered on a modest metal stage to view the launch.

Ayla was the only senior member of BISE amongst the group. Sheng was in charge of Operations Control, dug into a nearby hillside. The site was positioned some distance away from the launch facility further along the plateau at a point where the desert abruptly ended, giving way to the Lurish Mountains.

"Operations to Captain. Green across the board, three minutes to release."

"Captain to Operations. Confirmed."

Speakers on each corner of the platform tore through the empty desert, muting the low murmur of conversation. The light hum of broadcast cameras circling the gathered guests provided a constant background.

"You've no idea what a fight it was to be the announcer today." Ayla told her father during a gap in transmissions.

"Who won out?"

"Sheng's communications head, May. I heard her practising in her office the other day. She just finished an interview with Laaro."

"Your favourite celebrity friend! Do I get a sense of jealousy?"

"Ha. I wish I had time to be jealous."

"Two minutes to release. Vacuum holding strong. "

"Confirmed."

A gust of wind barrelled across the plain, muffling the speakers.

Operations Control was a converted underground military base. Less than two decades ago it had been a closely guarded secret. No one in the room would have known about its existence. Let alone be able to step near the site.

The control room had three rows of desks circling a central bank of monitors. Each desk had its own cluster of monitors tilted towards their operator.

Sheng paced the outer rim. He scanned from desk to desk. Now and then he stopped to peer over at scrolling figures from the litany of sensors on Orus and Spinlaunch.

"Air pressure within the craft is a little on the high side." He told an operator.

"Ninety seconds to release."

"Within normal bounds, sir!" The operator yelled over the loudspeaker.

Jonah and Tomias were magnetically strapped into their seats. It was a snug affair. In the early days of planning, Orus had been designed to hold a larger crew. Improvements in AB technology, balanced by a constant risk to life, had led BISE to cut the crew from six to two. It was an all-or-nothing approach.

The extra space hadn't gone to waste. Every nook of the craft was crammed full of specially designed experiment transport cases. The metal cases perfectly filled the interior.

The sole connection to the outside world were two narrow oblong windows on either side of the control monitors in front of the two men. Lights came on to illuminate the Inner Coil. The walls were smooth, covered in a pearlescent white paint. The tunnel gently curved, guiding two metal ribbons along its base.

"Sixty seconds to release. Confirm sequence."

"Sequence confirmed. Air pressure is stable." Jonah checked one of a hundred dials littering his plane of view.

Ayla took a few steps away from the gathered crowd. During the briefest of pauses in the transmission, she whispered into a small monitor in her collar "Stay safe, Tommy, I love you"

She slipped back next to her father.

"Thirty seconds to release. Confirm 'go.'"

"Go confirmed."

"Get ready for a show, Kala." Ashok spoke over an alarm ringing out on the platform.

"All ready." Kala held on to a rail at the edge of the platform, his gaze fixed on the distant mountains.

"Fifteen seconds. Release clamps."

A line of magnetic clamps holding Orus in place retracted into the ground. Jonah and Tomias felt the enormous vessel hover in place. They looked at each other and winked in tandem.

"Ten seconds. Safe journey, Captain. We're with you."

"Five."

"Four."

"Three."

"Two."

"One. Spool up."

The craft started to inch forward. The first feet forward were a silky glide. Orus began to pick up speed along a carefully designed acceleration curve. It was important so that the two budding Explorers retained their form, more or less.

"Mach 1."

Tomias felt an overwhelming sense of release. So much planning and training building up to this moment. Soon they would have to take Orus by the reins but right now, right now he could sit back… Mostly. "Jonah, do you feel the vibration from the tip?" Tomias sensed a light shudder in his fingers.

"Operations, there is a mild agitation coming from our leading edge."

"We see it, Captain. Monitoring."

The vibration morphed into a gentle oscillation. The vessel swayed what must have been millimetres from side to side as it ramped up speed in the Inner Coil. It felt like the swaying of a ship in the sea.

"Mach 6. Vibration stabilising. Release to Stage 2 in thirty."

The smooth walls of the Inner Coil gave little indication of their speed. The only hint was a gentle rightward force, pushing them towards the outer wall.

"Mach 12. All stable. Release in ten."

The vibration returned. Jonah's moment for contemplation was over. Time to focus.

"Three, Two, One, Release."

The ship began to glow. A mild sapphire light glazed the walls.

A gate in the Inner Coil opened out to the Outer Ring.

Orus blasted through the ring. Jonah and Tomias felt a violent shove to one side as the craft transitioned. Before they could orient, the ship emerged out on the final ramp.

Gathered on the platform, the leaders watched a silver streak flash across the long ramp, launching into the sky. Ayla held Ashok's arm as she watched, her gaze tracking ever higher.

A red ring flashed around the central monitors in the control room. A loud alarm rang out.

"Overpressure alert." An operator told Sheng as he ran to his desk.

"Are they aware?"

"Yes. Tomias has already reset it."

The red alarm disappeared.

"Sensor malfunction, take note." Sheng ordered.

"Yes sir."

Thin wisps of clouds spread across the cobalt sky. A white streak cut across from the crests of the Lurish Mountains. It had a rightward parabolic arc. The gods must have been right-handed.

As Orus disappeared from view. It left a neat pinhole in a nearby cloud.

A successful launch.

A wave of celebration rang out on the platform, in Operations Control and across a world watching in awe.

****

"Systems stable."

"Confirmed, Captain. You are on your way through the edge of our exosphere."

"Thank you, Operations."

Orus 5 sailed silently through the outer fringes of Earth's atmosphere. As per protocol, Jonah and Tomias decoupled their harnesses shortly after clearing the exosphere.

Hela lay ahead. The men watched their target on the monitor in front. Earth lay behind and out of sight. On either side they could see feint arcs of blue light seeping away.

"Focus up, Captain, there's your target." Tomias raised a hand towards the monitor. His pointed finger lay suspended up in front. He turned his hand, the first realisation of weightlessness.

"Not sure it's me who has to focus up." Jonah smiled.

Operations Control had remote command of the craft.

Looking out, Hela was no bigger than standing on Earth gazing up. Her colours were, however, far more vivid. Her forests emanated an intense emerald green. At the edges, the oceans shimmered. Every passing minute brought her closer.

"Captain. Prepare for Glide to engage."

"Confirmed, Operations."

Jonah set his sights on a square control module across from his left hand. He pressed a protruding rubber button and a small display flicked on. The monitor showed two waves out of sync running across a flat axis.

"Captain. Glide engaging. Confirm when active."

A light hum came over Orus. It rode up and down the length of the craft in what felt like the crests of an evening tide. One of the waves on the display drifted to the right until they were on top of each other. The combined line became thicker. The hum slowly settled into an imperceptible purr coming from every side of the capsule.

"AB Glide engaged." Jonah turned to Tomias and rolled his eyes.

"You never really got the point of the Abaryonic System, did you?" Tomias looked over.

"I get the point, but it always felt like its inclusion was more politics than practicality. The first two Orus missions used compressed gas to navigate and land. That seemed to work fine."

"Come on, it's pretty incredible. We're riding on proof that our universe is made up almost entirely of massless particles. AB creates mass from the massless. Tell me that's not incredible?"

"Sure, yeah. Still, it seems unnecessarily complex. The ship could reach Hela easily without it. One more thing to think about."

"Your enthusiasm is infectious. Let's hope Hela perks you up." Tomias smiled.

"System stable. Start journey checklist and enjoy the ride, Captain."

"Will do, Operations, thank you."

Jonah reached to the side of his seat and undid a strap holding a thin binder with an aluminium back. He briefly let go of the binder, watching it drift across the capsule with a light wobble. Tomias caught it and passed it back. Jonah turned to the first page and went through their homework for the trip ahead.

An advantage of the Abaryonic System was its ability to switch from attractive to repulsive force. A disadvantage was that it took a long time to slow the craft in space. Orus had been slowing gradually for the past ten hours of its journey.

Jonah undid his harness and drifted to a window. Instead of the expected darkness he saw a pearlescent milky mist below him. He immediately coasted back to his seat.

"Tommy. Are you seeing this?"

"Seeing what?"

"Come over here. Below the craft, a white mist. Operations can you see it?"

"Negative Captain. The cameras are clean."

Tomias unstrapped and headed over. He looked out of the narrow window but saw only the black of space illuminated at the edges of his view by the sun.

"It was as clear as day. Are you sure?"

"Yes, Captain. The view below Orus is empty. Check again and report."

"Nothing in sight now, Operations. Only a slight glow ahead."

"Likely a reflection, Captain. Check your main monitor."

Jonah and Tomias headed back to their seats. Strapping in, they stared at the monitor. The small turquoise pebble had grown to fill the entire display.

They couldn't take their eyes off of her.

"She's stunning." Jonah had studied the topography and features of the Hela's surface during his training. This was different, she was alive, really, truly alive. He could see clouds above the continents, oceans now clearly marked by their varying shades of stunning blues, turquoise and lapis.

"It's unreal," Tomias reached out to touch the monitor.

The approaching corona of Hela's atmosphere had a familiar glow. Unlike Earth however, the moon had a slight tint of green to it. In any case, she was real, and she was right in front of them.

"Captain. Prepare for the final approach and landing."

Jonah flipped to the corresponding checklist, "Starting separation sequence."

"Landing thruster power check initiated." Jonah flipped a series of toggles controlling valves for the landing system. "Systems stable."

"Actually. Operations, readings from the Egg's suppressant module are a bit erratic."

"We see them, Captain. They are within normal ranges, carry on."

Jonah flipped the toggles back. "Check complete. Tomias, please run the Nest's final check."

"Confirmed Captain, Glide disengaging."

"Glide disengaged. We are in Hela's orbit, Captain. Orienting Orus in a separation position."

Tomias tilted the craft to its side. Through their right window, they could see a beautiful distant blue marble. The Earth floated in a sea of darkness. All three billion inhabitants covered that little ball.

His left window was a new world. Jonah and Tomias practically stuck their faces to the cold glass. They each gripped a grab-handle on either side of the pane. Mesmerised.

Hela filled every inch. There was no edge, no horizon in sight. So much to take in. Clouds casting their shadows across grasslands. Rusty river estuaries splitting up islets of jungle trees. The muddy waters mixing with aquamarine ocean currents. Even a trail of clotted grey smoke emanating from Hela's largest volcano, Irephus.

Sheng stood with his arms crossed. He watched the feed running across the main control room monitors. The Nuwa probe, in constant orbit around Hela, had sent close up images before but they paled in comparison to the view now. The technology was better, clearer and crisper.

Ayla had made her way to mission control. She sat near Sheng and imagined Jonah and Tomias, now so close to Hela. *The first people in history to see her from orbit. She must be beautiful.*

May was stationed next to Ayla, "Captain, you have command of Orus 5 for separation and final approach, confirm."

"Confirmed, Orus 5"

"Make us proud."

Tomias took a deep breath and pulled his gaze from the window, turning to Jonah. They both let go of the grab handles and hugged.

"See you soon, Tommy."

"Go make history, Jonah. I'm always next to you."

"Let's not make it too close. That first step is mine!"

The private moment between friends was only mildly dampened by most of humanity looking on at them from their homes.

Jonah pushed off and sat in the command seat. "Ready for separation."

"At your pleasure." Tomias strapped himself into a chair in the Nest. Ahead of him was a secondary command monitor and a window facing Hela.

Jonah looked back at Tomias one more time before initiating the separation. A bulkhead sliced closed in between the Egg and the Nest like a giant camera aperture.

He listened as a series of bolts whirled. The final bonds holding the craft together. *A week alone on Hela. Bring it on.*

Orus split in two. The Egg edged away from the Nest. Jonah looked at his monitor. The Nest drifted away, an ever-smaller silver shimmer.

The mission plan called for Jonah to leave Tomias and the Nest in stationary orbit above his landing site. Upon completing the mission, he would launch the Egg from Hela's surface. Orus would once more become whole and, reunited, they would make their way back to Earth. As Jonah carried out his mission on the moon, Tomias would provide support, serve as a communications relay and execute a series of orbital experiments.

Over eighty landing sites had been considered. The site had to be scientifically interesting, but it also had to be safe to land. Over a year the list had been curtailed and curtailed until something approaching a consensus had been reached.

The primary site was near the edge of a large lake on the Rodinia continent. It was separated from the Tethys Ocean by an isthmus no more than a mile thick at its narrowest.

A number of rivers were believed to be draining water from the lake and into the Tethys Ocean though they seemed to be covered by dense vegetation.

Two back-up sites deeper inland were chosen should there be an issue with the primary target.

A water landing was to be avoided at all costs.

Ayla rested her head on her arm and looked on as various telemetric plots showed the craft's trajectory down towards the moon's surface.

She was startled by a news crew rushing by. They pushed up next to her to hear a press update from May who was sitting expectantly at her desk next to Ayla.

"We are entering the last and most challenging phase of the journey. Captain Jonah has completed a successful detachment from Lieutenant Tomias. He will now begin his final descent to Hela. All systems and processes have been smooth and stable. We expect him to reach the surface within..."

A sharp garbled hiss came from the Egg, cutting across the monitors.

May turned away from the crew and sat on her desk.

"Captain, please repeat?"

A silence followed.

"Operations to Egg, please repeat."

The monitor buzzed again.

"Orus 5 to Operations. A flash of light seemed to come from Hela, but it has not repeated. Commencing final approach procedure."

"Thank you, Captain, confirmed."

May swivelled around to face the news crew as they pointed their camera towards her.

"As I was saying, we expect Jonah to reach Hela's surface within 15 minutes."

An alarm echoed out from the central monitors.

Ayla signalled over to Sheng. "The craft is askew, it is off-course." A thousand thoughts ran through her head.

She heard the monitor hissed with static as the control room erupted with noise.

"News crew – leave the hall." Ayla pointed to the doors.

The hiss continued, punctuated by an occasional distorted word.

"Low, lower, what did he say?" Sheng paced over to Petra's station.

"The audio is unclear. Sensors show that the craft is still descending at a steady pace however it is askew."

"Operations, the Egg is corkscrewing towards Hela." Tomias relayed footage from the Nest to Operations.

"Lieutenant, do you have a connection with the Captain?"

"No. Only static."

The monitors relayed a view from the crest of Hela's surface. Her blue-green glow saturated the display. Cameras panned and refocused, blurring the moon in an attempt to get a fix on Jonah.

Out of the blur emerged a terrifying view. The landing craft was not only spiralling but also tumbling about its length, heading ever downward towards the surface.

"Can we stabilise?" Sheng gripped the monitor.

"Not from here." Petra's voice trembled. "The delay is too large. On-board control is the only option."

Cameras showed the odd burst of mist sprouting from the craft's sides. Either Jonah was attempting to regain control or the autopilot was trying to stabilise.

"...Too fast..." Jonah's voice cracked across the monitor. Its hiss was so loud the volume had to be dialled down.

"Spin is slowing." Petra pointed to a monitor.

As the Nest's camera showed Jonah stabilising, a surge of blue flame shot towards the lens. The flame cleared, leaving a coating of soot which obscured the view. The camera tilted to one side. It caught a blurred edge of fiery metal before settling on the darkness of space.

"Get the craft back in sight." Sheng shouted.

"The exhaust must have pushed the Nest aside. It is still firing. Lieutenant, are you alright?" Petra shouted into the monitor.

"Yes. Nest stabilising."

"Get it back up on the monitor!" Sheng gripped his station.

The Nest's own stabilisers could be seen pushing mist into space as it tried to reorient itself.

Eventually, the moon came back into focus.

"Where is the craft? Where is Jonah?" Ayla poured over the monitors.

"We've lost data." Petra attempted to reconnect. "Captain. Status?"

Static engulfed the room again.

"Lieutenant?"

Tomias scanned the monitors for a sign of Jonah. Seeing nothing, he moved to the window. "I can't see anything."

Cameras strained to find focus against Hela's glow.

"Three... free..." A final incomprehensible message leached out from the noise.

"He is still fighting the lander." Tomias was glued to the window.

"We have lost all data links." Petra stood from her station.

Suddenly, the static stopped. It was as if the whole control room went through a void.

Silence. Silence from the monitors, silence from the team and silence from Tomias.

Everyone stared at the empty monitors in disbelief. No one dared move.

Sheng placed a hand over his forehead.

"Lock the doors."

TEN

On the streets of Flavia, people drifted with their heads stooped, fixated on the ground. It had already been two weeks since the accident, but everyone still acted as if the air had been sucked out of their lungs.

Ashok walked through Flavia Park and on towards BISE. The park was calm and empty. Birds sang as they flew. A light hum of bees and bugs filled the air. The sun still shone.

The people of Flavia were also out but they seemed empty and devoid of life. The usual buzz of the great city was absent.

The corner of a small side-street across from the park held one of Ashok's favourite cafés, Café Canvas. A constrained space, it tried to pack as much as possible between its two oak entrances, one on either side of the street corner.

Inside, the focus was on a green marble L-shaped counter. It ran the length of the café. At the end of its long side stood a small coffee roaster surrounded by two stands of steel boxes. The boxes were filled with the previous days' roasts.

A classic bronzed espresso machine was placed on its short end. The grand machine usually fussed without pause. It served a constant stream of pundits who filled a dozen tall chairs dotting the marble bar. A monitor was perched in the top-rear corner. Its sound was always off.

Ashok stepped inside and sat on a soft round cushion atop the stool. "Good morning, a short espresso, please."

His usual at Canvas was a quick shot followed by a second, slower espresso. One to scratch the itch and the other to enjoy the flavour.

The barista nodded and pulled a shot. Brown syrup slid out of the spout and into an octagonal crystal cup used exclusively by the café.

"Here you are, Ashok."

"Thank you." He picked up the crystal cup and took in the sweet aroma. 'Focussing beyond the coffee, he glanced around.

He looked to his left. Then to his right. Only then did he realise the café was as full as ever. All but two seats were taken. A line of people sat, staring either at the reflections of light in their cups or vaguely towards a spot on the opposite wall.

As Ashok turned, the other customers seemed to immediately avert their gaze. Even those not looking in his direction turned a little more to the side. He downed his first shot. The glass clinking on the hard counter.

"Could you make the second one to go, please."

"Of course." The barista took a small cardboard cup from a cabinet behind the bar and pulled a second shot.

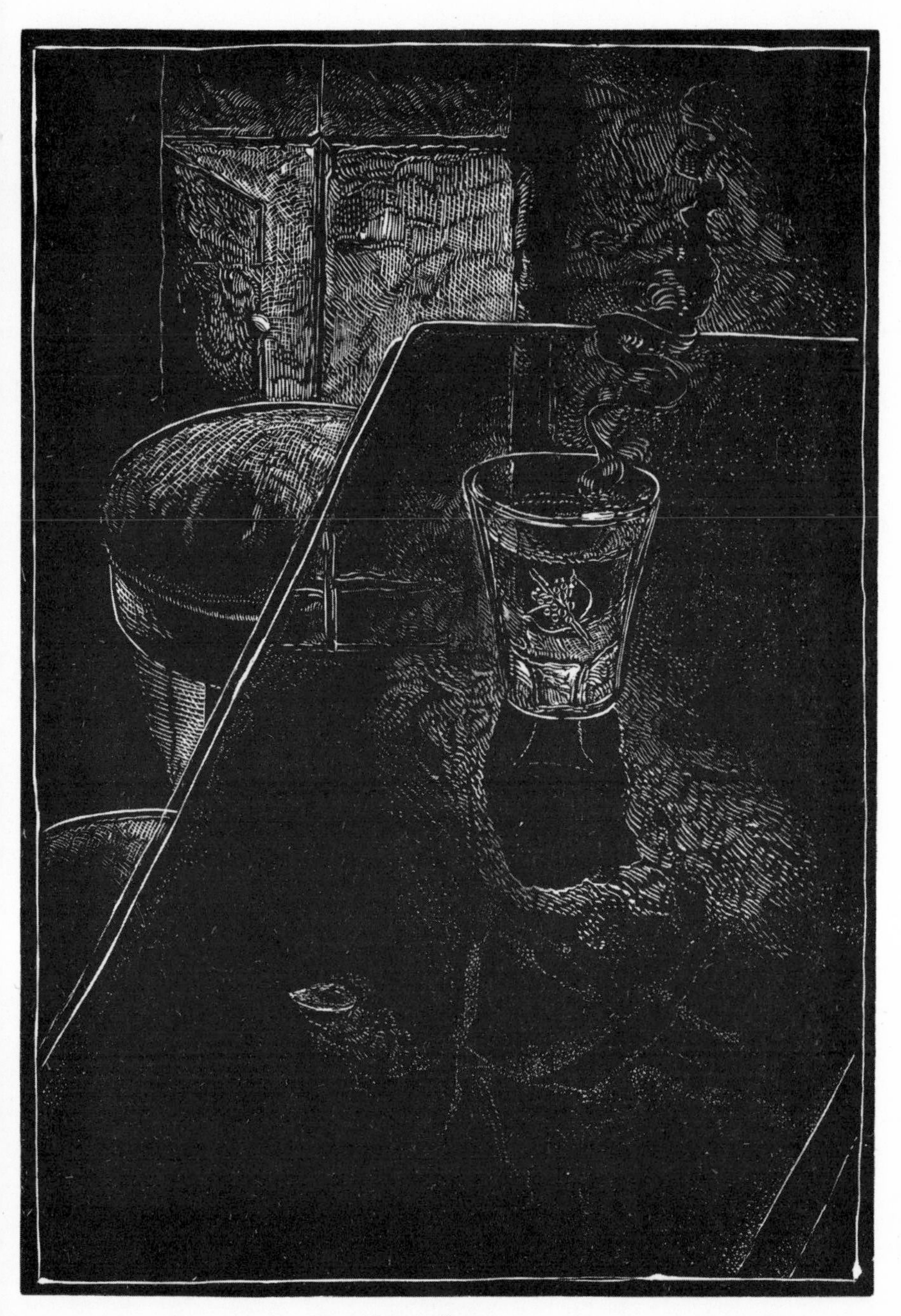

Café Canvas

"Thank you," Ashok tapped a token on the counter's underside, took the cup and stood to leave.

"Take care." The barista raised a hand.

Walking out, his eyes took a second to adjust between the dim interior and the glaring sun. The cup radiated through his fingers. It had a pronounced lip and a contoured, corrugated surface. Ashok ran his thumb across the rim and continued his walk towards the institute.

****

"They're waiting for you inside, Ashok." Mito stood by the side of a double door leading to a conference room within BISE.

"Thank you, Mito."

The doors were carved with abstract scenes depicting the institute's achievements from the early space programme.

Two thin arcs converged at the top of the split between the doors. They pointed to a representation of Hela. At their base, two larger semi-circles came together to form the Earth, carved with its continents. The globe was aligned with Flavia at the central divide.

Ashok opened the doors. The expansive room contained a single long table. The table widened and bowed towards its centre. It had been fashioned from an experimental prototype skin for the first Orus mission.

Opposite the entrance sat Sheng with Ayla and Petra to either side. They stood as he entered and shook hands. The group sat and Mito closed the doors behind them. Ashok placed his worn cardboard cup on the table.

"After two weeks of analysis, it seems we have a clear picture of the situation." Ashok started, "I have read through the technical reports and watched the debrief given by Tomias."

"There has been a deluge of data to go through." Sheng wore a buttonless charcoal grey shirt. It was held by a single electrum pin on the chest in the form of a long palm leaf.

"Following the crash, we have been trying to get our heads around the situation. While we all have a desire to mourn, it is important to understand what happened." Ashok ran a finger around the cup. "It is clear that a series of judgments were made which ultimately placed Jonah and Tomias in a situation of disproportionate risk."

Sheng placed his hands on the table, crossing his fingers, "If we can take solace in anything it is that Tomias made a safe return."

Ayla turned sharply towards him.

"I don't think we can take particular solace in that, Sheng." Ashok flicked his cup aside. "The boys were both in extreme danger. It comes down to luck that he came back at all."

"I disagree..."

"I don't." Ashok interrupted. "It is normal to try and appoint blame after failure but all of the information we have reviewed points to a clear and almost calculated breach of safety. After so many years of planning I find it incredible that this could happen in the final straight."

"There are many aspects of this mission that I've found lacking but... " Ayla placed a hand on the table. "We have been under a lot of pressure... You know how it was."

Ashok nodded, "Yes, Ayla. But you very well know that isn't an excuse to risk life. Sheng, you single handedly took the decision to deviate from the landing sequence, taking no counsel from your technical teams nor running proper testing before launch."

"With all due respect, it had to be done. There was no other option." Sheng stayed firm.

"After reviewing all of the information at hand, I have made the decision to relieve you of your position. Effective immediately."

"So, I'm a scapegoat for your own failings? You've pushed this mission forward at any cost for the last twenty years. All I have done is fulfil your demands."

"A full and proper investigation will be made to assess any and all liability. It will be handled by a review panel independent of BISE and independent of my authority. I have put myself forward for review too."

"I'll be happy if this decision lets you rest easier, Ashok." Sheng pushed his chair back and stood.

"It will take a long time before I can rest easy, Sheng. We're finished here." Ashok stood and left.

Sheng looked down towards Ayla, "At least you're happy."

"Why, Sheng? Because you've been removed? Do you think it matters? I would much rather you stay in the job for life and have Jonah back." Ayla raised and stared directly into Sheng's dark eyes. They stood motionless, a couple of inches apart.

"His death is on all of us, you included, I hope you realise that."

****

"Dad wants to see me in the morning." Ayla stepped over tender twigs on a gravel path.

"Do you know why?" Tomias walked next to her, his fingers laced through hers.

"I don't know, imagine it's to do with the investigation."

"There won't be an end to this anytime soon."

The forest was dim, lit only by Hela's faint blue glow. Their path opened up onto a peaceful meadow. Tall grasses arced over in unison, commanded by a light breeze. Ayla took a detour into the field, running her hand over the soft grass.

She stopped at a wildflower sticking out above the meadow. Its colours were bleached by the moonlight.

"No, imagine it won't. I think about it all the time. I should have stood up to Sheng more."

Tomias dropped down and sat among the grasses. His head peeked out over it. Ayla bent over to smell the flower, he pulled her down to sit on his legs.

She laughed and embraced him. Tomias fell to lay flat on the field. She rested on top of him.

Tomias's face grew serious again. "We still don't know what happened. With all my respect to your father, it is a little soon to be making conclusions."

"We know it's over. It's a sad conclusion to a poorly written book."

Together, they stared up at the sky, at Hela.

"Jonah was aware of the risks. You know that."

"Of course." Ayla focused on a large cloud over Hela's southern hemisphere. "We all knew the risks but, after so much preparation, they felt almost academic."

Tomias held her hand. "It's a little surreal." He rolled Ayla over and stood up. "Come on." Pulling her up, they stepped back towards the path leading up Mount Rhoda.

Soon, the forest cleared and the mirror's rim came into view. During a normal clear night, the basin was an intimidating sight. A chasm of darkness sank behind a sharp curving lip like a cheeky smile into the abyss. Every so often a ray of light would bounce off of the polished surface within, giving off a diffuse glow.

Ayla climbed over a wooden fence marking the path's end and continued up to the rim. She sat on it with her back tilted towards the city, peering into the giant bowl.

From its edge, the view changed completely. Hela, still rising in the night's sky, reflected cleanly off of the smooth basalt. A puddle of bluey-green light flowed from her feet and focused on the moon's South Pole towards the mirror's centre. Around her, clouds and stars bent and warped about the giant mirror.

"My father sat me here, a long time ago, must have been no more than twelve. He told me stories about Hela. Heroes, gods, everything so close, so vivid. I was in awe. I said, 'let's go, let's go there'. I'll never forget his reaction. He didn't laugh, he didn't even pause. He placed a hand on my head and said, 'I'll support you.'" Ayla leaned back, "I feel like I let him and everyone else down."

"You've done so much for this mission. Some dangers were unavoidable." Tomias sat behind her, his legs over the side towards Flavia. "Jonah and I would talk about it before he was even chosen to go down. We made a decision."

"What decision?"

"We knew that if the mission failed, interest in reaching Hela would disappear for a long time to come. We agreed that if one of us didn't make it, the other should immediately put a request in to go back. To do everything we can to get there."

"The thinking behind that is?"

"Fall off the horse, get up and get back on the damn horse. Give up and you give up for good. Either we do it now or we won't see Hela's surface in our generation. The day I was released from quarantine, I gave Sheng a formal letter stating my desire to go back immediately."

"What did he say? Also, why didn't you tell me?"

"I wanted there to be more to tell. He didn't even acknowledge it."

Ayla took a close look at Hela's bowed reflection. She could make out the fine edge of Rodinia on the Tethys Ocean where Jonah was supposed to land.

She swivelled around to face Flavia, "I'm not sure anyone would listen now."

"They'll listen a lot less in the months and years to come. Kala has been all over the news. He will push his own agenda. Nussa is already seizing this opportunity. We will become more and more irrelevant, BISE, Flavia, even your father."

Ayla stared out over the city. Far below them, lights from The Residence gently illuminated Flavia park. She kissed Tomias. "Perhaps no one will listen to you alone but maybe they'll listen to us..."

****

The desk was littered with lenses and clamps. A maze cut sporadically through the mess as if a hurried mouse had pushed equipment out of its way.

Tilted mirrors were positioned on every turn, a succession of lenses broke the straights like hurdles. The maze led to a cylinder sat at the centre of the table. A perfect crystal cube was placed opposite. The cube was backed by a curved wall of sensors.

Petra made small adjustments to the setup, hurrying about the table, tweaking and nudging the lenses. Every so often she would stop, take notes and continue. The mouse was frustrated not to fit down on the maze.

The central cylinder had a glass outer shell and a machined base. Inside, two metal cores almost met in the middle. Each core tapered into an extremely sharp point capped by a diamond tooth. The ends pinched a tiny black grain. It was caught between their mandibles. Topping the outer shell was a copper end-piece with a tangle of tubes emerging out of it in loops.

Petra entered a series of numbers into a monitor on the table's edge. Nothing happened. She entered a second series, and the complex cylinder began to hiss. A sharp stream of frozen gas sprayed out of a copper pipe. She quickly pressed the monitor and the pressure dropped.

Using a jeweller's wrench, Petra tightened a small copper nut at the pipe's tip. After entering the sequence again, the machine was silent. A positive confirmation lit the monitor.

Pressing a button on the wall of her office made solid blinds slowly descend over the room's high windows. A thick black curtain then spread over the blinds. It covered the room in darkness. Petra stood by the monitor and brought the maze to life.

A narrow green light illuminated most of the clamps and lenses. The light stopped abruptly after a sharp corner. Petra stepped over and carefully aligned the angle so as to let the light continue its journey.

The beam shot through the central cylinder, around the black grain and ended in the crystal cube. The cube projected a feint rainbow across the arched bank of sensors.

Finally, she placed a pair of oval protective glasses in-front of her eyes and entered a final sequence of numbers.

"Go-time."

A last tap on the monitor and the central cylinder frosted over in an instant. The soft green laser disappeared. The room was momentarily devoid of all light.

A piercing sapphire beam shot through the system. It gradually picked up intensity. The beam narrowed in on the pinched black grain, caught between its diamond anvils. Soon it began emanating an irate maroon glow.

The monitor let out a light beep as Petra looked towards the cylinder. Three seconds later an immense pulse ran through the maze. Vaporising the grain, it caused the diamond jaws to clinch shut with a loud smash.

Silence.

Petra opened the curtain and raised the blinds. She walked over to the crystal cube and picked it up. It radiated a mild warmth. Raising it up to a window, she peered in.

At the very centre of the cube a ghostly violet sphere had appeared. Looking closer, she could see an ethereal purple ball surrounded by wisps of vivid blue, magenta and red. Minute, irregular breaks in the sphere came in to focus.

Petra smiled from cheek to cheek.

"You didn't say much when I removed Sheng." Ashok stood by a lacquered cherry wall in his office. The wood veneer had been cut into carefully matched lengths which formed a series of repeating panels spanning the entire wall. Separating each of the sections was a thin vertical strip of electrum.

"You expected a little dance?" Ayla walked up to the wall and ran her fingers over the panes. She focused on the polished metal strips.

"I figured you might have something to say on the topic, the two of you rarely saw eye-to-eye."

"My thoughts are elsewhere."

"Did you think it was the right decision?" Ashok pressed the edges of two central panels. They moved out smoothly towards them.

"We all made mistakes, Dad, we're all culpable. I deserve to go as much as Sheng does."

Ashok slid one panel to the left. Ayla, observing the fluid motion, followed suit with the right. They revealed a hidden bar made from a single plank of cherry wood. Its unhewn edge curved in and out along its length. On top of the bar sat a glistening steel espresso machine with a waffled chrome surround. Next to it, a stout steel grinder.

"There's a fair amount you don't know about Sheng's actions."

"Like what?" Ayla started opening and exploring the contents of three drawers underneath the bar. The first contained a row of four electrum jars seated in forms cut out to their shape within the wood.

Ashok removed the second jar and unscrewed its top with a light twist. He pointed the open jar at Ayla, the rich tangy smell hit her immediately. Inside, glossy chocolate coffee beans.

"It's not important at this stage. I need to talk to you about something else." He placed four scoops of beans in the grinder.

"I need to talk to you, too." Ayla spoke over the whirr.

"I'll go first if you don't mind. I'm making the coffee, after all." He removed the portafilter, dosed the first shot and carefully pulled it using a slide level on the machine before placing it in front of Ayla.

"Difficult to argue with that." She picked up the octagonal crystal cup, taking in the spicy aroma. "Though it looks like you've stolen from Canvas again."

Ashok continued, ignoring Ayla's accusation. "I need you to head up BISE..."

Ayla didn't feel the heat from the cup until it overwhelmed her. She placed it back on the bar. "That's what I wanted to talk to you about. I want us to mount a second mission, immediately."

She picked it up again and took a sip, "We have perfected Advanced AB and Petra has a production vessel ready. We can go back and make it to the surface within a few months."

Ashok pulled his coffee. "Unfortunately, that's not the mission I had in mind." They walked out to a table in his enclosed garden. The air was filled with the scent of roses, brought out by the morning sun "It is very likely that we're going to have to shut down the Hela programme."

Ayla sank into a chair, "We can't give up now!"

"It's not about giving up. Tomorrow I'm going to Nussa to meet with the others. I expect there will be no support for BISE's continued efforts. The best we can do is salvage the institute and refocus its efforts."

"So, you want me to kill the thing I love?" Ayla jumped up and paced around the garden.

"No. I want you to save it."

"Save it with a swift bolt to the head, great idea."

"At least let me finish. The coffee is good but it's not that strong." Ashok savoured his cup. "I will need you to close down the mission. In doing so, I want you to do a review of the technology created during your work. Afterwards, create a strategy to redeploy it for other uses. If you have Advanced, great, let's use it for something else."

"In your head, did that feel like a consolation prize?"

"It's the best option we have. The alternative is that everything is shut down and all of your work goes down the drain. BISE could be disbanded and all of the talent it currently contains will be dispersed. Who knows what they could end up working on." Ashok went up to Ayla and placed his hand on her shoulder. "I need you to do this. Once you calm down and think it over, you'll see there's no other way."

"I disagree, Dad. There's always another way."

ELEVEN

"Mito, could you ask Ayla to come over to Nussa? We left things a little tense." Ashok stood at the tip of a Glider, leaning on its panoramic monitor.

The craft began to slow its speed as Nussa came in sight. Little by little, as the velocity declined, his field of view grew out from the narrow centre. Ashok stared out at the Imperial Capital's suburbs. People going about their daily lives.

"Of course, Ashok, what should I tell her?" Mito's voice came from the monitor.

"Tell her I'd like to spend some time with her. We can stay the night in Nussa."

"I will pass it on and give a heads up to the embassy that you're staying."

"Thank you, Mito."

The Glider slowed further as it entered the city proper. Soon after AB Drive was implemented Kala had cleared a strip running along the middle of Nussa's main boulevard. It allowed

Gliders to drift through the city, all the way up to the Residence grounds.

No more than thirty feet above the busy road, Ashok looked on at the traffic below, making its way across the city.

Coming to a halt, the craft lowered, alighting on a cushioned clamp built into the ground. Ashok stepped out on a fresh lawn where he was met by Frey.

"Welcome to the Imperial Residence, Ashok."

"Thank you, Frey, you've been kind to host this meeting."

"Always an honour." He pointed Ashok in the direction of a path leading up to the main house. "The others are already here."

Walking up, Ashok could see The Council leaders seated inside through the Residence's impressive arched windows

He waved but didn't notice a response.

Stepping inside, it took his eyes a second to adjust. The conference room was dark, despite the windows and the light outside. Kala sat at the end of a stout rectangular table. His seat was a smidge larger and more ornate than the others.

Frey pointed towards a chair on the side, next to Ra-bia.

"Welcome, Ashok." Kala slowly rose to greet him.

"Thank you, Kala. Hello, everyone."

Ra-bia shook his hand, Matias smiled, Yana and Arun let out a lax hello and Khin barely reacted.

"We might as well start." Kala continued.

"Let's." Ashok leaned over the table.

"Following the mission's failure, the System has taken a clear hit.

"A bigger hit than we could have expected," Arun added. "Morale is low, our people feel let-down."

"This is one setback." Ashok turned. "While I am heartbroken by our loss, it was a known risk. We have to move forward."

"*Our* loss? Jonah was *our* son. Nussa lost a son. What you are losing is our trust." Kala opened his palms towards Ashok. "For your sake, for the sake of all of us, we have to restore belief amongst the people."

"Kala, the world is fine. Yes, this was a tragedy, but the System is stable. No one on Earth is starving, no one fears conflict or strife."

Ra-bia turned to Ashok, "I'm sorry but I disagree, Ashok. We put our faith in this path. We believed the mission and its technology would be a beacon, a milestone. It didn't work. Our people are anxious about the future. We're anxious."

"I understand why you could feel that way. I believe the best course of action would be to try again."

Matias couldn't hold back his laughter. "Try again, are you crazy? We need to take a long hard look at the world and decide what we do next. Whether this is the right direction at all.

"What are you saying?"

"He's saying that perhaps it's time to rethink this experiment, Ashok." Kala interrupted.

"It's an experiment now? Is this what you all believe?" Ashok panned around a silent room.

"We want the Core System to work, Ashok," Arun spoke up. "We're all here because of you, because of your vision. But there's only so far we can go, so far we can push before something breaks."

Kala stood. "Power is too concentrated, too rigid. There's no flexibility and no give. No way for voices beyond this room to be heard. While the seven of us sit here and run the world, individual city state leaders are nothing more than glorified mayors."

"What do you propose?"

"When a bridge heats up, it expands. If you don't anticipate that expansion it will crack and fail."

"Poetic, Kala." Ashok continued to study the others.

"Poetic or not, it's true. Societies are not static. Like most everything else in the universe, they are prone to entropy. If that lean towards disorder is not anticipated by the system, it can only last so long before it cracks."

"So again, what do you propose?"

"I believe the city states should have more say in their own affairs. We could create another council, a chamber of city leaders. They could cluster and collaborate between our Cores."

"And the risks of indecision, responsibility, all those things we came together to avoid?"

"We can neither create, nor sustain a perfect world. All we can do is ensure there are no excesses. People are safe now, they're fed." Kala lent forward. "But they're not happy. They have to be able to directly impact their world."

"That's why we have the Kap. To provide the education necessary for anyone who wants to lead, regardless of their background"

"The Kap is an incredible institution but it is currently built on a false promise. All but a handful of its students will lead castles of sand."

"This is something I've dedicated my life to..."

"So have we, Ashok. That's why we need to make a change. It would be a fallacy to expect the Core System to work perfectly in perpetuity. What about when we're gone, when the system morphs and entropies? If you want to leave something which lasts beyond your lifetime, it has to embrace change. Even with a dose of creative destruction built in."

"I understand. And I see you are all aligned. Please give me some time to consider." Ashok sat back in his chair, resting his arms on the sculpted supports. "In return, I ask that you at least give a thought to a second mission."

"Before we continue," Kala brushed off the request, "let me show you all a short demonstration from our own engineering team here in Nussa." Still standing, he gestured to Frey.

Frey slid open a panel on the wall behind them. It opened an enclosed square room with a round steel table at its centre. Below the table, two black canisters were placed on either side of a charcoal grey box. Curled golden wires led to the top of the table where a large gyroscope sat motionless.

The leaders turned to face the rig.

"Go ahead."

Frey pressed a monitor mounted to the grey box. Soon after, the gyro started spinning up. Slowly at first, it rapidly gained momentum. An initial drone soon turned into a sharp shriek.

"What you see is an active – " Frey's speech was almost lost in the noise, "an active energy cell connected to a one megawatt Abaryonic dynamo." He walked up to the machine and swivelled the table. As he did, the gyro tilted to compensate. "At full power, the field created inside can propel the dynamo to point zero one C."

He pressed the monitor again and the speed increased further. A piercing pulse shot through the room. The machine went near silent. Only light vibrations from the table could be heard.

"What's that?" Ra-bia pointed to the gyro. Its central wheel began to glow a pale blue.

"This is Contained working as it should. It is a rapidly pulsing AB field capable of pushing the dynamo faster. The glow comes from electrons racing ahead of light as it is held back by the field." The device continued to increase in brightness until it bathed the previously dark room in an iridescent blue glow. "By containing the field in a sort of bubble, we can use it for virtually any function. This small device could power an entire town. With a couple of transmitters, it could power a valley of villages."

The table's vibrations became uneven. Frey stepped over and pressed the monitor a final time, shutting down the machine. Its brightness reduced and dissipated. Another pulse of sound pierced the air. The gyro slowed and quietened.

****

Two soldiers in parade uniform opened the Residence's main gate and Ashok walked out onto a lively road. "Has she arrived?"

"She has. Alya said she will meet you by the Central Broadcast Building. Is that okay? Do you want us to take you there?"

"Thank you, Mito, I'll go over by myself."

Several lanes of vehicles hummed along in each direction of a busy boulevard. He walked through the first three lanes of traffic.

Ashok stopped on a lush green ribbon of bushes splitting the boulevard. Vehicles in the other direction immediately stopped to make way. Their passengers gawked. He waved awkwardly. Nussa's traffic brought to a halt, he crossed and disappeared down a side-street.

"A quick change of scenery?" Ayla was waiting by the corner of the Central Broadcast Building.

"We left it a little tense yesterday, I thought it would be nice to spend the day together."

"This isn't Flavia you know, there must have been some odd looks."

"A few lanes of befuddled traffic," he smiled.

"As long as we're here, let's get some wine." Ayla walked forward.

"The embassy has plenty."

"Not like this." She led the way through Nussa's ochre sun-drenched streets towards Hallough's shop.

They soon reached the barrel-shaped door.

"Quaint." Ashok paused as he stepped through.

"So sarcastic, you haven't seen inside yet."

Ayla stepped in, followed by Ashok. Hallough was arranging bottles into their holders, carefully turning them to accentuate their hand-painted labels.

"Surprise, Hallough."

"Princess!" Hallough half-heartedly replied, though he was more focused on her companion. "Emperor Ashok, an honour. If I had known."

"Yes, yes, very good. Ayla has talked about you since her Kap days, let's drop the formal stuff." Ashok stuck out a hand.

"If you insist." Hallough ignored the hand and engrossed Ashok in a warm hug.

"Though I suppose you're the one responsible for introducing my daughter to wine."

"As far as I remember, she came quite acquainted. I simply introduced her to good wine."

"That's a fair assessment." Ayla wandered around the shop. "Hallough knows about every good vineyard in the world."

"Perhaps that's a stretch, Princess."

"Well, you definitely know a lot. Remember the one you gave me last time, from the caravansary out of Nussa?"

"Verbesh, near the village of Nyore, of course."

"How is your friend? You said it wasn't easy for her there."

"It has been difficult. I spoke to Tisa the other day. She told me that the people in the village were growing rather restless."

"Why is that?" Ashok asked.

"They live a static existence, Sir. Existence is probably the right word. While they don't need anything, the people have little reason to push or strive. Life is very different there to the cities."

"So I keep being told." Ashok wandered in a loop opposite to Ayla. He inspected the columns of bottles. "You think the Core System doesn't work?"

"I'm a wine-seller, I listen to people who come to my shop and talk to those who produce this elixir. What I hear over and over is that our cities are alive while our countryside wilts."

"I will have to visit sometime."

"Let's go now, Dad." She sprang over.

"What do you mean?"

"You didn't have any plans for the evening, did you?"

"Not as such, no."

"Right then, I've been wanting to go since Hallough told me about the place, let's go now. How far away is it?"

"Nyore is a couple of hundred miles out of Nussa. Verbesh is directly on the Great Trade Road. The village itself is a little further up in the hills."

"I thought you said it was by a desert? Clever marketing, Hallough?"

He smiled, “It is. The Masra desert starts nearby. It’s a pretty magical place, Ayla. Worlds collide. You’ll see if you go.”

“Come on, Dad. We can be there in less than an hour.”

“Right, fine, I’ll sort a couple of things and I’ll ask Mito to prepare the Glider.”

“Great! Now then, Hallough, it seems like I’ve robbed you of a sale. Don’t hold it against me!”

“I’ll choose to see it as a reason to come and visit again soon” Hallough hugged her once more and opened the barrel-shaped door.

✱✱✱✱✱✱✱✱✱✱✱

Antiquity produced a number of Great Trade Roads criss-crossing the world. They connected far-flung empires way before those empires could directly contact each other.

Mediator kingdoms would arise to act as conduits for trade and exchange. The Empire of Nussa started out as a simple trading post, its location near the shores of the vast Lake Naya, made for a perfect stopping place along the route. Over time, Nussa leveraged its position to expand, taking control of the routes as well as all of the states along them.

At its peak, the Nussa Empire controlled a two-thousand-mile swathe of land. Dubbed ‘The Bridge of Oceans’, Nussa stretched all the way from the Western to the Eastern Oceans.

Its grip on these lands led The Great Trade Road to emerge as one of humanity’s largest ancient construction projects.

Over centuries, the road was hewn out of the hills, forests, jungles and deserts which lay in its path.

Today, the artery tied together a string of powerful states which sat like pearls on a necklace stretching across the continent.

These days, travel along the road itself was rare. Most now used the Tube to move between states. People and cargo shot through along the thick double vacuum cylinder constructed along the entire length of the road.

Fading from its former glory, the Great Trade Road now served largely as a connector between villages along its route with villagers walking or cycling at most a couple of miles along it.

With the afternoon rolling on, Ayla and Ashok's Glider skated fifty feet above the Tube. Every so often the outline of a container would shoot off below them near the speed of sound.

"There! I think I can see it." Ayla pointed to a smudge in the distance as the Glider began feathering its pace.

"Your friend was right about the scenery, it's rather impressive." Gradually, the caravansary started coming into view.

The building stuck out in the landscape. Four high limestone walls with rounded turrets at its corners were marked out by the afternoon sun.

"Beautiful, isn't it?" Ayla placed her hand on the panoramic front panel. The building sat pretty much directly on the Trade Road. On the other side, a scrubby desert plateau spread out towards distant jagged peaks.

Verbesh from Nyore

Behind it was a different world. A perfectly ordered vineyard fanned out on all three sides, gently sloping up into rolling green hills. Up amongst the verdant folds, they could see the reflections of glass from windows in the small settlement of Nyore.

Reaching their destination, Ayla peaked into the building from her high vantage point. A large courtyard was cut out of the seemingly impregnable block. The Glider came to rest between the road and the building, in-front of a lofty rounded entranceway framed by a square stone outer border.

A tall lady woman emerged between the gates as Ayla and Ashok disembarked. A light current ran through the open portal. It caught on her floor-length crimson cloak.

"Tisa, I assume." Ayla reached out to shake her hand.

"Tisa indeed." She took her hand out from a deep-cut pocket. "Hallough gave me barely enough warning, I haven't really prepared. We don't get many people coming out here, never mind super important guests like yourselves. Princess Ayla, Emperor Ashok, it is a pleasure and an honour, please come in."

"We're so very grateful you invited us." Ashok followed suit in shaking her hand. "Though, from the sounds of it, you might not have had a lot of choice."

Tisa let out a broad, warm smile, "It is far from a chore." Her cloak swirled as she turned. "Come on, follow me, I have a little something prepared."

They walked through giant studded wooden doors. They led to a short passageway lined in stone. Doors on either side opened up to smaller tunnels. “We store the wine in these corridors.” Tisa pointed with her palm. “I’ll show you later.”

The passageway opened onto an uncovered square courtyard. It was an enclosed oasis. The stone walls were covered in ornate art and dotted with arched windows leading to internal corridors. Decorated wool rugs with vivid colours were draped over parapets under the windows.

The courtyard itself had a flowing fountain lined in turquoise tiles at its centre. Around the fountain were four square patches of grass. At the centre of each stood clusters of three fig trees. Their short canopies frayed out to create a natural smattering of shade.

“Welcome.” Tisa turned with a smile and pointed to a table next to the fountain. The sun had set over the high walls, leaving a mellow heat lingering in the air. Enough to draw the scent out of the trees and flowers in the courtyard.

“You have an incredible place.” Ashok turned from side to side as he went to the table, trying to take in every detail.

“It was a hell of a lot of work.”

“I bet,” Alya sat at the table, leaning to dip a hand in the fountain.

The wrought iron table was topped with inlaid tiles delicately shaped with abstract mango fruit and leaf patterns. On it, Tisa had placed an arrangement of local fruits, nuts and wine, of course.

“It’s always a pleasure to show this place to anyone who comes.”

“We can both see why.” Ayla tried a raw cashew misted with ginger.

“How long did it take you to get here?” Ashok pushed Ayla’s hand out of the way to reach the cashews.

“Going on eight years now. When we came, the land around the building was mostly dust and rocks. This place was a shambles. We started with the well and installed an atmospheric water generator. Only then did we begin the renovation. Half of the village got involved.”

“Yes, Hallough told us about Nyore, would we be able to go?” Ayla eyed the wine.

Tisa opened the bottle and poured a glass each. “If you would like to see Nyore, we could walk up there for dinner. I’ll tell them to expect guests.”

“Great, don’t let them prepare anything,” Ashok raised his glass.

“All in due time, first, cheers. This is a young wine, a test from our second harvest.”

“You’re very right. No need to rush. Cheers.”

****

“Sir, you came within seconds of a critical breakdown.”

“The experiment was a success, I shut it down when the vibrations became irregular.” Frey circled the gyro with a group of engineers within the empty square room.

"The data shows that by that time it was extremely unstable. The technology is not ready, Sir, the speed was well-above any current limits."

Frey stopped. "It's a pretty bad reflection on you to be telling me what I can't be doing with this."

"Yes, Sir, but we have a lot more work to do before Contained is stable." The lead engineer knelt as he inspected the canisters below the gyro.

"You've been saying the same thing for months."

The golden wires curling up from the canisters to the gyro had sagged.

The engineer tapped one of the wires with his fingernail. It disintegrated and crumbled to the ground. "Unfortunately, it will be many more months still."

"Unacceptable. This technology is the cornerstone to our proposal. It will give cities their independence."

"Yes, Sir. But it has to be stable before we make such promises – and it isn't. We were relying on the data from Sheng."

"It's my job to say what promises we can make and when we can make them. It's your job to make this work."

"It is also my job to try and keep you safe. The data shows you were less than ten seconds from going critical. If that had happened, this room and everyone in it would have been vaporised."

"I think I made myself clear. You do your job, I'll do mine. We're done here." Frey walked out of the room, leaving the engineers to pour over the crippled machine.

✱✱✱✱✱✱✱✱✱✱✱✱

With the caravansary behind them, Ayla, Tisa and Ashok made their way up towards Nyore. The sun was about to dip below the horizon behind the Masra Desert.

The trio meandered along a zig-zag path up a grassy hill leading up towards the village. The path was far from a straight line.

Steep rises gave way to flat sections, quickly moving to more steep inclines. From up close, the whole hillside looked like a giant game of snakes and ladders stomped out of the grass.

"Why would they make such an inefficient path?" Ayla looked out over the hill.

"It depends who you mean by they. If you think the villagers made it then, yes, it would be a terrible path."

"They didn't?"

"Not quite, these paths have been more chewed than stomped."

"Chewed?"

"Indeed. Millennia of goats wandering up and down the hills, looking for something sweet to nibble on."

"In that case, they've done a great job," Ashok walked behind them. "Even goats have a feel for engineering."

Behind them, they could see Verbesh with the Glider perched next to the Great Trade Road and the Tube cutting across above it. Now and then, the silence would be broken by a container or a pod zooming by with a distant swoosh.

They crested a fold in the hills and Nyore appeared out of the green. It was a compact village. No more than three-dozen houses nestled together around an open pasture.

The houses were squat, round single-storey buildings. They had tall pointy roofs. Some made of thatch, others made from stone and tile. All of the houses were painted in different shades of saturated honey yellow.

Walking to Nyore's edge, they saw six villagers sat around a small fire to one side of the central pasture. The sun had set, leaving behind it a rolling warm breeze.

"Hello, everyone, I mentioned I would bring a few guests."

"Of course, Tisa." A croaky voice emerged from the huddle. "Come, join us."

Ashok and Ayla shook hands with the villagers and sat on a woven rug by the fire. Tisa greeted the group and joined them.

"My name is Hire, I am the chief of Nyore." Hire had high cheekbones, accentuating a natural smile. He was no more than fifty, with grey curls in his coiled hair.

The villagers wore robes closely matching the colour of their houses. Generous light wool cloaks were tied by loose woven belts.

"Thank you for making the time for us, Hire." Ayla watched the small fire, fixated on the pulsing flames.

"Make the time? We don't often get guests here. It is a treat."

With the sun set, stars began to emerge. Hela crested the hills, a crescent of green and blue peeked above distant trees. Ayla looked over at her glow.

"It looks like you have a peaceful life here." Ashok felt the rough weave of the rug below him.

"Yes. Peaceful. A little too peaceful. If it wasn't for Tisa, we would go crazy."

"Now then, Hire, don't exaggerate. You have a comfortable life here." Tisa accepted a small shapely glass of tea.

"Humans weren't made to be comfortable." Hire passed the tea to Ayla and Ashok, the heat of the glass slightly burning them. "Was that uncomfortable, was it unpleasant?"

"Not at all." Ashok shook his head.

"You're being polite. It was unpleasant." Hire continued between sips. "But so what? I look forward to that sensation because it tells me that sweet tea is in my hand. I like sweet tea. So what if it burns a little to get it?"

Ayla laid out across the rug with her legs behind her father. "I don't know, Hire, I am quite comfortable here."

"You're comfortable now because you come from somewhere else. This is new. Twenty, thirty, fifty years. The hills are still beautiful, but you become sedate. No! Humans have to create. We have to push. We have to destroy!"

"Why destroy? Why can't we just create." Ashok asked as he leaned back on Alya's legs.

"There's no such thing as creation without destruction. The pressure has to go somewhere. If we can't destroy it stays within us, it builds, it is unstable."

The group was interrupted as a shooting star fired across the clear sky above them.

"I don't know if I can agree with you, Hire."

"You know exactly what I mean, Ashok but you haven't found your balance yet."

"So, you recognise your guests." Ashok raised up towards the fire.

"We might be villagers, but we all have monitors!" The group laughed.

"Perhaps you're right, Hire, but what kind of leader would build destruction into their system?" Ayla fixed on the fire.

"Whether you build it in or not, the system will find a way. And it won't be neat or tidy. It's inevitable. As inevitable as Hela rising every evening." Hire signalled to one of the villagers who placed a large steel pot on the fire. "We can continue this later. Now, join us for some food."

TWELVE

Sheng's former office spanned the width of BISE's top floor. A broad seating area was framed by floor-to-ceiling windows facing the campus parks. Sheng's desk was, however, positioned at the opposite end of the long space.

A thick padded chair was pointed away from the rest of the office and towards a rear wall of windows looking across the vast fabrication halls.

Ayla looked around for three folders of documents. Finding them in a drawer, she rolled the chair to the opposite side of the desk, stacking them to one side. She quickly gave up on the gloomy setting and went over to the soft, sunlit seating area.

Placing the folders on a low wooden table, she opened them up one by one, taking out a series of documents from each. Pretty soon she sighed and fell back into the pillowy seat.

Petra knocked once and walked in. "Trying to make some changes?" She sat across from Ayla, placing another, thicker, folder down on the table.

"I never really liked the guy..."

Petra laughed, “You can say that again.”

“I never really like the guy but, I didn’t imagine things turning out this way.”

“None of us did. I need to show you something.”

“Any chance we can do it later? I’m trying to get my head around the operations of BISE and it’s not particularly straightforward.”

“You’ll probably want to hear this sooner rather than later.”

Ayla stared out to the clean-cut lawns and neat paddocks. “This is such an amazing organisation. So much talent and knowhow in one place. And we have to wind it down.”

“As I said, you’ll want to hear this.” Petra opened her folder.

“Sorry. I’m listening.”

“Look at this.” She showed Ayla a document dated three days before the launch. “This is a command to change the landing profile of Orus 5. It is signed by Sheng and cleared through a confidential path.”

Ayla took the page, “What does it mean?”

“For some reason, Sheng changed the landing protocol at the last minute. He reverted back to an early version we deemed dangerous.”

“With what explanation?”

“None. It was tagged on to the mission sequence, obscured by a bunch of other parameters. No-one apart from two flight engineers knew. They were under strict secrecy.”

"Why the hell would he do that?" Ayla reviewed the landing arc plotted on the document. "We all agreed this would place a strain on the landing craft."

"Perhaps he wanted Orus down faster. Less time descending, less exposure to risk and so on."

"So, this might be the reason we lost Jonah?" Ayla stood.

"Yes, the profile could have artificially put more strain on the lander than it could handle."

"I knew our technology works. Sheng has to be prosecuted for this. I'll pass it on to the investigation panel."

"Is that your only conclusion?"

"What do you mean?"

"You said it yourself. The technology is sound. It works. There's nothing stopping us from going again. We can reach Hela."

Ayla placed the document back on the table. "Our orders are quite clear. We are to close down the programme and refocus."

"When have you cared about orders, Ayla?"

"I understand what my father is trying to do, he's trying to save the institute, Flavia. Besides, we don't have the equipment. We don't have anyone on our side."

Petra jumped up from her seat and ran off towards the other side of the room. "Come over here, let me show you something."

"Two secret things in one day, my."

"To be fair, this one has been right in front of your eyes. So it's more on you."

They went up to the windows beyond Sheng's desk. The fabrication halls stretched out into the distance. Components and gear expanded out along row after row of stacked shelves.

The halls were dimly lit, especially in comparison to the view from the other side. A handful engineers wandered amongst the broad isles.

"After the failure of Orus 3 we had to scrap the original design." Petra looked on, searching with her gaze. "Spinlaunch didn't manage to get it into orbit."

"I remember, yes. It made quite the mess."

"But it later turned out to be a software control issue, Spinlaunch was fine."

"Sooo..."

"Soo... there was a second craft, what would have been Orus 4, virtually complete. It was going to follow soon after Orus 3 but the mission was shelved while Spinlaunch was investigated. By the time it was cleared, the craft was superseded by a new, improved Orus 4"

"It's here? A whole Orus system is somewhere in there?"

"Bits of it, yes. It's in bits all over the world but look." Petra pointed in the distance to two giant arcs of wafered metal placed on their side. "That's part of the rear assembly. Half of it is here. There might be some components in Kamrun and maybe even some in Nussa. It won't take more than a few months to put together if we wanted to."

"That's not fair, Petra." Ayla almost placed her face to the window. "It's so close. There's no way anyone would support it. No one believes the technology even works, not even Dad."

"I've kitted out a BISE Glider with the newest stable Advanced AB. We could ask a test pilot to run a demonstration. It would be hard to argue with it if the system works on our gravity."

Ayla turned to Petra. "Where's the Glider?"

"In the old military base behind Mount Rhoda – I had it placed in a storage facility."

"Did you now?" Ayla's eyes sparkled.

****

Still sleepy, Ashok yawned as he observed a ray of sunlight shoot through a thin linen curtain. Its radiant morning glow flickered across a crumpled satin cover by his side.

Irnes turned towards him, "Good morning."

Ashok smiled. "That it is."

He walked to the window. Looking out over Dvor, the breeze felt cool on his skin.

"Are you not a little concerned your citizens will see you?" Irnes raised her eyebrows.

"Their treat."

"So it is. Hungry? The staff can bring some breakfast in the next room."

"Good idea. Do you have sampita somewhere in this castle?"

"That's a solid block of sugar and egg white, it really isn't breakfast food, Ashok. I asked for fruits." Irnes turned and walked to a closet.

"Fruits?! And fruits are a breakfast food?"

"Our fruits are fantastic."

"Not a big cube of meringue though, are they?... I'm sure they'll be great."

"Always a pleasure to see you, Ashok." Irnes buttoned up a fitted ash grey jacket.

"You too, Irnes, you too. If the Core System does change, I'll likely end up on the side-lines. Maybe I'll spend more time in Dvor."

"If it does change, Dvor might change. I know the patchwork of states around us wouldn't mind joining up."

"You'd look to form a new Core?" Ashok threw on a cream cotton shirt, slipped on a pair of loose linen trousers and tan sandals.

"It might make sense. Dvor is a historic centre of power. I don't see why I shouldn't explore it."

They walked through to an antechamber. Irnes' staff had placed a glistening crystal bowl full of perfect fruit on top of a carved wooden table. "If you take a step back from Flavia, you could help me consolidate the region. The Balkania Core is too big, it makes sense for it to split." Irnes pointed to the bowl.

Ashok looked on at a ruby red apple perched on top of the pile. "I'm not sure my work is done, Irnes, plus Flavia is my home."

"Power is power. Whether it is Flavia, here, Pacha or wherever."

"Maybe. But the reasons for holding it can differ. I really do feel like that sampita. I'll walk down to the city before going."

****

"Laaro, could you come over to Flavia with a crew?"

"Ayla, an unexpected surprise, what do you mean?"

"I need you to be here at the end of the week, can you do it?

"It will be a little difficult to coordinate, especially when I don't know why."

"Please trust me and help me with this."

"What do I tell my producers, my crew? What do we need to bring?"

"Tell them you have a scoop."

"What year do you think this is, Ayla? A scoop, really!?"

"Whatever. Tell them you have a secret exclusive from the Residence. Take a large zoom lens and set aside global broadcast time in the afternoon."

"What? Ayla, you need to give me more."

"I can't Laaro. Do this for me, please."

****

The granite cobblestones down to Dvor were slick with morning dew. Ashok spotted the nearest bakery and darted inside. He pointed to two heaving sampita's, taking them to go. The cubes of white fluff barely squeezed into the baker's box.

Ashok continued his walk through the old bazar as it awoke for the day's trade. Shopkeepers opened their stores and began to lay out an assortment of wares from ceramics to hand-crafted copper. As he passed, some waved, some greeted him but most simply got on with their day.

Turning on his favourite side-street, Ashok found himself in-front of Sabil's roastery. The main entrance was closed, its wooden shutters firmly boarded over the door and windows. Ashok listened through the thick slats. He could hear something inside. All was not lost.

"You there, Sabil?" He knocked twice. A muffled grunt echoed from inside.

"Was that yes, yes, I'll be there right away? With fresh coffee?" He knocked again. Coarse shuffles came up to the door, bolts and latches were undone with little finesse.

"It's true what they say, you have no heart!" Sabil groaned behind the shutters as he finally unfastened their latches.

"You know, we do have automatic locks with sensors and stuff. This could open up in a second." Ashok teased.

"No taste as well as no heart. I feel sorry for you!" Sabil gave Ashok a long hug, the box he was holding almost squeezed out from his hands. "It's a coffee shop in the old bazar. Do you not think it would lose a bit of its charm if everything were made with lasers and force fields?"

"This isn't a sci-fi wonderland – as far as I know, there's no such thing as force fields." Ashok pointed his box at Sabil. "Though, lasers do add class to any situation."

Sabil peered inside, "You're the only one who eats those things." He closed the lid. "They're deadly. I can't eat more than half."

"Come on, for me, I have wounds to lick."

"Because The Council wants change? Oh, boo hoo."

"And how do you know what The Council wants?"

"Oh, right. Heartless, tasteless and judgemental. What? Just because I have a humble roastery doesn't mean I can't possibly know what happens in the corridors of power?" Sabil went inside and soon emerged with two small spoons. He flung one towards Ashok, reopened the box and began to scoop out his sampita.

"I suppose that's what I was inferring." Ashok pushed his hand out of the way and took a scoop. "It's pretty boo hoo, don't you think?"

"For whom? For the states, probably not. For you, no. What they're suggesting might finish off what you started."

"Shouldn't I finish off what I started? Shouldn't you be making coffee?"

"Come on, old friend, you've become a little complacent," Sabil went inside and checked his espresso machine. It was a huge copper contraption. Curling pipes glimmered from the few rays of sun entering the shop. With loud, targeted shoves and pulls, he knocked out two thick shots of espresso. Their crema crept up the scratched octagonal cups.

"At least this way it's easier to take the abuse." Ashok inhaled the tangy aroma and took a sip.

"What abuse, it's true. You've achieved something amazing; you really have. But it's not done yet, it's not stable. You're flapping about pretending the project is complete, but it isn't. For the world to avoid repeating the past there has to be some give, some freedom."

"People keep telling me that." Ashok took a big scoop of sampita. "What if these freedoms destroy everything?"

"Why? Because people will have the freedom to choose their own destinies? To decide how they're governed?"

"...Yes."

"They'll make mistakes, of course they will. But the more rigid the system, the bigger the impacts of those mistakes."

"So, build the system around managing the inevitable failure. That's optimistic."

"Don't skew my words." Sabil threw a patterned rug over the now-open store windows. "Allow it to expect change, allow others to have a voice, a real voice."

"So where do I fit in? I'm redundant?" Ashok helped him straighten creases out from the rug.

"Some will seek to take advantage of the changes; you need to provide balance."

Ashok leaned on the rug and stared into his cup. Sabil stood by him.

“Look at me.”

“Yes, yes.” Ashok looked up.

“You need to go out on a peak. To provide balance you need to be trusted by all sides. If you push too far before you let go you’ll lose the trust.” Sabil placed a hand on Ashok’s shoulder. “Go out on top, my friend.”

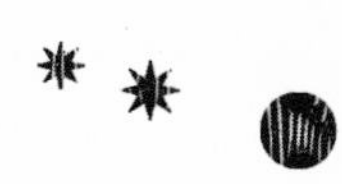

THIRTEEN

"Last chance. Are you sure you want to do this?" Tomias stood by a tall hangar door.

"Wouldn't it be strange if I said no now?" Ayla opened a service entrance built within the main hangar doors. Lights blinkered on as she stepped through.

"And Petra prepared the technology?"

"Yes, it's all ready. This is pretty much launch-ready Advanced AB fitted on to a Glider." She walked up to the craft. The last few lights to come on bounced off of its crimpled skin.

"It's a prototype. See how the skin is uneven to increase surface area." Tomias reached a hand out to touch the Glider.

"Yes, yes, come on, let's get inside. Do you have the cameras ready to mount?"

"In the bag. Since you didn't tell Laaro what to expect, he only sent a few."

Ayla rolled a steel step ladder over from the side and placed it up to the Glider's entrance. The wheels screeched and the hangar echoed as they slid across the concrete floor.

"This place hasn't seen action in a while." Tomias kicked the ladder's rubber wheels before climbing up.

"Now then Tommy, if you prefer, show me how it works, set up the cameras and I'll go by myself." Ayla stood face to face with the Glider's metal skin. The outlines of a door slowly cleaved out of the surface as if cut by a fine scalpel. The door slid to one side and they stepped inside.

"Not sure I'd live that down. Especially not after watching Jonah go down in flames."

"That's the spirit!" Ayla ran over to the control desk. An arc of monitors fanned out in front of her. "Set up the cameras and spool up."

"What does that even mean? It's just a geeky way of saying 'switch it on.'"

They clamped two cameras to each side of the control desk and pointed one towards the wrap-around front window.

Prototype Gliders had their control desk built within the craft itself. It was virtually all they contained. No lounge, no soft seating. Not even any sashimi. A control desk and two jump seats for the test pilots.

"Press your back and bum into the seat until you feel a series of clicks from the magnets." Tomias sat down and locked in.

"See, off to a good start already."

The magnetic clamps tightened on their flight suits leaving only their arms with free motion.

"Test. Operator, test. Can you see me?"

A woman's voice came through the monitor. "Operator here. Yes, I can see you and hear you loud and clear."

"Ayla! Will you tell me what's going on?"

"Ah, Laaro! Great to have you with us."

"I'm going nuts, Ayla. I'm stood here at the side of the park with my crew and have no idea what's going on. There's a crowd gathering. Where are you?"

"Nearby, Laaro. Don't worry about it. I'll see you shortly. Ready to broadcast?"

"What does that mean? Ayla, this is crazy!"

"Are you ready to broadcast, Laaro?"

"Yes, we go live in two minutes."

"Thank you. See you in a bit."

Ayla pushed a button, bringing the hangar doors to life. They began to slide in opposite directions. A ribbon of warm sunlight broke across the laser white light inside.

"Tommy, please power up and get ready to leave."

"Alright then, spooling up, if you will." He activated the control desk and toggled the Glider's power to hover. The craft pushed up against their seats as it rose silently off of the ground. "All systems operational, she's stable."

"Laaro, are you there?"

"Don't test me, young lady."

"I need you to place one camera with a close focus right at the tip of Mount Rhoda. Train another with a wide pan on Flavia Park. Can you do that?"

"There are three cameras with me."

"Well, leaves one for you then, doesn't it?"

"How gracious. Static shots or should we expect action."

Ayla smiled. "It's fair to say you can expect some action. Thank you Laaro." Ayla turned to Tomias, "Tommy, take us outside."

Tomias directed the Glider out of the hangar. They emerged into the golden afternoon sun. The hangar was located in an old military base behind Mount Rhoda. The towering mountain partially eclipsed the sun's rays. Their craft crept along, hovering a few feet above the warm concrete.

"You'd think there would be more people at this facility."

"You would, wouldn't you? But as head of BISE, I thought I'd send them on a super important training today."

Laaro's voice cut in before Tomias could respond, "Ayla, you're on in 15"

"Thank you, Laaro. Tommy, taxi to the far end of the runway. Then follow the plan."

"Alrighty." He nodded and started steering the Glider.

As they picked up speed, the Glider's rounded nose dipped down before levelling out. Many years ago, the facility had been a test site for ionjets.

Since the primitive machines required ground contact to launch, the runway was still perfectly clean and flat. The only imperfections were at the seams where the large flats of concrete joined one another. They stretched out in a line for over a mile out from the base of the mountain.

"Good afternoon, everyone." The camera focused on Ayla. "Dreams are worth fighting for. A fight can take many forms."

Monitors in homes around the world altered between Ayla, strapped into her seat, the view from her cockpit window and the concrete rushing ever-faster underneath.

"All of us have fought for too long to see this dream die. Especially when its success is so close and so attainable."

A billion eyes watched as the end of the runway came in sight. Tomias throttled back, briefly tilting the camera towards the sky. As it reached the end, the Glider came to a near halt.

Ayla continued, "We have to try, we have to push. Right to the very end." The craft turned a sharp hundred and eighty degrees.

The back of Mount Rhoda came into sight.

"And I know you're with me..."

Cameras cut from her face to the window.

Tomias toggled the throttle to full power. The craft accelerated violently towards the mountain. It pushed Ayla and Tomias back hard into their seats.

Edges blurred from their vision leaving only the green of Mount Rhoda's slope ahead. It neared with every second.

"Dear viewers, we have no idea what to expect." Laaro voiced the scenes as leaves on the trees at Mount Rhoda's foothills came into view. "Stay safe, Ayla."

The Glider hurtled into the mountainside. As it reached the sharp incline, it gripped Rhoda's contours, pointing up into a steep ascent. Every so often viewers across the world were startled by the sound of a protruding branch hitting the Glider's base as it soared no more than a few feet above the tree line. The craft screamed relentlessly up towards the peak.

Laaro trained his team to centre on Mount Rhoda's tip. The second they grasped focus a silver droplet shot out from behind the ridge.

"My god." Laaro stared open-mouthed.

The Glider launched vertically into the sky, no longer controllable, no longer pushing against the ground. A silver needle fired into the blue.

After a few long seconds, its ascent slowed rapidly. Coming to a brief stop miles above the city, the Glider tilted down. The cockpit's view filled with the buildings, streets and squares of the city. As they hurtled back down towards Earth, Flavia Park appeared to be their impending bullseye.

"It seems they are in an uncontrolled freefall." Laaro and his team stood firm as the craft fell towards the ground. Countless families looked on as the sunlight reflecting from its rippled surface briefly illuminated Mount Rhoda's Hela mirror.

A thousand feet above the park, their freefall seemed unnatural.

Pointing square at the ground, the Glider suddenly looked like it was slowing.

"There, there in the grass!" Laaro pointed to the spot in Flavia Park directly under the falling mass. The grass was bending, forming a small bowl. It pushed further and further into the turf.

Two hundred feet and the craft was clearly braking, the ground beneath it was now noticeably cratered.

Thirty feet and it was almost hovering.

Five feet above the ground, the Glider stopped. It looked like a raindrop fallen down from the sky, perched above the grass.

It levelled off and came down to rest. The craft's bulbous tip hung over the depression made by their descent.

Laaro, his team and several hundred stunned onlookers ran over as the door slid open. Ayla appeared from the shadows, her hair messy, her face red. "We can make it to Hela. He *must* make it to Hela!"

She sat on the edge of the door and pushed off to the park below, landing with a tumble. Tomias came out after her, landing on his feet.

The crowd swarmed them. Laaro pushed through. "What have you done, Ayla, what have you gone and done?"

She looked straight down the camera, "We proved it's possible!"

****

The sounds of a thousand birds, bugs and beasts was near deafening in the evening twilight. They chirped, swooped, cricketed and croaked like the liveliest of days in the middle of Merkum.

This clever analogy was lost on Hire as he made his was down the hills towards Verbesh. His pace was slow but steady. Every so often, he would pause and take in the sights and sounds around him.

A rolling breeze diffused the nectar of exotic flowers into the warm air. Again, to him, they were simply flowers. Their velvet perfume filled his heart nevertheless.

As he reached the outer rim of the vineyard, Hire spotted Tisa tending to a vine not too far away.

"You can't stay away from your vines." He laughed.

He lifted a broad lime-green leaf and examined a bunch of young grapes. The berries were starting to gain colour. The bunch was uneven in sizes and shades. Some of the berries were a dark pink, others a light violet. A few still carried their greens.

"I feel I know every bunch here."

"Did you see her?"

"The young princess? Of course. It was quite a spectacle."

Tisa cleared the odd blade of grass sticking out of the red earth near the vine's roots. She stood, unfurling a thin linen cloak as she stepped over to the next root.

"You think she has a chance to pull it off?"

"That girl has the power to do anything she wants. You saw her."

"There's a fire burning in her, yes. It's been a while since I've seen it."

"Plus," Tisa looked up at the sprawling vines, "she has a good taste in wine."

"I don't know what kind of person approves a stunt like that." Kala shouted. "Risking his own daughter?"

"You know Ayla well enough to know she did this on her own." Ashok leaned against his desk. He looked across a wall of monitors showing other Council members, "It was shocking for me to watch, too."

Ashok turned away from the monitors and peered through his open balcony. An eagle swooped over Flavia Park down below. The sun was setting behind Mount Rhoda. It cast a smooth shadow across the park.

"It is absurd that the incident could have happened in the first place, regardless of how or who encouraged it." Kala sat behind an ornate desk made of streaked ebony. It was inlaid with the Nussa coat of arms.

"Tell me, all of you, what has been the fallout in your Cores?" Ashok insisted.

"That's a little beside the point, don't you think?" Kala retorted.

"No. I think it's pretty relevant. Do tell me. Arun?"

"Well, we have received reports of celebrations and gatherings of support across the Core."

"Matias?"

"Likewise, Ashok, the people seem to have come alive."

"What are you trying to prove with this, Ashok, why does it matter?" Kala tapped on his desk.

"Yana, what has been the reaction?"

"We have received several calls for a resumption of the programme and a new mission, Ashok."

"Right. Matias?"

"Here too. People are fired up."

Ashok walked over to his balcony. A camera followed him at a fixed distance. "While I don't agree with her approach, I see the reasoning for her actions."

"How are you going to respond? How will you reprimand her?" Kala leaned forward.

"I think the question is, how will you respond? How will we all respond?" Ashok rested his hands on the stone parapet. "These events have crystallised my thoughts and I have a proposal for you all."

The eagle soared up. It took a wide approach to the park, circling around the end and coming back towards the Residence. Ashok watched on as it swooped in towards a tiny dark spot in the corner of a green lawn, talons breaking through the wind. "All of you see the public reaction. They are excited, emboldened. They believe again. It would be a historic misstep to ignore that."

"Tell us what you're proposing." Kala sat back.

The bird caught the dark dot firmly in its talons and arced back up towards the mountain. As it came closer, Ashok could see it was a rather unfortunate field mouse about to make its smooth transition to dinner.

"We go again."

"What!? No. No!"

"We go again." Ashok repeated, "Before Ayla's stunt I'm sure you all received the same documents as I did. We have the equipment ready, the technology works, our people all want it. We have to go again."

Kala stood from his desk, "Ludicrous! We closed this chapter. Ashok, let the world move on. How many lives do you want to risk, how much hope do you want to dash?"

"This is far from an easy decision, Kala. You saw what she wants."

"All the more reason to stand down."

"Yes, on that." Ashok turned, leaning on the parapet. "I have also made a decision to support The Council's desire for change. There are some amendments that I will need to see but, after a successful mission to Hela, I am prepared to accept most of your requests."

Through the door Ashok could see The Council's eyes widen. "In order to ensure such a successful transition period, I will, at that point, step down as leader of the Balkania Core."

"What are you saying? We support you on a new mission and you give in to our request?" Kala sat back down.

"No. This isn't a trade. We're going to the moon. The people's voice is clear, we have to give them a new mission and reach Hela successfully. Second, I'm not giving in, I've come to the conclusion that these changes are necessary. After stepping down, I will focus on building lasting stability to the Core System."

"You still spin like a pro, Ashok." Matias smiled. The Southern Ocean stretched out to the horizon behind him. Harsh waves crashed into the cliffs below his office.

"Spin or no spin, that's my proposal. Please tell me your answer in three minutes." The monitors went dark. Ashok took a final look back across Flavia and went inside. He opened up the hidden bar behind the wall of wooden panels.

With a little less focus on detail than usual, he fashioned a quick espresso and stepped over to his enclosed garden, waiting for the connection to resume.

"We have discussed your proposal, Ashok." Matias spoke with a slow unease. "The magnitude of what you're saying requires more time to look into the details..."

Ashok took a slow sip of his aromatic coffee.

"...But we agree to support you in principle." Matias finished.

"I want to stress that this was not a unanimous decision." Kala spoke up, "You're putting us in a corner, and you know it."

Ashok nodded with a smile.

Matias continued, "Please have your staff prepare a full plan and let's all convene within a week."

"Does anyone have any other comments?" Ashok took the rest of his coffee as a shot and stood straight.

"What happens if the mission is unsuccessful?" Ra-bia asked.

"If it is unsuccessful, Ra-bia, I will step down for good. You understand what 'unsuccessful' would mean for me, I hope?"

A timid knock barely resonated through the heavy oak door. Ayla pried the entrance open and stepped through.

"I was expecting you to come charging in." Ashok still stood at his balcony. "Push something over, at least."

Ayla walked towards him. Her steps were careful and light.

Ashok shook his head. "No, no. Not so fast."

"You'd rather not see me?" She stopped mid-way and began to turn.

"I always want to see you."

"Well then?" She took another few steps forward.

"This conversation will go a lot better if we have a drink. Pick a bottle from the bar next to my desk and bring a couple of glasses."

Ayla darted across the room to Ashok's desk. Her mission proposal documents were strewn across the imposing bureau. Ashok had littered the pages with notes and comments. His writing was completely illegible. There was no way to tell if they were positive or a stream of angry scribbles.

To one side of the desk she saw a beautiful but rather innocuous heptagonal pedestal. Slightly shorter than the desk, it had seven sharp cut faces and was topped by a round lid. Every surface of the masterfully made stump was covered in a golden olive burl. She pointed to it.

"Yes, yes, that."

Ayla searched for a door or latch, but the panels were perfectly mated. She tapped them one after the other. The third tap was followed by a satisfying click. A section of three panels opened up revealing a stack of crystal tumblers and half a dozen bottles of fine whiskey from around the world. Ayla took them out and examined them one by one.

She held one up, "Sinmi 40. You and Uncle Kala used to love this." She poured two glasses, returned the bottle and went over to her father.

"I suppose we still do. Good choice."

Ayla placed the glasses on the thick stone parapet. "There was no other way. I couldn't let the mission slip through our fingers."

Ashok grabbed her by the shoulders and pulled her in for a long embrace. He could feel her relax as they hugged.

"Come on, cheers."

"Cheers, Dad."

"How did that thing even land?"

"Petra has been working on ABD for a long time. We had told Sheng, but he didn't want to listen."

They turned to look over the city. Streetlights barely shone through dusk's ruby glow. A warm breeze ran up from Flavia Park.

"It seems a little unnecessary to go through some sort of back and forth. I know why you're here and, ultimately, I support you."

"Thank you, Dad. It means a lot."

"You have to understand the cost. You forced The Council's hand. Good work, by the way. But it does mean we can expect little to no support from them. Any missteps and, at the very least, BISE will be history."

"At the very least?"

"I don't want the Core System to break down before it's had a fair chance. It's is all you've ever known but it's still quite fragile."

"I know we'll succeed."

"And make sure you take care of yourself, Ayla. Promise me you won't take any unnecessary risks. I care about the mission, but I care a lot more about you."

"And Tomias?"

He winked, "Yes, yes. That guy. Him, too, of course."

They smiled and raised their glasses once more. Ashok placed his tumbler down and fumbled around on his wrist.

Undoing a clasp, he removed his chronograph. The electrum case shimmered in the evening light. He gave it a quick polish with his linen sleeve.

"I want you to have this. Take it up there with you."

"But it's your watch. *The* watch. You love this thing."

"As I said, I love you more. Take it." He gave the timepiece a final wind and placed it on Ayla's wrist. "You'd be surprised how useful a manual chrono can be. Just remember to wind it every few days."

FOURTEEN

"I can't wait for the launch." Sirem looked up at Hela. The clear Himavan night showed the moon's every detail.

While Hela's seasons were more nuanced than those on Earth, they did broadly line up. Autumn on Earth was mirrored by patches of gentle golden foliage seeping through Hela's forests. They ran across in veins and spots across her continents. Clouds were plentiful and, on clear nights, storms could sometimes be seen dampening the reflection from her surface.

"It would be great if they make it this time." Noake also stared up at the night's sky. The two lay on the side of a steep hill above the Kap. They were covered with a light wool blanket. Next to them, a fire pit was cut out of the hillside. Firewood was neatly stacked next to the simple hole.

"If it were you, you'd have made it in one go. Wouldn't even need a craft." Sirem laughed. Dry lengths of fir crackled and spat into the sky, held aloft by the fire's heat.

Noake nudged her, "Look at the drama that unfolded. Surely a little more prep and they could have avoided it."

"Indeed, the most complex thing humanity has ever done would be fine if Noake were on the case."

"Not sure I'd say the most complex, but maybe."

"I hope I'm not interrupting." Adroa came into sight from a little way down the hill, "I was taking a walk and couldn't help but overhear."

She came and sat next to the two. Sirem raised up and offered her a corner of the blanket.

"Why do you say that, Noake?"

"About the complexity? I think we've done more in the past. The mission is visible because it's happening now."

"Hard not to be visible." Sirem pointed at Hela and laughed.

"We have overcome huge challenges in the past and made it through. I'd argue they held a greater degree of complexity."

Below them, the Kap campus lit its lights. At once, a labyrinth of open courtyards and connected buildings illuminated.

"You're the history buff, what do you mean?"

"I do think our history sets the stage for our world today, yes. I've always found civilisation's early evolution fascinating. The coastal kingdoms gained a huge amount of power and influence. Their ability to pretty much control tidal power meant they could specialise. They could create. As always, that creation focused on weaponry, war and conquest."

"Why as always?" Adroa hunched over and warmed her hands over the pit.

"They subjugated the inland territories. The whole First Period was defined by powerful coastal states absorbing swathes of communities, forming the Four Great Empires. But they reached too far. As the empires grew, they required more resources. Yes, Pacha and Giro had, for the times, unlimited access to energy, but there wasn't so much they could do with it. Inland states soon realised they too had power. They controlled the food supply."

"It was an unstable world." Sirem pulled the blanket from Noake. A ceaseless expanse of dramatic peaks was bathed by Hela's soft light.

"Change was inevitable. The First Period ended violently as the oppressed states rose up against the coastal kingdoms. It was chaos. I can't imagine how people lived. Emerging from the FIP came the Second Period. Old rivalries were still there but now they aimed to reach a balance of power. Inland states formed nations, coastal states merged. Trade kept them civil for almost five hundred years.

"This uneasy balance began to shift when Saphan started exploring wind, solar and eventually atmospheric power. Now they had little need to be civil. Age-old wounds reopened, stoked by a desire for revenge. The start of The Collapse."

"You're too young to remember but I can recall the very tail-end of those conflicts. It was a difficult time."

"The world descended into chaos yet again, easily forgetting the pain of their ancestors."

"It's easy to say we should remember our past, it's harder to practise it when you're placed in a difficult situation." Sirem sat up.

Noake thought for a second, “I don’t know. Over fifty years, a billion lives were destroyed during The Collapse. That’s a long time to hold anger and hate.”

“But I don’t understand how it all stopped?” Noake focused his gaze on the flames. “Generations of people grew up knowing only conflict. Then it stopped. How did that happen?”

“It’s easy to take our world, however it might look, for granted.” Adroa rubbed her hands. “Sometimes everything changes overnight. It might feel like it comes from nowhere, but the building blocks are often laid down long before.

“We know that The Collapse was defined by hostility, but we shouldn’t envision that it was constant chaos everywhere, all the time. Life, as it always does, finds a way to adapt. If anything, our conquest over the nine continents is testament to that.” Adroa looked over the silent valley.

“Why is that relevant in this case?”

“Well, during that turbulent century, a great deal of progress was made in fields from energy to medicine, communications and food production. All of this culminated with the discovery of the Phions.”

“The enmity ended because we discovered some particles?” Noake threw a branch into the dancing flames.

“Humanity had reached a tipping point like no other in its history. Up until that point, the more work one put into something the more value was generally created... the more you farmed, the more you produced. The notion of value became decoupled from time and human input.”

"And you criticised me for a vague statement." Sirem leaned into Noake.

Adroa smiled. "The world reached a point where there was far more to be gained through collaboration than confrontation."

"And The Collapse stopped collapsing?"

"Not quite. After so long, the various hostilities had degraded into a battle of interests. Ashok came at the right moment. Those in power weren't so much interested in 'winning' as they were in holding on to power itself. He got them to realise two things. First, that the world had reached a point where they could have more by not living in perpetual fear."

"Bribing warlords, classic." Noake prodded the fire with a stick.

"A little bit, yes." Adroa stretched and stood. "Second, he showed the futility of their current situation. What's the point of supporting a system where the most powerful place their children in a state of constant risk?"

"So, the world Sirem and I know was built to satiate the very people who had terrorised the Earth before?"

"It's not a one-sentence answer, Noake. I suggest we dig in on the way down to the Kap."

Noake and Sirem stood and took a copper pale of water from the side of the pit. They poured it over the burning fire. Embers hissed and stirred, shooting off clouds of warm ash before settling down.

Adroa continued, "In a way, yes, you could say that."

Every so often a couple of marble steps stood out in the darkness, lit by Hela above.

"It was a by-product of the transition. Ultimately, self-interest won through. It was clear that the world had reached a point where far more could be gained through peace. After that, change happened rather quickly. As one of the first steps, The Kap," Adroa pointed down towards the campus, "was created to prepare future leaders like you, for the complexity of what lay ahead. You know the steps that followed in establishing the Core System."

Sirem held Noake's hand as she walked ahead through the darkness. "We've studied it over and over again. But it feels incomplete."

"How?" Adroa asked.

"From everything I know, the world transitioned towards a near-deification of knowledge."

"Quite the sentence." Noake sprang up from behind.

"But really. The whole system aims to perpetuate some form of monotony."

"What do you mean?"

"Take the Hela mission." Sirem continued.

"I was five years old when it was announced. It was a masterpiece of communication, relentlessly holding global focus. Everyone trained on one topic, on one goal. But, if you take a step back, is it really all that important?"

"I mean, it is the moon. The thing humanity has been striving to touch for all of our existence." Noake kept pace. "To discover whether life really started out in the heavens and came down to Earth. You know the spiel."

“Of course. And it’s exactly that. A spiel. I don’t disagree with the desire to go up there. I want to know as much as you do. It serves a purpose. It focuses our attention, our will, on a global level, while bigger things happen.”

“And what are those bigger things?” Adroa turned as she walked.

“I think Ashok, The Council and you, Adroa, see the value in having a common focus like the Hela mission to shape and galvanise a global mindset. Using the mission as a tool to drive the transition from the old system to the Cores.”

“If that were to be the case Sirem, at least in part, how would you feel?” Adroa looked at her through the night.

“That’s a good question.” she stood her ground. “I guess, I guess, I would understand the need. At the same time, I would be a little sad that we can’t simply do things for the reason we say we’re doing them. It seems duplicitous.”

“Actions can have more than one outcome, Sirem.” Noake jumped in. “Why not be aware of all of them and design appropriately. I don’t think secondary motives would make a successful mission any less impressive.”

The Kap came closer into view as they descended down the hill. Its amber glow illuminated the path ahead.

“There is no one conclusion from this discussion.” Adroa walked on.

“It seems there rarely is.” Sirem jumped over two steps in front of her.

“We can discuss history all we like. We can understand the mechanics and question the outcomes but, until you’re faced with the need to make a decision, you really don't know how you will react. Sometimes, the magnitude of our decisions is obvious. All too often it becomes clear only after the fact."

"And we're back to hindsight." Noake smirked as they neared the Kap's rear gate.

"Hindsight and perspective. If there's one tangible thought I can leave you with it would be to consider perspective. There are a dozen phrases like 'put yourself in someone else's shoes' but they very much diminish the significance of perspective." Adroa unlatched the heavy wooden gate and held it for Noake and Sirem to pass through. "It is amazing how different the world looks to each and every one of us. Tenets of our world. Things we take completely for granted can be turned on their heads. Perhaps the mission will show you what I mean."

Sirem walked through the gate and looked back, "Seems like you have something in mind?"

FIFTEEN

"Do you have the craft configuration at hand? The one that was used for the tests."

The engineer brought up a table of parameters and showed it to Petra.

"Exactly! The older Orus craft have slightly thicker shells. I'm pretty sure the safety margin overlaps." Petra left the engineer holding his monitor, making sense of the data. At least this time she took the lift on the way up to the top floor.

With a half-knock Petra stumbled into Ayla's office, "We need to talk."

"Sounds ominous." Ayla had rearranged the office. Her desk was now placed by the wall of windows. "Come sit."

"Ayla, we have to cancel the mission. We have to delay."

"A little late for that, don't you think, why would we?"

"I was comparing the data from tests on Orus 3. Sorry, Orus 6, and your stunt over Rhoda. There's an issue with the thrust."

"It's a lot of Oruses. What do you mean? It worked fine."

"Yes, Drive worked fine on landing, but the craft has a chance of rupturing on the take-off from Hela. Craft's skin is thicker than on newer vessels. There is an overlap in the uncertainty curve of the Phion resonance."

"What does that mean?"

"The resulting resonance can corrode the skin. It could weaken or even rupture it."

Ayla got up from her desk and stared out of her window. She looked out over campus gardens. The summer heat had lightly yellowed the meadows. Patches of violet flowers and dashes of poppies freckled the calm landscape.

"How big is the risk?"

"It's difficult to say. Looks to be at least 10%, maybe 20, even 30%. In any case, it's unacceptable."

Ayla paused, "We would be able to land safely?"

"Yes, but the thruster would be too corroded to do much else. You would be stuck there on Hela, unable to come back."

"Can you show me the issue?"

Petra thought for a second. "Yes, we can run a test sequence on the basement rig. It already has a scale thruster mounted."

They headed down through BISE's meandering underground corridors to the small engine model test room. Ayla smiled as they entered, "I see you didn't repair the floor."

The concrete was still cratered from Petra's earlier demonstration of the AB Drive. "No, it made me smile each time I looked at it so decided to keep it."

A new model stood clamped firmly in the rig. Its grooves were shallow and fine. The engine's skin was almost indistinguishable from a flat silver surface. The model looked similar to a Glider in its form. The main difference was that it was more evenly rounded on both ends, in contrast to the Glider's teardrop tail.

"The problem is one of structural integrity. The earlier Orus systems were designed to be landers, without too much attention paid to their return. The aim was to make them strong."

They walked up to the model. Ayla ran her hands over its surface.

"When reviewing the power output of your flyover in Flavia I saw that the numbers don't add up. When the Phions resonate, they uncouple a huge amount of energy. Most of that energy is channelled out away from the skin. In whichever direction we want it to deliver thrust. But due to uncertainty, some of it ends up within the skin itself. It's a kind of corrosion. Random baryonic particles within the skin will degrade the structure."

They stepped back to the doorway and Petra initiated a test sequence using a monitor by the door. She gradually toggled the power. "This time, it's clamped quite firmly in place." She pointed to the rubberised claws gripping the engine.

Soon, the rig began to creek and the engine started pushing up. "The vice has been set to contain the force; we're looking at the engine itself here."

They began to feel a turbulent wind creeping across the floor, meandering around their feet.

"We're on a typical landing curve."

"Looks good."

"Yes, it's perfectly fine now. Now, look at this." Petra reconfigured the test. "Let's run a vertical launch curve a little above normal power. Put these on." Petra reached over to a bench and grabbed two pairs of tinted glasses.

The gust of wind picked up again. It slid past their feet like an incoming tide. The model began to vibrate. Soon, the wind became erratic, as if stirred up by an unseen swell.

"What's that?" Ayla pointed towards the base of the model.

"Our problem."

The model's pill-shaped base started to glow. A pockmark of white light began to shine through the solid surface. At first, it resembled a faint spill of varnish. Quickly, the spots began to burst through as sharp shafts of concentrated white rays hitting the floor. Petra flipped a kill-switch by the monitor, immediately stopping power to the rig. The wind died down and the light faded.

"Come, look." Petra went up to the rig and signalled Ayla to touch it. Ayla ran her hands over the engine. It was smooth and clean. When her hand reached the oval base, she felt the surface flex. Pressing a little harder, her index finger pushed clean through, the shiny metal surface crumbled, creating a jagged hole. Small pieces of the skin sprinkled down on the floor.

"That's not good."

"No. This rig was set up at 50% above normal power. Even at the normal launch curve there is a non-zero chance of something similar happening. If it doesn't break apart, Orus' skin could be compromised. Your re-entry back to Earth would be near impossible."

"So, either we're stranded on Hela or we break up on re-entry."

"Yes. We need at least nine months, maybe a year. We need to make a new craft. Advanced is essentially modular, but the skin has to be refabricated."

"Impossible, if we don't go now, the mission will be scrapped."

"Ayla, if you go you would be making a one-way trip. Returning in this craft would be too risky."

"Give me a few days to think. In the meantime, carry on as planned. Please keep this information to yourself."

****

"Do you remember when you were drawing the designs for this space?" Adroa walked through her quarters in the Kap. "You were so funny. I think we had to get two senior engineers to work out what everything meant."

"You laugh but you use it, don't you?" Ashok reclined back in a woven hemp hammock stretched between two short cherry trees in his enclosed garden in Flavia.

"Of course, I love it. All the more because of the design process."

The school's tuition and housing structures were made of a polished local marble. Its creamy white hue emanated a tranquil tone. Adroa's quarters sat within the main Kap complex. Her space stood in stark contrast to the calm, stoic, college buildings.

The main structure resembled an upturned nest. It was constructed from a dark red perforated metal structure. Plants, shrubs, flowers and even small trees grew out of the frame as it rose a full storey above the other buildings.

In the middle, partially enclosed and partially open to the elements, a series of seating, working and living spaces were broken up with gardens, brooks of running water and fruit trees.

"Well, it wasn't easy to make it all look so natural." Ashok pointed to the monitor, outlining Adroa's green backdrop. "The trick was to make it seem like it actually *hadn't* been engineered."

"Ahaa, of course. Genius, as always." Adroa smiled as she walked through her gardens, stopping to smell the occasional flower.

"A week to go."

"Yes. Excited?"

"It's balanced out by worry for Ayla. She hasn't left and I can't wait for her to return."

"She's determined. She'll be fine." Adroa sat on a perfect green mound, drizzled with wildflowers native to Dharma.

"I was thinking." Ashok looked at a chestnut-headed sparrow balancing on a thin branch. "We need to do more. We've been so focused on getting to Hela. There's a whole universe out there."

"What are you thinking?"

"When she comes back, I want to work with her to create a network of satellites, probes, missions, you name it, all over the solar system – and beyond. We can make a base on Hela and use the lower gravity to launch from there. We have so much down here, it's crazy we haven't done more."

"Not sure if crazy is the right word." Adroa stood and walked through to her bedroom. The room was surrounded by bushy hazelnut trees. Its wide glass door was framed by two inlaid columns of onyx green marble. "The world changed completely over the last twenty years. We've had plenty to do down here."

"It will continue to change. We have to think ahead. Hela has led us to look up at the sky since humans have existed. Our future is up there. Once we explore and settle the moon, we have to go beyond."

"One step at a time, Ashok, one step at a time." Adroa took off her long linen gown and slipped under the covers. "Our first mission is to sleep. Good night, Ashok."

"Good night," Ashok smiled. "Think about what I said."

****

The road bent and curved out into the distance. A toothed mountain silhouette framed the horizon. Chips of limestone gravel littered either side of the tarmac as the motorbike tore forward.

"We're racking up the sanctions." Ayla sat back with her arms around Tomias.

"True, but then again, who's going to sanction us, you?"

They rode along with the autumn sun warming their dark suits. The noise of the wind rushed by their helmets accompanied by a light hum from the motor. Tomias kept an old electric cruiser at the base in Kamrun.

During training it was strictly forbidden to ride the bike but Tomias and Jonah would sneak out early morning, head over to Saphan, take a short break and come back before they were noticed.

"Quite the machine." Ayla spoke into a microphone set within her helmet. She held him tightly.

"It is, you can feel every bump in the road. You need to pay attention all the time." Tomias sped around a soft bend. They leaned in as the bike tilted on its oversized tyres. "After Rassi pushed us through some heavy drill, we would race out here right as the sun came up."

"I miss him."

Tomias leaned back into her and whispered, "Me too."

The barren landscape was broken by tufts of grass poking up through the chalk ground. The odd bush spouted out by the roadside. Squat trees could be seen here and there in the distance.

"We're getting close." Tomias let off the throttle and looked on as their view was consumed by green. Rich pasturelands replaced the rocky desert. Neatly ordered plantations of palm trees sprouted up in the distance like great bushels of wheat bound together.

Slowing, they turned off of the main road. A laser-straight boulevard, wider than the intercity road they were on, shot out in front. Flanking either side were squadrons of soaring cedar trees. Riding through the centuries-old formation, they felt a cool breeze run along their suits.

Up ahead, looming larger with every second, a broad stone platform extended across their view. Ten feet tall, with its ends barely visible, the granite base was made of mammoth blocks - precisely hewn together into an imposing shear wall.

They stopped in front of two wide staircases jutting out from the wall, diverging up away from each other. Their sides were carved with ancient scenes of battle and triumph over animal and man. Ayla and Tomias placed their helmets on the bike and ascended the steps.

"I haven't been here since I was a little girl, it's awe-inspiring."

"Impressive, yes, the Imperial Palace."

"To think it was the seat of power, pretty much for the world, a thousand years before Nussa."

Coming to the top, the impenetrable stone face opened out onto a vast complex. Immediately ahead of them was a towering hypostyle hall held up a decorated roof. The columns were shaped in the guise of the same cedar trees that lined the boulevard. They were painted in a rich ochre. Each column was topped by a griffin enfolded in silvery-gold leaf. The hall led to a single gate.

"The original Gate of Nations." Tomias pointed ahead and smiled.

"It has a rather more daunting look to it than ours, don't you think?"

"Oh yes, your father definitely improved on this world wonder."

The sprawling site was near-empty. The palace had been maintained and restored over the years, but its sheer size meant that keeping it pristine was near-impossible. Here and there, the electrum leaf on the griffins was peeling back.

Walking through the gate, they entered the grand complex. A series of ornate buildings were connected by covered pathways held up by the same red columns. On either side of the paths, wildflower beds and dry fountains dotted the gardens.

"I want to show you something." Tomias took Ayla's hand and led her off of the main path. They walked through a higgle of grass and flowers to the side wall of one of the buildings.

Tomias searched the stone blocks making up the building's base. Looking closer, Ayla could see the blocks were smeared in graffiti. Names dates, monikers, all scored into the stone with knives, flint or the edge of a sword.

"What are you looking for?"

"Aha! Here it is." Tomias pointed to a dotted rectangle marked out as neatly as one can with a knife. The number 1310 stood at the top of the border. The cartouche was filled with writing, each letter comprised a series of dots forced into the stone.

"It says, 'I, Sergeant Willo was here in the year 1310, for Hela in her wonder'"

"Willo is an old name from around Giro, I think. But what's that number?" Ayla touched the letters.

"Yes, the inscription is from a general who came here from Giro. Almost 3000 miles, by foot, by horse, whatever."

"So, the date, it's from the First Period?"

"Exactly. It's nearly 700 years old. Isn't that insane?"

"It looks like it was carved yesterday." Ayla placed her palm on the script.

"Your decision is made, Ayla, and I support it. We've been looking up in awe and amazement for thousands of years. We're no different to Sergeant Willo. We have a chance to realise his dream. To change humanity for ever. We have to go, regardless of the risk."

Ayla looked up and saw the moon in the open sky. Her green forests and blue oceans paled, bleached by the mid-morning sun, "We have to go."

Petra ran through final checklists.

"All check. Orus, expect final countdown in two minutes."

"Confirmed, Operations. All check and ready on Orus."

Tomias' voice came through the monitors. The central monitor in Operations Control showed a split view of the craft's interior. One side trained on Tomias and the other on Ayla.

Both were strapped in, magnetically locked to their seats. The giant vessel sat in darkness with only the interior lighting providing illumination. Ayla's flight suit had been assembled in haste. It was a dusty snow colour to the captain's matt grey.

"Okay everyone. Commence final sequence." Petra stood by Sheng's old control position. She ran through the live sensor data to ensure system stability as the Spinlaunch powered up.

This time the facility was relatively calm and quiet. Outside there was no plinth for The Council. No media were permitted within Operations Control. Several cameras passed along predefined routes within the large round space.

"Are you ready?" Petra looked over to Ashok.

He sat at a desk not far away. Periodically he would stand, look around the room and then sit back down.

"It's not me that has to be ready. Good luck, Petra. Ignore me."

"I will have to, don't take it as intentional."

It was a hot day at the facility near Kamrun. The heat radiated off of the Spinlaunch coil's outer skin. Seen from above, it looked like a giant coiled stovetop, abandoned in the desert.

"Operations to Orus, final countdown initiated. Two minutes to release."

"Orus to Operations. Confirmed."

"Good to go, Ayla?" Tomias stared forward as his helmet was locked to the seat.

"Let's do it!"

The lights within the Spinlaunch flashed on. The windows on either side of the control monitors looked down the pristine white tube of the Inner Coil. Two silver strips ran along the tube's base as it curved ever so slightly to the left.

"Vacuum holding and stable." Petra signalled to the operators. "Spool up."

Orus began to creep forward in silence. The creep grew to a jog. Ayla thought it curious that the view from the windows stayed the same, despite the distinct feeling of acceleration.

"Operations to Orus, systems stable, increasing speed."

"Orus to Operations. Confirmed."

The craft reached Mach 2 within the vacuum centrifuge. Ayla imagined the thrust would be more aggressive.

"All stable. Ten percent, increase to fifty."

"Thirty seconds to release."

Ashok leaned forward, resting his hands on the desk. On the monitors, Ayla and Tomias stared straight ahead, their eyes looked focused and ready.

"Mach 9. Release to stage two in ten."

Orus 6 shot through the Inner Coil. The craft began to vibrate and jostle from side to side. A light purple glow covered the craft's chrome shell.

Three, Two, One, Release.

Ashok gripped the desk. Orus exited the Inner Coil at Mach 14, firing into the Outer Ring like a bull released from a pen.

In less than a second, they covered the four mile coil. Despite their firm magnetic harness, Ayla felt a powerful pull to the right. *That wasn't part of the training.*

To be fair, her training had been rather thin.

Before she could fully comprehend the feeling, it was subsumed by an overwhelming rush of excitement. Orus volleyed through the last, inclined straight resting on foothills of the Lurish Mountains.

In the control room, Petra and Ashok watched as secondary monitors displayed the view from the final launch stage. The silver projectile fired out of an oversized gun barrel dug into the hillside. Cameras immediately fixed onto Orus, straining to keep focus. The craft disappeared into the sky. It barely left a mark in the thin clouds.

"Trajectory stable, speed stable. Drive active."

Ashok stood and turned his attention to the main monitor. The Explorers were temporarily and expectedly knocked unconscious.

"Orbital waypoint in eight seconds."

Ashok pointed towards the monitor as Tomias opened his eyes.

"Orbital waypoint passed."

Ayla unlatched one eye before releasing the other and blinking. Her pupils briefly dashed from side-to-side. She knew she would likely go unconscious, but she was still irritated to miss the ascent.

"Operations to Orus. Confirm your status when able."

The monitor opened with background static before Tomias spoke up.

"Captain, check."

"Co-pilot, check."

"Orus, you are currently two-hundred miles above the Earth, on your way to Hela. Welcome to space."

In frantic unison, the control room broke its silence and exploded in celebration. Ashok rushed over and hugged Petra, taking her off her feet.

✱✱✱✱✱✱✱✱✱✱✱✱✱✱✱✱

"It's incredible." Tomais stared out through a viewport pointing towards the Earth.

Orus 6 was longer than Orus 5. Built with the aim of more extended missions in orbit, the craft had a cylindrical living and working area behind the control deck.

"I could get used to this." Tomias floated over to another window and gazed out into the darkness.

"I agree on the view." Ayla rose out of her seat, drifted over and clutched a grab handle by Tomias. "Not so sure about the space. Could perhaps use another room or three."

"Well, that's the main takeaway from this mission." Tomias grabbed her by the waist and spun her around. "You should have seen Orus 5, we were strapped into those seats for most of the trip."

Ayla went to a monitor embedded in the wall. "Right then, enough silliness, we have work to do."

"You know, I am the captain up here." He noted with mock reprimand.

"Save that for your fantasies, captain, come on." Ayla sat down in front of the monitor.

"Pretty sure we're broadcasting." Tomias pointed.

"Operations to Orus... confirmed, you're live."

"...Given the timeframe, it's impressive we managed to include so much of the scientific agenda." Ayla swiped through the lists of experiments ahead of them.

"What's up first?" Tomias drifted over to Ayla and put his arm around her.

"In a few minutes we will approach the waypoint. We need to ensure a small cube is released as planned." The monitor displayed a set of release instructions.

"What does it do?" Tomias scrolled through.

"It's part of Petra's refraction experiment, I think. Operations?"

A short pause followed before Petra spoke up over the monitor. "Correct, it is a multi-part refracting interferometer to be installed between Hela and Earth. An atmospheric analysis tool."

"Tomias, stand at that window and confirm when the payload is released." Ayla weaved around him to settle back in her seat, monitoring the release via the instruments.

A signal sounded right on schedule. It was followed by a simple instruction stating the experiment code and its successful deployment.

Tomias watched as what looked like a crystal cube spun out of Orus' belly. A tiny, flat AB thruster atop the cube adjusted the trajectory and position of the device.

Its other end was covered in a dull black solar panel. The glistening payload appeared to reduce its spin and began tilting to one side. As it did, once each rotation, it seemed as though it shot out a ray of brilliant white light towards Hela.

The cube had two hair-thin channels running through its length. They passed through a sphere cut through the core.

"Ayla, come see this."

Finalising the release confirmation, she slipped out of her seat. "What?"

"Are we expecting that?" He pointed towards the ray and waited for the cylinder to rotate. Sure enough, when it aligned, a dazzle of brilliant light flared out across the darkness.

"Operations, we're seeing an unexpected light emission from the cylinder. Please advise." Ayla wrapped her arm round Tomias.

"Orus, the module is incapable of emitting light."

"Petra, I know what we're seeing!" Ayla stared through the window.

"We can't see anything on the external cameras. You're clear to investigate. Rotate Orus about its axis to see whether it is a reflection from the sun."

"Thank you, Operations." Tomias accessed the craft's controls from a monitor next to the viewport, initiating a slow rotation.

As Orus turned, the ray of light disappeared. It no longer flashed up as the lens rotated.

"Operations, the light has stopped."

The ship continued its rotation. Their view from the window approached an alignment between Orus, Hela and the Sun behind them.

"Confirmed Orus..."

"Wait! Stopping rotation." Tomias halted the turn.

He switched off the thruster so suddenly that it stopped with a jolt. "Wow."

Ayla was thrown aside by the sudden stop. She made her way back to the viewport. "What..."

"Orus, please update your status."

"Operations, it's beyond words. The sun seems to have illuminated a path. A brilliant, diamond path, towards the moon."

"Petra, are you seeing this?"

"We are adjusting the exterior camera."

Ayla and Tomias looked on, holding hands, as the most beautiful ribbon of shining light stretched ahead of them towards Hela.

"It's just like the old story." Ayla placed a hand on the glass. "What is it?"

"Orus, we have the feature in focus. It is impressive. Seems you are travelling directly above it. Captain Jonah did mention a sighting, but we never established what it was. The ship has a set of particle sensors. You have clearance to release one into the feature for analysis."

"Confirmed, operations."

Tomias signalled Ayla to release the sensor.

She accessed the system, fumbling to enter the commands, not wanting to take her eyes off of the otherworldly apparition. "Sensor launched. Tomias, look."

As they trained their eyes on the light, it was as if a wafer-thin stream was running through empty space, lit up by the sun.

"Petra, it looks, it looks like a current, flowing back and forth." Ayla strained to make sense of the celestial river. It seemed to flow in both directions at the same time like a gentle brook with eddies and swirls.

"Orus. We have solid dataflow from the sensor."

"What is it?" Ayla asked.

"It seems to be mostly ice crystals, water. The ice is reflecting sunlight." Static flared across the monitor. "There's more. We see organic molecules. Orus, it looked like there could be bits of life within the ice. Incredible. Incredible. We will have to investigate further to confirm for sure."

"The crystals are flowing. They're flowing from Earth to Hela and back towards the Earth. There are stunning whirlpools of crystals in between the two flows."

"Orus... It looks like your namesake was right. The diamond road is real. And it could be a pathway for the exchange of life between Hela and Earth."

"Amazing." Tomias put his arm around Ayla.

She nestled in closer towards him. They watched on in a warm embrace.

****

Hela filled their monitors. Operations broadcast the view across the world. Thirty miles above her surface, one could easily mistake the moon for Earth. A subtle green tinge to the bluey atmosphere was the single giveaway.

"Approach stable, AB stable." Tomias monitored the controls.

"All clear on this end, Orus." Petra sat by her desk. Once more, Operations Control waited in quiet anticipation.

The landing site for Orus 6 had been chosen near the first mission; somewhat closer to the lake on Rhodina than the Tethys Ocean. In honour of the previous mission, the lake had since been named Lake Jona. The h taken off, leaving the name unfinished - an old convention to denote deceased namesakes.

Even at this high altitude, it was clear that the Tethys Ocean had knots of agitated waves cresting near its shores.

"Orus, Nuwa is reporting surface winds at roughly thirty miles. Prepare for a turbulent ride down."

"Confirmed, Operations."

"Ayla, time to strap in." They adorned their helmets and activated the magnetic straps. The clamps immediately snapping them back into the seat's contours. After sixteen hours of near weightlessness, it was odd to feel such a strong tug from the back.

As they lost altitude, the outline of Lake Jona came into view. Its edges were ruffled by what appeared to be thick tree or plant cover.

"You're entering the Helletic atmosphere, Orus."

The ship descended tail-down. Ayla and Tomias could see only space through their windows.

The black began to gain tone. It mixed with a milky glaze before brightening to a translucent teal.

A pen Ayla had left floating in the work area pinged off of the back wall as the moon's gravitational hold strengthened.

Periodic puffs of white mist blew upwards, accompanied by a buffeting vibration increasing in intensity.

"We're ionising the atmosphere from the friction." Tomias gestured with his eyes.

"Doesn't AB create a film around the ship?"

"Throughout the journey, yes. During descent, it focuses on the bum, so the sides get buffeted by the atmosphere."

The view from their windows and monitors went white as they plunged through thick clouds. A light purple haze emanating from the ship's skin illuminated the clouds.

Emerging out on the other side, they could now clearly see Lake Jona. An uneven band of beach ran around its kidney form. It was repeatedly interrupted by chubby tree canopies, jutting into the water.

A strip, no more than a few miles thick, separated lake from ocean. While Tethys was still choppy, Jona seemed tranquil and calm. Nearing further, Ayla noticed the web of rivers, squirming through the surrounding forests, feeding into the lake.

Orus was jolted from its smooth descent right as Operations called out five miles of altitude. Strapped firm into their seats, Ayla and Tomias shook with the craft. The jolt transformed into a violent shake.

"A lot of shaking, Operations." Tomias struggled to speak.

"Strong windshear, Orus, you're losing altitude, fast."

The view started to flicker. The rich teal sky came in and out of view, between blurred clouds. Orus 6 was wobbling.

"Operations, initiating an avoid manoeuvre."

"Confirmed, Orus."

"Two miles. We're coming in too fast." Tomias pushed the craft to the side, aiming to escape the windshear.

"We're off-course, might end up in the water." Ayla gripped an armrest.

"Operations, AB to full, assisted descent."

"Confirmed. Prepare for a potential water landing."

The craft felt like it fell into honey. Its rate of fall slowed in an elastic embrace. Their view upwards stabilised. It then gradually panned to the side.

"We're stable but drifting. Landing site missed." Ayla looked at the monitor showing the approaching ground. The chosen landing site was a relatively open field ten miles inland, not far from the lake. It momentarily darted across their view.

AB had allowed Orus to reduce its vertical speed, but they were now drifting uncontrollably.

"Continuing slowed descent, we'll land where we land."

"Confirmed. A thousand feet."

"Ayla, prepare for landing. It might be hard. I love you."

"I love you, too. Looks like we're heading for the isthmus."

At two hundred feet, the craft scraped across something soft.

"Tree?"

Ayla had no time to answer as a loud buffeting came from the vessel's base. It felt as if hard brushes were smacking them.

Landing on Hela

They listed and banked, pushed around by the encroaching treetops.

For a moment, the noise stopped. During a brief second, they fell silently through Hela's atmosphere. Abruptly, the calm ended as Orus slammed into the ground. It was a sudden smash preceded by a transitory grind as they buried in from every side.

Silence.

SIXTEEN

"Ayla, are you okay?"

"I think so. You?"

"Yes. Operations?"

"Both of your vitals are stable. Captain, Ayla, you have touched down on Hela. Orus appears to be twelve miles East of its initial target landing site."

"Thank you, Operations."

Still strapped to his seat, Tomias felt a lean to his right. The monitors were off. Two shafts of light from the windows broke the darkness in the cockpit. Out of the left window they could see a teal sky peeking through thick tuft of clouds. The right seemed to be obscured by a weave of what appeared to be thick grey branches. Tiny sharp leaves poked out through the knit.

"Looks like we're tilted, can you feel it, Ayla?"

"Yes. Can you right the ship?"

Tomias attempted to activate the monitors. They flashed and blinked but refused to cooperate, remaining decidedly off. "We've probably tripped a breaker."

"Orus. AB and main electrics are down but the ship has auxiliary power."

"In that case, let's release the straps and assess. I'll open mine first, I'm closest to the side if I fall out."

"Let me go first." Tomias began to unfasten his straps. "I'll catch you."

As he finished his sentence, Ayla disengaged her fastenings. Popping up and out of the sculpted flight seat she slid to the right. Momentarily she managed to get a grip on to a central armrest, but her hand slipped and she fell straight out of her seat.

Ayla dropped to the ship's sidewall. It was an unnatural, gradual fall. She barely bumped into the metal skin, knocking a few instruments and sliding down towards the base of the craft. On the way down, Ayla reflexively grabbed on to a couple of handles but, as the slide was neither fast nor uncontrolled, she let go each time.

"Hela's gravity is rather funky. You can release and fall straight down from your seat, you'll be fine."

"Right then. So long as you're okay splinting a broken leg on the moon." Tomias released his fastenings and fell into the central armrest. He manoeuvred around to the far side of his seat and sat on the backrest with his legs dangling over.

"Come on, jump, I'll catch you. It'll be romantic." Standing at the ship's base Ayla stretched out her arms.

"No time for silliness." Tomias signalled her to stand aside and he pushed off of the seat. He fell down steadily, lightly bashing his helmet on a viewport handle part of the way down.

"Smooth, Captain." Ayla embraced him as he reached the base.

"Operations, we're both unhurt and our suits are still sealed. We should leave Orus and assess the situation. Please equalise the pressure and open the side-hatch."

"Nuwa is reporting a clean atmosphere, Captain. Retain pressure in your suits as a precaution."

"Confirmed, Operations."

"Pressure equalised, hatch opening." A brief hiss of air preceded the sound of a lid popping off a jar.

As the hatch disappeared, the craft was engulfed in light.

Two camera pods broke off of the porthole's rim and raced out, focusing back on Orus.

A warm draught ran across Ayla's suit. The heat made her realise how cold their cabin had been. She wiped a layer of condensation off of her visor. "Go on then."

"It's all you."

"Of course."

Grabbing on to the side-handles, Ayla pulled herself up to the hatch. She positioned her legs outside and she sat on the edge, looking out, "Incredible. Are you seeing this, Operations?"

"Crystal clear." A rumble could be heard in the background of Petra's voice.

Ayla gazed ahead. They had touched down at the start of the isthmus between Lake Jona and the Tethys Ocean, right at the point where the land started to thin.

The ground was composed of sandy gravel. Oddly bulbous trees fanned out on each side, peppering low dunes guarding a thickening forest.

The trees looked as if they had been moulded by a bowl. A crescent crown of featherlike leaves was supported by a thick mesh of winding branches. The branches led to a stubbly fat trunk.

The trees by the beach stood no more than twenty feet tall. Those in the forest seemed to rise far higher.

Ayla looked on at the curving shore of Lake Jona as it swept around in either direction. The expansive lake disappeared out over the horizon, with its calm waters reflecting the sky above.

"Is it safe?" Tomias looked up at her back.

"Let's find out." Ayla let go of the hatch and shimmied down the side of Orus.

"You're live in 5."

"Thank you, Operations."

Ayla stopped at the craft's base. It had dug into the loose ground. She managed to stand up on its rippled metallic skin.

"We take these steps standing proudly on the shoulders of countless generations who have looked up in awe."

With those words, Ayla stepped off of Orus 6 and onto Hela's surface.

Her boots left light prints in the gravel.

Tomias raised himself up to the hatch and sat on its lip with the intent of launching off. He was taken aback by the sight ahead and stayed frozen on the edge, gawping forward.

Refocusing, he knelt and shuffled down the shell. He jumped off of the edge and planted himself next to Ayla. They embraced facing towards the two camera pods floating ahead.

"Welcome to Hela!" Shouts of celebration sounded out around Petra as Ayla and Tomias stood and held each other, observing their new domain.

Tomias held her tight. "We did it!" he whispered.

****

"Tomias, Ayla, I want to congratulate you on this historic moment." Ashok's voice boomed out through their earpieces. "You are the only human beings not watching this right now."

"We have a pretty good view ourselves, thank you, Dad." Ayla waved to the cameras whilst still holding Tomias.

"The world is proud of you both. I'm very proud of you. We will leave you to establish a base ... while we go celebrate."

"Very kind of you!"

"And we're clear. Ayla, Tomias, congratulations once more. Give yourselves some time to adjust and let's get on with the programme." Petra spoke with an uneven cadence. In the background, Operations Control was still audibly abuzz.

"Thank you, Petra. First things first, let's see about these helmets." Tomias looked over atmospheric results on a monitor wrapped around his wrist. "Looks stable. Removing my helmet. Ayla, keep yours on for a moment."

He disabled the helmet's seal and raised it above his head with both hands. After a cautious breath, Tomias filled his lungs with the moon's air. He held it in as if savouring a fine wine. Slowly exhaling, "It's so warm, so humid."

Ayla released her helmet and placed it on the ground beside her. "It's beautiful." She took deep breaths, in and out, "It feels like a summer's day in Nussa after a rainstorm, like a honey syrup."

"The air is clear and there are no particulates or organic particles detected in any significant quantity. You both have respirator masks in your left trouser pockets. Should the need arise, an alarm will sound, as per your training." Petra was calm and focused.

"Thank you, Petra," Ayla looked out over Lake Jona. As she did, the clouds above began to thin and clear. While scanning the horizon, she saw a feint round object appear in the middle of the lake. Focusing on it, Ayla rapidly realised it was a reflection. Jerking her gaze upwards, she tugged on Tomias' arm.

"Wow."

Earth appeared, though breaking cloud cover.

"I'm so used to seeing Hela in the sky. I always imagined the Earth would look the same. It's so large, so imposing." Ayla sat on an eroded boulder by the lakeside.

"Incredible. Three billion people…" Tomias sat by Ayla on the rock. A few flakes rubbed off and dropped on the ground below.

"Right, Ayla, how do you feel?"

"Good, a lot of adrenaline but all good. You?"

"Good, all good. Let's go through the checklist."

"Operations, would you give us a few minutes of radio silence so we can get organised?"

"Yes Ayla, back with you shortly." Petra closed the monitors.

The two cameras landed on the lakeside some distance from their site.

Ayla sprang up off of the rock. "We need to see the other side of Orus, to check for damage." She held out her hand to Tomias and turned with an aim of sprinting around the ship.

Not yet adjusted to the lower gravity, she tripped on her first step and fell on her knees.

"Are you okay?" Tomias picked her up.

"Yes yes, come on."

They walked around the ship. Orus had sunk unevenly, several feet into the soft ground. Its bulging rear end sat like an egg slanted in the sand. The top of the ship rested in the thick canopy of a tree.

"What do you think?" Tomias dug around the sunken base.

"This subduction is from AB, not from impact. It burrowed like this in the lab as well," Ayla placed a hand on the grooved metal skin. "If it were from the impact, we wouldn't be here."

"Looks solid from here."

"We need to check closer to the base." She nudged Tomias out of the way and stuck her hand deep in the gravelly beach.

She felt the ship's outer layer through her gloves. "There! Come, confirm."

Tomias reached down until almost his entire arm was under Orus. With the tips of his fingers, he could feel a jagged rim on the skin. It caught and snagged on his gloves.

"That's not good." He removed his arm and dusted off his suit.

"No. Drive has corroded the skin." Ayla walked back to the shore side and sat on the ground.

Tomias went to sit with her, "What's the plan?"

"We don't mention this to Operations on a public channel. Let's use our downtime to work out a plan and set up a secure line with Petra."

The cameras beeped and rose back up in the air. They hovered in concentric circles around their landing site.

"The connection is back on. How are you settling into your new home?"

"It's a lot to take in, Operations. So far so good."

"You look a little dusty, Ayla, everything okay?"

"Still getting used to the gravity here, Petra. All good."

"A lot to take in."

"It is, Mito." Ashok sat at Ayla's desk. He monitored the broadcast on a panel of monitors. "And it's only the start."

"It has been a long few days. I suggest you go get some rest. They're not going anywhere."

"Thank you, Mito. I'll relocate to The Residence."

"That's a good idea. Might I suggest a shower and a shave, too? We're gathering with The Council in Dvor tomorrow."

"I'll have you know I'm sparkling clean... You might be right about the shave though."

Ashok walked out of BISE, towards The Residence. The city's streets were alive like he'd never seen before. People smiled as they passed each other along Flavia's tree-lined boulevards.

Ashok's mildly scruffy appearance, an unkempt beard and a crumpled linen tunic, made him less recognisable than usual. Upon marking him, people waved and yelled.

Why not stop by Canvas? It's close enough on the way.

From the other side of the street, Ashok could hear a tumult seeping out from within the cafe. Laughing, screaming, clapping, Canvas burst at the seams.

Worming his way through the side-entrance, Ashok aimed for the bar. It was tough going at first. Sixty or more were crammed into a space made for twenty at most. Everyone was glued to the monitor in the top-rear corner. It displayed scenes from the landing. Ayla and Tomias embracing on Hela's surface, Operations Control erupting in celebration and scenes of joy shot around the world.

As he continued to mine on through, a couple of people noticed the shabby vagrant parting the crowd. Their puzzled look was followed by a short wave of silence. It didn't last.

"ASHOK!" The café erupted.

People hugged him, whistled, and shouted.

These are scientists! He thought.

A partition hurriedly opened up. It led to a hastily vacated seat at the bar. The moment he sat, a procession of phantom arms wrapped around, patted and squeezed him on the shoulder.

The barista came up and shook his hand across the marble, "Something special today, Ashok?"

"The usual, please... But make it two shots up-front."

Despite the crowd, Ashok could feel the reassuring heat radiating from the espresso machine. It had been put to good use throughout the day.

Two perfectly pulled shots appeared in front of him. Momentarily oblivious to the crowd, he sized them up, took in their aroma and hit them, one after the other. Canvas erupted in cheer again.

"Come on people!" He laughed.

"You come on!" A burly man in his fifties shook Ashok's hand. "Take it in, Sir, take it in. We've been here all day. It's the same across the world."

The monitor showed clips of raucous street parties and celebrations from Pacha to the Far-East-Steppe. Between each shot, the feed cut to Ayla and Tomias embraced on Hela with Orus and the forest in the background. That one intimate moment, so distant and yet so human, had taken Earth's heart.

"Excuse me," Ashok signalled the barista, "I'll take my last shot to stay, please." He swivelled around on his seat and plunged into conversation with the exalted mob.

****

"We're still working on getting the power back. You can sleep within Orus for the first cycle or establish the Exopod."

Ayla pointed to the shore-side.

"We'll prepare the Exopod, Operations. A few experiments to install first."

Tomias had neatly ordered a dozen titanium boxes of gear and supplies along a raised piece of ground, far away from the lake's light waves.

Nearby, Ayla had piled a similar collection of labelled experiment parcels in something resembling the start of a game of pick-up sticks.

"The sun is already cresting." Tomias gestured towards the sky. "We have two research items to set up for day one. Let's get them done and inflate the Exopod."

"Yes sir, Captain, sir!" Ayla saluted.

"Is the gravity making you lightheaded?"

"More the idea that we could be stuck here for a long, long time."

"Operations will be back in a few minutes. Unpack the scouts and we'll worry about the damage later."

"How very productive." Ayla checked over the experiment labels. She placed her index finger on a large cubic box at the bottom of her pile.

Ayla shifted the boxes above. "I could get used to this." She lifted an otherwise fifty pound box with one hand.

"You just wait for the three hour daily exercise routine."

"Take a girl for dinner first. I didn't realise romance didn't exist here."

Tomias rolled his eyes, "Literal exercise. And a lot of it."

"We'll have time for that." Ayla opened her box and removed three mirrored spheres from its padded interior. She activated them with a few taps of the monitor on her wrist.

The largest sphere was an oxidised silver colour with no visible markings.

Coming to life, fine strips of blue lights scattered across its surface, distributing evenly around the sphere. It purposefully rolled over towards Lake Jona. Lightly touching the gravel ground, the ball left no trail.

Smallest of the three was a pearlescent white sphere with angular grey lines criss-crossing an iridescent shell. The Aerial Scout vectored straight up. It hovered fifty feet above the landing site and shot off to its distant perimeter.

Lastly, the anodized ultramarine Ground Scout trundled off, making its way into the thick forest.

"We see that the scouts are active."

"Yes, successfully deployed."

"We'll tell you if any relevant data comes out of them."

"Next up is the moon section of the refracting interferometer experiment." Tomias scrolled through his checklist.

Ayla found the right box. This time it was on top of the remaining pile. "As long as it's on open ground, it doesn't matter where we set it up, right?"

"Yes. Open, stable ground. The beach isn't ideal, but we can anchor it up there." Tomias directed Ayla to a flat piece of open ground next to the beach.

From where they were standing it looked as if the field were covered by low grass. As Ayla carried the box over, she saw that the ground was actually topped with a thick layer of spongy moss.

"A few hours in and we're already destroying the environment." She placed the metal case on the moss and deployed its anchoring spikes.

Four titanium alloy rods screwed through the moss and into the soil. Water seeped through the moss as they pulled the box perfectly level.

Ayla walked back to the beach and activated the experiment. Panels on the outer box unfurled like petals. They overlapped in a sharp, circular pattern on the ground.

On the inside, the panels were lined with dark grey solar panels. At the centre of the unfurled array sat an intricate clump of lenses and mirrors encased in an elongated glass belljar.

"Looks like an alien flower." Tomias watched as the equipment calibrated itself, lenses and mirrors turning and pivoting.

"A little ironic, given the context, don't you think?"

"The module is operational, thank you. Stand back as it activates the rangefinder."

"Will do, Petra."

Several seconds later, the contraption stopped aligning its various components. The largest lens within the belljar angled towards the sky. A narrow green laser light fired out through the lens and over the lake. It was stopped by the layer of frothy clouds.

Ayla and Tomias looked on as the light searched around the sky. It darted from point to point in wide systemic sweeps. Eventually, it settled on a narrow patch of sky. Pulsing twice, it extinguished.

"Pretty cool." Ayla stepped towards the device.

"Yep. Help me get the Exopod up please." Tomias dragged the largest container in his line-up onto the edge of the beach. "Let's put it here. So it doesn't damage your precious moss."

The sun was already setting as they undid a series of latches on the sofa-sized box. Taking a few steps back, they activated the module. Its sides unfurled neatly, unrolling a wide flat doughnut of silver fabric.

"We have a knack for origami, as you can see." Ayla smiled.

The fabric began to inflate. It rose higher and higher, gaining volume and girth. Over a few minutes the Exopod had ballooned to three times their height and half of Orus' length.

In its final state, the habitation pod resembled a bulging white wheel of cheese with a single porthole as an entrance. A round metal lid flattened it from the top.

"Welcome to your home for the next week." Ayla sprang towards the porthole.

"Have a comfortable first night on Hela, guys."

"Thank you, Petra." Tomias followed Ayla towards the hatch.

"For your information, Ground Scout picked up an unexpected trace of metallic residue. It's likely from your landing. We'll keep you posted."

"Thank you, Petra. Please do."

Operations out

"Corrosion fallout from Orus. Let's set up a secure connection with Petra tomorrow morning." Ayla opened the Exopod's porthole and climbed in.

SEVENTEEN

"As we have already seen, the mission is delivering stunning revelations." Ashok sat at the head of a sprawling walnut table. "BISE has confirmed the preliminary observations made during the journey."

The Council Leaders sat on either side of him. As the host, Irnes sat at the end.

"It seems Earth and Hela exchange organic molecules as well as atmospheric matter. Life on Hela is life on Earth." He continued.

Adroa joined the table, a seat was always made available for the head of the Kap. Chiefs of Staff and their executive teams sat on a ring of desks behind the leaders. Each team perched over their respective head. Everyone, including Ashok, was adorned in formal attire, befitting Dvor Castle's Grand Hall.

The hall was a glistening example of literal excess. Easily capable of hosting five hundred, no surface was left uncovered by a rare type of charcoal-streaked marble.

The High Table was placed on a raised base in the exact centre of the space. Thick square pillars flanked the walls. They rose three stories up.

Lions sat primed on top of the columns. They supported an intricately carved marble roof. At the end of the long rectangular room, a solid electrum dome hung on the wall. Sharp electrum rays extended out from the precious depiction of Hela.

"Do we have an insight whether life came from Hela to Earth, or the other way around?" Kala sat half-way between Ashok and Irnes. He wore an opulent wine-coloured collarless jacket with electrum piping.

"It's too early to say. Speculation beyond the established facts." Ashok took a sip from an espresso silently placed in front of him.

"In any case, it is an incredible achievement." Matias sat across from Kala. He wore a crimson cloak held on by a wide gold collar over a turquoise tunic.

"And it is only the start. Over the next five days the crew will conduct and establish a long list of experiments before preparing for their return."

"And their precarious landing?" The gleaming Hela sculpture was suspended behind Irnes like a giant crown.

"BISE are working on the power issue but they assure me it is temporary. It should be sorted in a day or two. The engineers are on it."

"And what of their return? How will the world be protected from anything they might be carrying with them?"

"Well, Irnes, initial analysis of the diamond road did show it contained various germs and viruses. Nothing alien to Earth.

We can assume that there is nothing up there that would be harmful down here. In any case, Ayla and Tomias will be placed in quarantine upon their return."

"How long will they stay locked up? When will they be able to come to us? People will want to see them." Yana asked.

"Two weeks, at most, less if the tests are clear. After they rest, we have drafted a tour around the Core States as well as a number of secondary destinations. Mito will distribute the packs now. Do tell me if you have any questions or issues."

Mito stood and handed the others a pack of documents.

"The world can't wait for their return." Kala smiled.

"Neither can I, believe me. After that we'll have years of discoveries to reveal and build on."

"Years? Ashok, have you considered The Council's previous requests?"

"Again, it is too early for me to comment, Irnes. There will be so much to do after the mission. I need some time to make a coherent plan."

The hall echoed as Irnes pushed back in her chair. Its legs screeching on the stone floor. "I think we all deserve an answer rather soon, Ashok."

"As I said, I will lay out a proposal when I feel it is the right time."

"That's not acceptable! The world doesn't revolve around you!"

"Irnes, perhaps we could table this topic at our next regular meeting. You're welcome to join." Kala turned towards her.

"No... We deserve to know now. He's holding us ransom."

"That's enough." Kala raised his palm.

"I suggest we focus on celebrating our joint achievement. You all have my word that I will consider your suggestions in my final decision." Ashok turned his palms towards the ceiling, "We're done here."

Irnes shoved her seat back and rushed out of the room.

****

"I don't know what follows. Before the landing, I had decided to agree with The Council's demands. Now there's so much I want to do."

Ashok and Sabil walked along the Lacka River. The winding waterway neatly separated old and new Dvor. On one side, the castle rose up with its steep gantry, surrounded by the ancient houses snaking through narrow streets. On the other, Dvor's market was the sole alcove of the old city. Beyond it, wide boulevards delineated rows of modern buildings.

"This is a rather good high to leave on, don't you think?" Sabil wore loose wool trousers with a baggy cotton tunic.

"Maybe you're right."

Centuries ago, the two sides of the city had been connected by three stone bridges stretching across the Lacka.

The two outer bridges were made of near-identical arches hewn from dark granite blocks. In the middle stood the Hara Bridge. It led up to Dvor Castle and comprised three arches, finer and narrower than the others, they were propped up by thick pillars breaking the rapid river waters.

The two men walked along a promenade set down by the water. It had been designed some distance below the busy street above.

"Irnes is becoming restless." Ashok waved as passers-by smiled and greeted them.

"I understand Frey has been giving her certain ideas." Sabil kept his hands in his pockets.

Ashok noticed a square form sunk in the walkway, right next to the water's edge. He walked over to investigate. "It's a backgammon board. I've never seen it before."

"Would you believe it is four hundred years old?"

The board was carved into the stone itself. It was as if someone ran away with a paving slab. The once-sharp edges were rounded and worn.

Inside, two rows of twelve triangular points stared at each-other. While the board was clearly well-used, the white lacquer paint on the points was only lightly scratched.

"We haven't played in years."

Sabil rummaged around in his deep trouser pockets. He presented a woven hemp bag in his palm. "I always carry a set."

"Seems productive." Ashok took the bag and undid a loose twine knot. He emptied its contents in Sabil's hand. A pile of flat polished pebbles tumbled out. Fifteen jet black onyx. Fifteen milky crystal. Two cubes of rainbow opal sparkled through the mix.

They sat on either side of the board. Their legs hung over the rushing water.

"You used to know how to play. I imagine you've lost it. Everyone letting you win all the time." Sabil teased as he placed the pile down and shuffled a pebble from each colour between his hands.

"I've played with three people for as long as I can remember. Adroa never stands down, Mito tries but it's not his game. Ayla. Ayla is more stubborn than her mother." Ashok tapped Sabil's left wrist.

He opened, revealing a smooth white crystal and proceeded to arrange the board. White for Ashok, black for Sabil. "And Adroa? You two have been playing at this for a long time. Don't you think it's time to make a move…? You're not getting any younger?"

Ashok rolled a four. "Thank you. She's here now, we're having dinner at the house."

Sabil rolled a five and played the first turn "Ah, perhaps you could settle in Dvor!"

"Can you imagine?" Ashok rolled a two and a one. "With Irnes here, it would be a bloodbath. I'm surprised there were no casualties today."

"Go on, it would be entertaining. I could use some excitement."

The waters of the Lacka River splashed around below their feet.

"You know." Ashok paused before rolling a double six. He smiled. "Her term here in Dvor is ending soon. It's probably one of the reasons she so agitated."

"Luck, pure luck." Sabil cursed. "And?"

"You've been outside of this world for a while. Perhaps it's time to come back in."

"What do you mean?"

"You know what I mean. Have a think. People here still love you. Not only thanks to your mediocre coffee." Ashok rolled a double three. "...And you're bored, so sad and bored! This is all lovely but there's so much more out there."

"If you cheat as much in your leadership, I can see why Irnes is agitated." Sabil rolled a one and a six. "And my coffee is the best in Dvor, jackass!"

"Sure it is. Think about it. There's still time."

****

Ashok kept a tidy estate in Dvor. Since introducing the Tube, he rarely stayed at the old house. It had been adapted into a public space for cultural events and public debates.

The two-storey mansion was surrounded by manicured grounds on three sides. It sat perched on a rocky bend of the Lacka River, a little way out of the city centre. Ashok kept a small apartment within the house. It had a few rooms and a softly lit terrace overlooking the fast-flowing water.

Adroa wore a translucent linen gown with a wide-open neck. It let the warm night breeze pass through and over her body.

"Beautiful night."

She looked up at the clear cloudless moon. Hela's features were sharp. Lake Jona was just about visible. A small blue blemish next to the great Tethys Ocean.

Ashok came out on the terrace in a pastel blue robe, carrying a bottle of wine. He placed it on a wooden table set with a cream candle and plates of light food. "When she comes back, I want to show you a very special place indeed." He poured a single glass.

"Wow." Adroa savoured the desert elixir. "Where's it from?"

She passed the glass to Ashok who took a slow, considered sip. "Long story. Remember that wine guy Ayla keeps going on about in Nussa. Hallough?"

"Vaguely, yes."

"Well, not him. But a woman he knows who owns a winery around an old caravansary on the Great Trade Road."

"Amazing story. Thrilling from start to finish. Did you write about it?"

Ashok put his arm around Adroa's waist and kissed her while still holding the glass. "Yes yes, as I said, it's a long story. We'll have to go."

"As long as there's more wine there."

Ashok leaned on a thick stone parapet lining the terrace. The city's glow diffused up from the river's sharp turns and out over distant hills. "I keep thinking about that place. Ultimately, Kala is right. We need to change."

Adroa sat by the table. She surveyed a silver plate containing small bites arranged in neat circles. "You do, but there are a lot of factors to consider." she picked up a slice of grilled aubergine from and dipped it in a sweet sauce. "You saw Irnes today. She clearly has her own ideas."

"She's been pushing hard for some time." he stretched over from the parapet, snagged a thin wedge of cheese and reached for the wine glass. "I had an idea for Sabil to take her seat again."

"What did he think?"

"Mostly rude words. But it did spark his interest. Plus, I've been thinking about my idea for BISE. It's becoming clearer. It makes sense. If I keep my seat on The Council, I can push to create a permanent base on Hela. A small city. From there we start humanity on a new path."

"You know you can't do everything, everywhere." Adroa squeezed the glass out from his hand. "You'll have to give up something."

Ashok pushed back from the parapet and came to sit on the table. "Sounds like you have a thought?" he placed a hand on her thigh, pouring more wine.

"Perhaps." She took a sharp sip. "I think you should step down from Flavia. Think about Kala's desire for collaboration between the states."

"And The Council?"

"Keep a seat, for now. But let someone else lead it."

"Who?"

"While you and Kala have your differences, you know he has the world's best interest in mind."

"We still have some way to go. And I don't trust Frey."

"Neither does Kala. It's time to make way for new blood. Both in Flavia and in Nussa. At some point, you have to let go."

"You have someone in mind?"

"As a matter of fact, I do." Adroa paused and took a strip of crispy baked pita bread, dipping it in a small bowl of hot, seasoned hummus. "Are you worried?"

"About Ayla? A bit. She'll be fine. But she is all the way on the damn moon."

They both stared up at the barely visible strip of land between Lake Jona and the ocean.

"And it's all your doing, too." Adroa leant over and kissed Ashok, lightly biting his lip.

"Again, hilarious. You've brought on a new comedy teacher in Dharma?"

"Yep, that's exactly what he's teaching me." She slipped a hand under Ashok's robe, gripping between his legs.

He stood, taking the glass with him. Adroa followed, trying to snatch it. Swinging back, he spilt a velvet swig on her gown "Oh no, how terrible, we'll have to have it washed straight away."

He slipped the gown off of her shoulders with the tips of his fingers, following it down around her body as it fell. With two hands on her waist Ashok pulled Adroa into him.

Ayla took some time opening her eyes. "I could get used to this."

Cocooned side-by-side in silver sleeping bags, Tomias had wrapped his arm around her. "It's not too bad, is it? Could have used a double bag though."

"I'll chastise Petra for not prioritising the development of double sleeping bags these past months."

"Rightfully so. The pod is a bit sparse, too."

The round, windowless interior of the Exopod was bright and empty. While there was ample space, the two huddled next to one another with their equipment scattered around.

Ayla's equipment scattered around.

Tomias had arranged his gear in a near-perfect cube next to the porthole.

"What's for breakfast?" Ayla wriggled out of the sleeping bag and scoured her sterile home.

Tomias stood, stepped out of his bag and opened their rations case. "Well, the pack says, 'scrambled eggs.'" He took out a vacuum-sealed foil pouch. "But it feels an awful lot like sand. Hopefully the boiled water will do something to it."

"You stay the hell away from the water boiler machine."

"Kettle?"

"Whatever. I have dibs on it first." Ayla poured water from a tall square jug into the open throat of a dark thermos. It had a stumpy spout at its side.

She pushed a button by its base and a puff of steam shot out of the spout. More importantly, it was followed by a thick brown liquid, oozing into a short crystal cup. Ayla's eyes lit up with delight.

"Right. I see. Didn't have time to sew two sleeping bags together but you did have time to develop a portable espresso machine."

"Well. Priorities."

Tomias reached forward. "Can I at least have one?"

Ayla pulled her coffee close. "I suppose. You're lucky we packed two cups." Pushing the button again, a whirring noise cleaned the machine and put forth a new brew.

"Imagine if I used a water glass for coffee."

"Insanity, right?"

After a reasonably edible breakfast, the two emerged out of the Exopod to find the rocky beach covered in fine dew.

The sun was beginning to burn through the clouds. It blanketed the damp ground in a coat of mellow light.

"We have a couple of hours to explore before Petra connects."

"Let's go see the ocean."

"The ground Scout is on its way back from its shore." He reviewed a monitor on the Exopod's wall. "It seems like it hasn't found anything worrying that way." Tomias turned and stared off into the trees behind them.

Ayla saw a trail of moss flattened by the heavy Scout snaking into the thick forest.

With the Aerial Scout circling above, the two headed through the isthmus and towards the Tethys Ocean. Leaving their base behind, they quickly plunged into dense shade.

The seal-grey tree trunks were tall and straight however the woven canopy obstructed virtually all direct sunlight. Their view was cut short barely a dozen trees in.

Their steps crunched through the uneven soil like iced-over snow. The ground was soft and sandy. The same chalky shale was mixed in as the shore.

The air was thick and humid. Their canopy awning acting like a natural greenhouse. Twenty minutes into their walk, they began to hear a low rumble. A vibration permeating through the forest and the ground.

"What's that?" Ayla crept forward.

As they continued, the rumble became more defined and rhythmic. The sound of waves resonated from the trees.

Soon, the shade was pierced by thin rays of pale blue light. As the forest began to ebb, the white crests of crashing water came into sight.

Emerging out on the other side of the isthmus, the two Explorers found themselves standing near a high sheer edge.

Below them was a straight fifty foot drop. Stretching out ahead was a violent, angry ocean. Its waves smashed halfway up the cliff. Every crash brought up a warm mist. It wet the ground under their boots.

The sound of Tethys roared along the battered coastline. It was accompanied by a punishing hot wind. It pushed them back towards the forest. The treeline resonated with crashes and thuds accompanied by the odd creak and squeal. Glancing back, Tomias placed a hand over the taser in his pocket.

"This isn't quite how I imagined it." Ayla stood facing the turbulent waters.

"The Earth is stirring it up into a frenzy." Tomias scanned the cliff's edge. Trees ended a few feet before the drop. Further down the winding coast he could see some of them bent, hanging over the precipice. "Look over there, it's the Scout."

Two bluffs away, behind clouds of mist, the dulled ball rolled along above the drop. Now and then it would stop, circle around a rock or a tree. Whenever it was intrigued, it would focus a cone of red light over whatever piqued its interest. After a quick scan it would roll on.

"Let's go to it." Ayla led the way around the coast, walking closer to the treeline than the edge.

The land between them and the Scout dipped before rising back up. At its lowest point, a rocky outcrop cut into the water. Tethys did her best to destroy it, battering the protrusion from every side.

Standing in the depression, Ayla and Tomias looked back, pointing to where they'd emerged from the forest. Directly below, they could see the open mouth of a cave punched into the cliff.

A stream fell out of the cave. It was instantly whipped into white scattering spray. The water mixed with the ocean waves as they surged upwards, repeatedly flooding the gaping hole.

Lost in the view, they jumped as the ground Scout zipped past their feet. Humans were of little interest. Startled, Ayla turned around.

"What's that?" She pointed to a sharp metallic edge sticking out from a curved root behind them.

Tomias walked over to see a torn foil sachet caught in the roots. "It's a food pouch. Must have blown over from the camp."

"As I said, two days here and we're polluting Hela." Ayla picked up the used container. "This is a fish stew. Sounds horrible, by the way... But we only had those eggs. In any case, I'm sure we left our pouch in the pod."

Tomias kneeled to the ground. "It might be from Jonah's crash. Maybe it's somewhere nearby." He jumped and ran, climbing to higher ground. "If it is, we have to find it. When Petra calls, we have to tell her right away. We'll make a secure line."

Ayla looked closely at the bag. "Wait, Tommy." Ayla showed him the bag, "It's opened at the top. This wasn't torn randomly. It's been deliberately unsealed. Eaten. By someone. By something."

EIGHTEEN

"All we can say for certain is that this is definitely a food pack from Orus 5" Petra reviewed analysis results from the find.

"Surely there is evidence that it was eaten, opened." Ayla looked at the report. The pouch was now placed in a sterile container at the Exopod's side.

"It's torn and empty, but we would expect the tear to be at the top, that's how the pouches are made."

"There's no other damage, only that clean tear."

"We'll look at it again, but you have other work to do before we go live again."

"Let's start with the refractor." Tomias stood by the metallic flower.

"Okay, we'll power it up from here." Petra had relocated to the main Operations Control station within the BISE campus in Flavia.

In contrast to the brutal waves and winds of the Tethys Ocean, Lake Jona was calm and tranquil. The teal sky was almost clear. A thin lick of clouds filtered the view to Earth as it loomed above.

"This will be a full run. Don't be surprised by the light."

"Confirmed, Petra."

Ayla walked along the shore from their exopod to Tomias. She passed him a pair of protective glasses.

"Range-finding on." a thin red laser shot out of the central dome. The beam itself couldn't be seen in the bright sunlight but, staring up into the sky, they could spot a feint red blotch dying the clouds.

"All modules locked, firing main beam." the red light disappeared. The device let out a long low tone. It increased in pitch to a loud nasal whine. Right at its peak, the noise suddenly stopped. A powerful sapphire ray fired out of the dome.

The beam was flat and wide. Unlike the red laser, it could be seen slicing a ribbon up through the sky.

Unimpeded, it punched a hole through the clouds right where the red spot had previously been. The light headed off into space and towards Earth.

No more than a few seconds later, the beam abruptly stopped.

There was silence on the monitor.

"Petra? Operations?" Tomias called out as they took a few steps back.

"Yes! I think we can call that a success. Thank you!" Petra's excited comments were again followed by silence.

"Shall we continue?" Ayla asked.

"... Yes, of course. We have a few minutes before we broadcast. The power issue has been sorted. Let's raise Orus and land it on its side."

"And the damage?"

"This operation is safe. When the ship is on its side, we'll assess the magnitude of the damage. From what you've said, it sounds quite serious. We're working on a range of options."

"Have you mentioned anything to my father yet?"

"Not yet, no."

"Alright. Make sure the bottom is out of frame when we go live." Ayla looked over at Orus as it leant on the thick trees.

"We have Aerial Scout in place. The manoeuvre should place the craft flat, right behind the Exopod. Afterwards, the Scout will move out to the other side and we will block that view from its route."

"Ready when you are." Tomias signalled Ayla to move further away from the camp.

Operations Control in Flavia was organised more like a cinema monitor than the doughnut-shaped hall in Kamrun.

Rows of desks were staggered facing a tall wall of monitors. The room had no windows, but it was as bright as an operating theatre. The entire ceiling emitted an even white glow.

Petra's desk was at the rear of the room. It was raised from the other posts. "Stand by. Orus is powering up."

For a few moments, Ayla and Tomias looked on from a distance at not a great deal happening. A few chips of gravel and sand rolled out from beside the craft's base. Orus' curved tip began to move out from its leafy perch. Gradually, the drawn-out shiny egg began to straighten.

When it was perfectly plumb with the ground, the ship started to raise out of the rocky nest it had burrowed in the beach.

Ashok flew into Operations Control directly behind Petra. He walked in right as the Aerial Scout projected Orus in its slow ascent across the main monitors.

She jumped up out of her seat and turned to shake his hand. Fixated on the monitor infront, Ashok missed her outstretched hand.

His smile disappeared as the scout showed rocky debris and metal fragments falling out of a pockmarked spot at the craft's base.

"What is that?" His eyebrows scrunched.

"It seems the AB corroded the hull on the way down."

"It seems?" All of the engineers turned from their workstations. "You knew about this. And you didn't tell me?"

Orus completed its ascent. It reached above the flat tree canopies. Briefly, it stood still, reflecting the bright turquoise sky. The craft then turned ninety degrees about its centre and pointed towards the ocean.

"Sir. We are working on a contingency plan."

"What contingency plan? The hull is compromised!" Ashok walked half-way down the room. "Ayla. How could you not tell me?"

"Dad. What are you doing there?" Ayla paused. "We'll work out a solution. There was no other way! The mission would have been cancelled."

Orus began a gentle descent. It came back down below the treetops. The vessel came to rest exactly as planned, with the oven-sized hole hidden from view by the Exopod.

"What solution? That thing can't leave Hela's atmosphere, nevermind re-enter Earth's. This is suicide, Ayla, how could you do it?"

"Sir." Petra walked up to him, "I'm very sorry but we go live in thirty seconds."

****

"Captain. The Water Scout has detected an unexpected substance in the lake. It is approximately three miles up the coast from your current position."

"Any more details, Operations?"

"We're looking at the data now, but it looks like some form of chemical leak. Ground Scout is inland from the same area."

"Thank you."

"Perhaps it's a leak from the crash site. Maybe it's nearby." Ayla was unpacking a series of experiments next to the Exopod.

The sky had covered over with layers of thick clouds. Their cover insulated the ground below, concentrating the humid air.

Tomias had removed the jacket from his day suit, leaving only a fitted vest. “If it is, we should find it.”

“Captain. Ground Scout has identified signs of smoke or smoke residue fifteen hundred feet in from the lakeshore.”

“Can we see a video feed?”

“No, the cameras are obscured, and Aerial has no line of sight through the forest.”

“May, could you give me authorisation to go and get a visual myself?”

“Please hold while I secure authorisation.”

“I want to come with you, Tommy.”

Tomias reached through the Exopod’s porthole. He took his jacket. “It’s against the protocol. We have a lot of work to get on with. I’ll go check it out, you continue with the experiment list.”

“You’ll have a constant video link?” Ayla gently slipped his helmet on his head.

“Captain. You’re authorised to get a visual of the site. The location has been sent to your monitor. Take your taser.”

“Confirmed, Operations.” Tomias opened a locked metal case and took out a remote control-shaped polished weapon “Yes. I’ll keep the video running. Switch to my channel on your monitor.”

Ayla synced the monitor on her sleeve with a camera built into his helmet. Aerial Scout circled far in the distance like a hawk surveying a find.

Tomias embraced her and slowly made his way up the winding shore. Though his first target wasn't far away, the route was slow and tiring.

Unlike their landing site, most of the lake's coast was a thin strip of gravel repeatedly cut by fallen trees. Their bulging crowns wedged deep in the water. Every twenty, thirty feet he would have to either climb over, duck under or vault the hulking grey logs.

Ayla watched as he navigated Hela's coastal assault course. Part-way along he stopped, turned and waved before disappearing behind dunes of broken treetops. Her monitor showed him steadily make his way up the shore. She left it on while working through the scientific tasks for the day.

Twice on the way he stopped to rest, each time leaning on a log to take a breath. The high humidity made for heavy progress.

As he approached his coastal target, Tomias noticed a shimmer on the water. Small waves lapped an oily residue. It covered patches of chalky pebbles with a grey metallic film.

"It looks like coolant, Captain."

"Thank you, May. There are drips leading into the trees. Several large patches of it are floating on the water."

"It is likely from the Orus 5 crash site. Please seal your helmet. The site will likely be contaminated."

"Confirmed, May. Switching to an air filter."

From the shore, he followed dabs of coolant towards the forest's edge. The first few lines of trees were spaced far apart, allowing a thick cover of sodden moss to grow between them. Tomias peered in but the forest rapidly thickened.

Stepping in from the sunlit coast, he found himself in near-darkness. A laser projector on his helmet lit the way ahead. Its beam was crossed by rays of sunlight which had managed to find their way through the dense canopy.

As he walked Tomias felt an odd sense of unease. It was the first time on Hela he had experienced any form of trepidation. A thick gust of wind ran through the treetops. They cracked in the dark. Twists and shivers rang out through the canopy above.

Deeper still, he saw odd patches of lights through the gloom ahead.

Coming nearer, the lights seemed to reflect off of something on the ground. A few steps on, not looking at his feet, he kicked something hard and nearly tripped.

He looked closer, "A storage box. It's smashed open."

"Yes. It has the Orus 5 markings. Careful as you go, Captain"

As he neared the cluster of lights, Tomias switched off his projector. It was darker than he thought. He broke through a weave of dry branches which had fallen to the ground. Not noticing a ledge on the other side, Tomias slipped and fell through the tangle.

He raised himself on one knee. A layer of branches had stuck to his suit. Dusting off, he could make out a series of angular silhouettes. Cargo boxes.

Coming closer, he stopped in his tracks. A chill ran down his spine.

They were arranged intentionally, not scattered. Two perfectly stacked rows of undamaged metal boxes.

They were clean and unscratched. Some were open and empty. Others still sealed.

"Are you seeing this? It doesn't look right. This is no crash site." He circled around the find.

"Yes, Captain."

Suddenly Tomias was thrown face-down on the hard ground. His helmet knocked and scratched against stones and roots as he struggled to understand what was happening. He realised a warm weight was keeping him from moving. It pressed forcefully on his spine.

He tried to reach down to his taser, but unable to move his arms under the weight. He was helpless.

With all his strength, Tomias pushed against the ground and turned. His visor was covered in dirt. He could roughly make out a human form looming above.

Wiping off the dirt with his sleeve, he saw two green eyes, wide-open, staring at him through a matt of hair.

"Jonah."

The spectre stood motionless while Tomias raised himself and removed his helmet. Jonah gazed at him as if in a trance. His sharp cheekbones poked out through a tangled beard.

He wore a torn white vest and trousers which had been cut into shorts. Their silver threads dangled out from the ends.

“Tommy?” Jonah broke his daze.

“How can it be? How are you here? How are you alive?”

“I’ve been waiting, Tommy. Waiting for months.”

“But you crashed, I saw Orus disappear on Hela.”

“No... There was a power issue. A thousand feet up Orus went dark, it pulsed. I forced Drive and landed. It was a hard landing. It blew all of the cells.”

Tomias lent forward to embrace him. Jonah, still staring into his eyes, slid out of his grasp and fell to the forest floor.

****

“A very good evening, viewers!” Laaro pressed his elbows over his glossy white desk. Video from Hela looped behind him. “In the space of a few hours, the nature of this historic mission has changed completely.”

Laaro’s monitor displayed footage taken from Aerial Scout showing the two men emerging out of the forest. Jonah was leaning on Tomias as he stumbled through the jumble of roots along their way.

“This momentous journey of discovery has quickly turned into a rescue mission.” Laaro leaned back in his chair. “We are yet to hear an official statement from BISE. All of our preliminary information shows that the mission will be cut short so that Jonah can return to Earth as soon as possible.”

The scene changed to show footage of people taking to the streets around the world. They held hastily made signs expressing a mix of joy and concern.

"While he seems weak, we have heard that Jonah is healthy. After the initial shock of his encounter with Tomias, the group appear calm and happy to have found each other once again. It goes without saying that I can hardly believe I am saying these words..."

The monitor showed Ayla running towards the two. She could be seen embracing Jonah and helping him over to their camp.

"Have you spoken with Ashok?" Frey watched the footage on a monitor in Kala's office.

"We talked earlier today."

"Do they have a plan?"

"Not yet. BISE is working to find a solution." Kala sat on a plush velvet chair in front of a stone coffee table in a corner of his office.

"The situation was difficult before. Now it is vital we get Jonah back."

"As well as assessing Orus they are considering sending a rescue mission."

Frey sat down on a seat opposite. "That would take months to organise. We can't have the world watch Jonah die up there."

"Ayla and Tomias are also there." Kala noted slyly. "But I agree, we can't."

"Before today, I was going to advise you to leak the hull failure. Ashok would lose any advantage he thinks he has. He would have to agree to all of our terms. But now. Now we can't. Not yet."

"That's not how we do things, Frey. Ashok might be stubborn, but he deserves our support. Now more than ever." Kala raised himself out of his snug seat and went to an open window. Hela shone like a great teal marble in the clear black sky. He turned towards Frey. "I understand you have been speaking with Irnes."

"We exchange ideas now and again, yes." Frey straightened.

"What have you been telling her?"

"As I said, we exchange ideas."

"It's mostly a rhetorical question. I know what you've been discussing." Kala went to lean on his mahogany desk. "You have no capacity to offer Flavia to Irnes. We're trying to create a world that can last – not play short-term power games."

"She is a good leader."

"You know that's not the point." Kala slammed a fist on his desk. "Consider this a direct warning."

"Noted." Frey stood. "But it would be unwise not to use this opportunity. Jonah is a son of Nussa. The fact that he is alive can galvanise our efforts."

"We can and we will. But there is a right way to approach the situation and this isn't it. In the morning I will speak with Ashok again. We will work out a plan for their safe return."

Frey nodded and left the room. Kala opened an ornate glass cabinet next to his desk. He removed a decorated crystal decanter and poured a neat smoky whiskey into a thick crystal glass. Resting at the window, he stared up at Hela.

****

The morning was cloudy and cool. A steady breeze ran over Lake Jona. Jonah and Tomias sat on storage boxes around an imaginary campfire by the shore. The forest whistled behind them.

"They're going to have to change the name of this lake." Ayla came from the Exopod carrying her espresso machine. She handed out freshly drawn coffee to the guys.

"Why? Because I didn't die? That seems a tad unfair."

Jonah had cut his hair into a more manageable nest. His beard was trimmed back to a light stubble.

"I guess they could keep it on hold for you." Tomias grasped his insulated cup with two hands and took a sip.

"Coffee was one of the first things I ran out of."

"Plus, yours was that instant crap. Let's not be making insulting comparisons."

"How much have you explored?" Ayla sat by Tomias and held his hand.

"It's tough. The forest is thick. There are no easy routes. A few openings, meadows and fallen trees. But I haven't found the expanse of clear land we were aiming for."

"Any animals?" Tomias laughed.

"I don't know." Jonah hunched over his coffee.

"That's not the answer I expected."

"It's probably the isolation. Something doesn't feel right here. I've never seen anything, but it often feels like something is around, watching."

"That's why you jumped me?"

"I don't know. When I saw your outline rummaging through the supplies I was overcome by some sort of primal instinct. It's hard to describe."

The sun broke through the cloud cover. Warming rays lit a fine fog suspended a few feet above the lake's surface.

"Team. Ashok is with me." Petra opened a line on the monitors. "We have a few minutes before we broadcast."

"Morning Petra. Hi, Dad."

"Jonah, how are you holding up?" Ashok smiled.

"Good, thank you. I had a good night's sleep for the first time in months."

"Happy to hear it. Gather up some energy, you'll need it. We're working on several scenarios to get the three of you back. In any case, the mission has changed. I'll pass back to Petra who will outline your next steps."

"Right." Petra sat at her command desk.

Ashok stood behind her with his arms crossed. "Our priority is to solve the compromised hull. For the moment, it is to be kept from the public. The mission will be cut short and refocused around your return."

"What are we to do in the meantime?" Tomias looked back at Orus. The ship's damage was still hidden by the Exopod.

"We have sent an updated list of priority experiments. Make sure they are completed. Otherwise, keep healthy and keep smiling for the cameras." Petra gave an encouraging thumbs up.

"Great pep talk, Petra, speak to you soon. Bye, Dad." Ayla stood and walked to the water's edge. Small waves slipped under the toes of her boots.

"Come on." Tomias jumped up, "We can't sit around all day. Jonah, take us to Orus 5. Where is it?"

"Not far from where you found me. There's a high hill with a deep natural depression. An old crater or something. It's overgrown with trees and weeds. The ship sank through the trees." Jonah stood and stretched. "I'll take you an easier way around."

****

"That gulley leads to the ocean." Jonah stepped down into a wide ditch. He pointed off to his side. At the deepest point the ground was soggy and soft.

"I think that's where we found your empty food packet." Ayla and Tomias walked beside him through a slippery maze of springy moss and protruding roots.

"When the weather was good, I'd sometimes go there. I'd sit for hours, looking at the Earth, trying to make out places I recognised."

"When the weather was good?" Tomias lifted a fallen branch so the others could pass under.

"You have no idea. It can change in an instant. One minute you can clearly make out reflections from the Hela mirrors in Saphan and Pacha, the next it's a horrible storm. I can't count how many times I've come back to my pod drenched and frozen."

"Maybe you should have picked somewhere closer to eat." Ayla patted him on the shoulder as they began a gentle climb.

The gulch soon widened and the ground hardened.

"These trees are different. They're like balls." Ayla examined the curious flora. Trunks flayed out in all directions. Their crowns were almost perfect spheres. Each tree varied in height like an eccentric piano organ.

"Come, it's a little more impressive around the corner." Jonah led them around a bend.

To their right, the slope became steeper. A warm breeze came from the trees on their other side. As they headed towards its source, the forest became brighter. Sunlight illuminated countless curves from the rows of tree trunks.

Stepping through the last few tangled roots, they appeared out on the edge of a sharp cliff. Ahead of them the landscape opened out into an unobstructed panorama.

"Wow." Ayla leaned on Tomias.

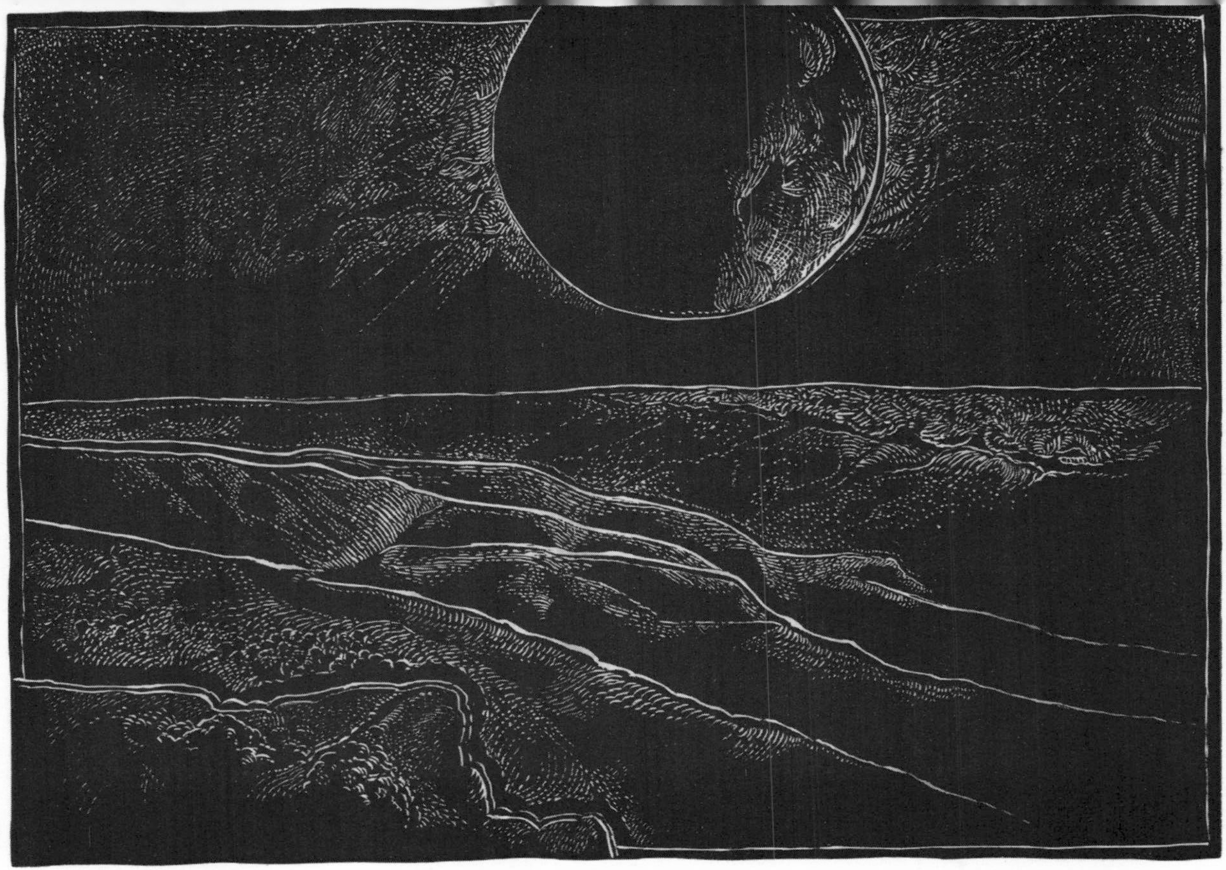

Earth from Rhodinia

"Yep. This is the other spot I'd come and sit."

"I can see why. It's beautiful."

An undulating emerald valley stretched out towards the horizon. Gentle hills were cut by flowing brooks leading west towards Tethys. Above them, the Earth hung low in the teal sky.

"So, the lake is suspended up above the rest of the continent?" Tomias put his arm around Ayla.

"Yes. The plate must have been pushed up. I lost count of how many earthquakes I've felt here. It feels like the ground is cracking around you." Jonah stood next to Tomias.

"If it wasn't for the cold nights, you could have slept here." Ayla looked out over the wild expanse.

"Actually, I often did. My heaters and all of my personal equipment still has power."

"But how? With the damage to Orus 5"

"It's only the ship's cells that are damaged so I couldn't transmit off of Hela. The craft itself is structurally fine."

Ayla leaned around Tomias and grabbed Jonah. "The cells are compatible. Could we take them from Orus 6 to 5?"

"No reason we couldn't. But Orus 5 is designed to land on the moon. Not on Earth. And it has space for two people."

"We packed it with so much stuff. It's crammed with all sorts of crap." Jonah glanced over his shoulder.

"A lovely way to describe two decades of work." Ayla turned towards the forest. "Come on, show us."

Jonah paid a lasting gaze towards the valley before they entered back into the forest. Reaching the hill, they started to climb. Jonah had flattened a clear path through the moss and soil. Halfway up, a row of regular depressions dug into the hillside.

"Did you dig these?" Ayla took each dent in large single steps.

"No, but they make for useful steps, don't they? A boulder must have bounced down."

"Yep." Tomias followed behind. "That's what boulders do."

"You know, Tommy. I kept my promise. This scraggy hill is officially called Tomias Knob." Jonah laughed as he climbed.

They ascended higher. The dense trees provided thick shade. The cool morning had given way to a sweltering heat. Their straight path soon stopped at a sharp lip of moss. The ground fell away on the other side. Only the crater's near edge could be made out. A sea of trees filled its entire bowl.

A patch of silver flashed between the undergrowth in the distance. As they neared, Jonah's improvised camp came into sight. His Exopod was half-inflated, its sagging skin propped up by several surrounding trees. Orus 5 sat nearby. The craft had dug itself several feet into the ground.

"Must have been a hard landing." Tomias stuck the tip of his boot into the soft soil raised out by Orus.

"It was surprisingly smooth. Barely an inconvenience. I managed to over-thrust right on touchdown."

"That's why it burrowed into the topsoil." Ayla touched Orus' smooth silver skin.

"It also destroyed the cells." Jonah went into his Exopod and came out with a large aluminium can of crème soda. "I was saving this for a special occasion." He poured out three cups. They toasted and laughed.

"Nothing says celebration like crème soda. Let's see what Petra thinks about the cells."

NINETEEN

Adroa kept a telescope at the edge of her bedroom. A brass tube sat atop a chrome tripod. Its position was carefully selected, pointed at Hela through a weave of green.

Her bedroom comprised a marble box with two glass sides. It was nestled in the corner of her quarters. On every side the room was surrounded by green. The dome of flowers and vines loomed overhead. There were precious few angles to peek through and see the moon.

Ashok played with a grooved electrum adjustment wheel, trying to focus on the isthmus of Lake Jona.

"It's hard to describe." He peered through the eyepiece. "A feeling perfectly balanced between sheer anger and worry."

"For me it was in waves." Adroa sat at the edge of her bed. She looked out to her gardens. The early evening brought with it a cool breeze which carried the scent of pine sap. "Ultimately, she made the decision to go consciously."

"I can't say I support it."

"Which is exactly why she didn't tell you about the risks. We would never have let her go."

Ashok managed to catch the faintest of flickers from Hela's surface. A brief silver shimmer from the edge of Lake Jona. Orus, perhaps.

"And now what? We wait here helpless?"

"Hard to say we're waiting helplessly." Adroa stood and went over to Ashok. "As far as I know, there are a few thousand people at BISE working around the clock to bring them back. I know Petra will do everything she can."

Ashok put his arm around Adroa as he still stared through the small metal eyepiece.

"Don't get me started on Petra. If times were different and I were a little more tyrannical, she'd be straight in a dungeon. An unpleasant one at that."

"It's good to have a spectrum of tyranny."

"Seriously. She lied, ignored orders, withheld information. Bam. Dungeon!"

"Perhaps I detect a smidge of jealousy? Petra is an incredibly dedicated person. Everything she's done has been with the mission in mind."

"I can't help but feel you're a little biased."

Adroa took Ashok's hand and pulled him away from the telescope. "A little biased, perhaps. But entirely backed by merit."

"I'll stave off the dungeon for now then."

"Indeed. Let's go out for dinner. It's so rare you come, there are some beautiful places."

"You'd better hope they quell my near-tyrannical fury."

"Yes yes, very scary. Come on."

They stepped out of Adroa's bedroom and into her sculpted oasis. The garden was quiet, punctured only by the sound of two bluetails chirping between the bushes.

Wandering out of the Kap, they walked down towards Dharma. The town centre was only a few minutes away, connected to the Kap by a wide path made from loaf-sized bricks of speckled grey marble.

Ashok had a peculiar practise of walking barefoot in Dharma. The sun-heated stone warmed his feet as they entered the town. The narrow streets were abuzz with life. Merchant's laid out a selection of wares from across the vast Himavan Mountains.

Above them, hidden out of sight and behind balcony parapets, families of rhesus macaques surveyed the spread. The monkeys were picky yet determined. If they saw something of interest, they would spring into action.

A lead would head down to create a commotion and distract attention. Two flanking furballs would swing across to take their loot. By this point, the locals had reached an uneasy truce. More of a passive capitulation.

The only sight of their resistance was buckets full of long canes placed on every few street corners – a warning sign to keep pillaging to within civilised bounds.

Adroa led the way through the busy streets, stopping in front of an unassuming wood panel door. They stepped inside to a small room with a tiled checkerboard floor. Simple tables were covered in patterned cloth and surrounded by wicker chairs. She smiled to the staff and continued forward to a door leading out onto a terrace.

The confines of Dharma's narrow streets immediately disappeared. The terrace had half a dozen tables pinned to the wall, each with two thin wicker chairs on either side.

In a broad bow, the scenery unfolded ahead. The town peppered rich green folds in the Himavan. A dense core of buildings stuck to the mountainside like milk spilling over a pot.

Pine trees wriggled and curved around through the tight spaces. Beyond Dharma's centre, the forest took over. The odd house poked out from an ocean of soaring trees. The view stretched over the valley for tens of miles.

"Not too bad, is it?" Adroa sat and Ashok followed.

"Perhaps I can see why you like it. But don't distract me. You lured me here for a reason."

From the corner of the terrace, they could see the Kap up above the town. Its lights had just come on. It was an island of marble, illuminated in the fading light.

"I did. It's time you know something."

A waiter emerged out onto the terrace carrying several plates. He smiled and arranged them neatly on the table.

"I remember this." Ashok examined the bowl in front of him. "Thenthuck. A fancy way of saying noodle soup."

"And momos. An even fancier way of saying dumplings." Adroa pointed to a plate in the centre of the table. "Since the early stages of the mission, I've been working with Petra on a set of experiments."

"What kind of experiments?" Ashok grabbed a crimpled dumpling and dipped it into a fermented chilli sauce.

"They seek to gain perspective. A look at our universe from a different vantage point."

The waiter returned with a pitcher of quince wine and two glasses. Adroa raised a brief cheers and took a long sip.

"We have this ingrained belief that we have a right to master the world. A right to understand how it works."

Ashok also took a sip. The wine was dry, with a pleasant honey aroma. "And we've been doing a good job of it."

"Have we? Perhaps from our existing perspective, we have. The discovery of the Phion particles changed everything. It showed that our world wasn't meant to be 'understood' by our senses. Perhaps we have to question our viewpoint."

"Our viewpoint on what?"

"On everything – matter, energy, even life. I've been exploring many of these ideas on a theoretical level. But the mission provided an opportunity to run actual tests."

Ashok grabbed a deep spoon and rummaged around his noodle soup seeking out small balls of marinated dough. "You've satiated me into listening. How have you usurped the mission I've spend half my life preparing?"

"Petra will show you in more detail, but comes down to time. I believe, we believe, that to truly understand our world, we need to form a new understanding of time." Adroa took a momo and placed it on the edge of her lips.

"Who's we?" Ashok focused on the tender bite.

"The Phion discovery created more questions than answers. A group of us began seeing parallels between the new science and age old myths. We've been bridging the worlds of science and mythology since."

"Why is this the first time I'm hearing of this!? You never thought it would be worth a little mention?" Ashok stabbed a momo with a chopstick.

Adroa stared over the valley. "It's all too easy to be labelled a quack. We needed evidence, hard evidence."

"So?"

"If we abstract ourselves from time, the universe starts to look like a very different place."

"How?"

"Oh, a full explanation will take far more than dinner," She smiled. "A couple of volumes, at least."

"Whatever that means." He waved the chopstick. "Go on."

"...Light, for example. We're stuck on the wrong side of a locked door, unable to see through." Adroa grabbed his chopstick and held it level. "In a way, light does not move, it has no speed. We move, through time."

She moved her finger along the smooth bamboo. "Our perception of light and matter is an illusion brought about by our senses. The refraction experiment tests this theory."

Ashok took a long sip of sweet wine, "That's a fair amount to unpack."

"It is. As I said, it takes time. Do you remember stories from Aaron, the mathematician?"

"Yes. He had a lot of abstract theories." Ashok hunted through his murky soup for more dough balls.

"He was onto something. All we have done is move from mathematical theory to the scientific process."

"And the experiment shows that the speed of light is a scam?"

"If you were in one of my classes, you would be sat right at the back," Adroa pinched his hand. "It is a shadow, a hint, from a perspective where time does not exist. Ask Petra to show you details of the refractometer tests."

"I will. First off, however, I'll ask how she's planning on getting our daughter back." Ashok reached over and held Adroa's hand. In front of them, the valley was dark. Dharma's lights, sprinkled through the forest, mirrored the sky above.

****

A sharp shard of shale clinked off of the Exopod's roof. Orus 5 shook from its nest.

"Keep going, he's moving." Ayla rested on one knee, focused on the craft's base.

"Increasing thrust." Tomias stood by the shore of Lake Jona, controlling Orus from the monitor on his wrist.

The chrome egg wobbled about its self-made crater in the shore-side. Its tip jostled from side to side, thrashing the stout treetops which gave it anchorage.

Free from the ground, Orus rose a few feet into the air. Barely clearing the Exopod. Tomias directed the craft to rest over the water.

Orus 5 rotated about its centre and calmly glided across the shore, stopping above the calm waters of Lake Jona.

"The damage is pretty significant." Ayla walked over to Tomias. They examined the craft's corroded base. Out from the gravel, a plate-sized hole was surrounded by a smattering of pockmarks and breaks.

Tomias watched a scoop of gravel fall out of the hole, splashing into the water. "There's no way we could launch into space, nevermind re-enter. The hull is completely compromised."

"Jonah, are you ready to receive?"

"Yes, Ayla, ready when you are."

"OK, Tommy, set Orus for his destination."

Tomias entered a set of instructions into his monitor. Orus pushed off from its stationary position above the water and slowly headed along the shore. A crested wave trailed behind the craft as it hovered ten feet above the lake.

"Orus 5 is on its way to you. Expect it within ten minutes. We'll follow behind."

"See you two shortly then."

The Air Scout whizzed past. It came from the direction of the Tethys Ocean. It flew overhead and intercepted Orus along the coast. The spherical scout trailed the ship like a moon orbiting its planet.

Seemingly eager to catch a glimpse of the move, the Earth peeked through the morning clouds.

Ayla and Tomias walked along the shore, manoeuvring through the maze of fallen trees littering the coast and on into the forest.

"Another food sachet." Ayla pointed to a piece of foil shimmering from the side of a tree trunk.

"Not the tidiest of boys is he?" Tomias carried on through a now defined path between the trees.

"Jonah, your rubbish is littering this whole forest."

"When the winds whip up, the last thing you'll worry about is littering. Orus 5 has arrived. I've taken over control and set the ship down next to Orus 6"

"We'll be there in a few. Don't you think the names are a little confusing? Maybe we should rename them." Ayla jumped over a root winding across their path.

"How about Salt & Pepper?" Tomias turned with a smile.

"I get it." Jonah heckled over the monitor. "Because one is pointy and the other one has a massive deadly hole in it."

"How positive. Good work, boys."

A short while along the path, the two reach the base of Tomias Knob. They made their way up the slope, emerging out above the treeline.

A foamy layer of mist rose above the flat canopies. Sharp peaks in the mist whipped up towards the sky.

An unfamiliar sight emerged as they crested the hill and descended into the crater. One pointy, one stout, the two Orus craft stood side-by-side in a small clearing the trio had made over the previous days.

“You know, they actually do look like salt shakers. Let’s not mess with a good thing though.” Ayla stepped down into the crater, towards the clearing.

As well as clearing a few trees, they had also repaired Jonah’s Exopod, bringing it back to a more functional state.

With the Exopod set up, equipment organised and the craft side-by-side, the bottom of the crater now looked far more like a makeshift base than a squalid crash site.

“It’s not that bad.” Jonah pointed to the hole in Orus 5 “We could probably buff it out.”

“Yeah, the whole hull has a purely cosmetic function, you’re so right.” Tomias sat on an equipment case at the side of the camp.

“Come on, let’s do this.” Ayla clapped into action “Did you prepare the resonance coils? No point transferring them if they don’t sync.”

“I’ve detached the cells on 5 and secured the receiver. We just have to attach the transmitter to 6.” Jonah shooed Tomias off of his seat and opened the metal container. He took out a stack of square silver pads resembling vacuum-packed sandwiches.

Tomias took them and climbed into Orus 5 “Detaching the cells and adding the transmitters.”

"I see them coming online." Ayla checked power levels on her monitor.

"All cells detached and transmitters attached."

"Right then. The moment of truth. Let's see if they sync."

Tomias emerged out of 6 and stepped over to Ayla and Jonah who were now standing behind a stack of boxes at the clearing's edge.

"Resonating and powering up." Ayla connected the cells in 6 to 5 using the transmission coils. "Run through 5's systems."

Jonah began bringing his ship back to life. "Power is flowing. Starting with low-energy circuits." He took a step forward. "Communication, navigation and sensor relays active."

The group exchanged a pensive hi-five.

"Cells holding and stable. Power up AB"

"Powering up." While upright, 5 was still wedged in the thick canopies. The trees began to creak as Jonah channelled power to the engines. A branch smashed under the pressure. It exploded like a firecracker, sending a cloud of leaves floating to the ground. "AB stable."

"Raise him up and set him flat."

The craft straightened, releasing from its wooden crutch. As it lurched out of the ground, 5 blew soil and moss over 6 from its self-made nest. Rising above the trees, 5 tilted flat. For a moment, the two ships aligned perpendicular to each other forming a giant silver T.

Jonah set 5 down in the clearing. The craft came to rest, taking up almost the entire width of the clearing. Manoeuvre complete, Ayla, Jonah and Tomias hugged and laughed.

"You made it look so simple." Tomias grinned.

"We'll have to do more power tests once the cells are transferred." Ayla patted Jonah on the shoulder. "But that was amazing."

"If only the resonators worked all the way to Earth! Now we have to lug those cells out and carry them over."

****

A dotted line plot towards an image of the Earth.

"We didn't want to cause concern back home."

"How could you be so sure that a solution would be found?" Laaro leaned back against his glossy desk.

"We're pretty resourceful up here. And, on your end, we have quite a few clever people who have put their minds together." Ayla mirrored Laaro's pose, leaning on an uneven felled tree trunk.

"So what happens next, Ayla? When will we have you here in person?" Laaro clasped his hands.

"We're in the final stages of prepping Orus 5 for return. After leaving Hela, we will head straight towards Earth orbit. During the trip we will run a series of tests on the ship's ability to re-enter. If he can handle it, we'll do a few laps of Earth and come in to land."

"And if it turns out you can't land?" Laaro lent forward. "I heard that the institute at Nussa has offered assistance."

"Good hearing. One of our back-up scenarios is an orbital rendezvous, transfer and descent." Ayla mimed the two craft docking in orbit. "The institute at Nussa have fitted a cargo craft with their new propulsion system. It is currently going through final testing."

"Is it safe?"

"So your hearing isn't that great. It is. Nussa has been working on the technology for years and the Imperial Residence has assured BISE that their technology is more than capable for the task."

"Well, I truly hope for the best, Ayla. I think I speak for everyone when I say that the mission has been a rollercoaster of emotions." Laaro pushed off from his desk and stood. He wore a long navy tunic pinched by a thin hemp belt at the waist.

"Thank you, Laaro. I'm looking forward to joining you in the studio soon." Ayla stood and walked towards the camera pod. As it followed her around, the frame turned to show Orus 5 sprawled across the narrow clearing. The craft's glistening hull reflected skewed visions of Jonah and Tomias as they tidied equipment from the site.

"Mixed bag, Ayla. I can't wait for you to return but I'm more than a little miffed at you and BISE. The whole world has been invested in this mission and it is more than a little disingenuous to withhold such critical information." Laaro circled his desk, sitting down hard into his chair.

The studio cut Ayla's audio before she had a chance to respond.

"Thank you, viewers, for joining me. In less than 48 hours we will begin our live coverage of this dramatic return mission. BISE and The Council have a host of questions to answer about the conduct of this mission. Our first priority will however be seeing Ayla, Jonah and Tomias safely return to Earth.

And we're clear.

The main studio lights dimmed.

Laaro – Ayla is still on; she wants a word with you.

"Put her through, thank you."

"What the hell was that?"

"What?"

"BISE withholding information and so on? Then stopping my audio."

"Ayla, we all want you back safe. That said, a lot of people here are angry at the way the mission has been handled. It's only fair to reflect their concerns." Laaro tidied a pile of notes on his desk and stood.

"I think you could have handled it differently. Perhaps given me a chance to explain."

"The distance doesn't help Ayla, get back and we'll clear it all up."

"Alright, take care."

Laaro stepped off of the raised platform surrounding his desk and on to the studio floor. He slid behind a hex of thin pipes which stretched the background to his shot.

Carefully climbing over slithers of tangled cables, he headed through a dimly lit door at the back of the set. It led to a thin corridor with a sharp turn no more than a dozen steps in.

A stout silhouette propped up against the corridor wall. Around the next corner, a dim light gave the doughy mass a modicum of form.

“Thank you, Laaro. BISE has been given far too much freedom in its handling of this mission.”

“Ayla has been a friend for a long time, I didn’t like that.”

“They’ve left us no choice.” The shadow turned. “Something has to be done. Nussa has stood on the side-lines for too long.”

“I hope you know what you’re doing, Frey.”

A jittery breeze pushed its way through a loose pane of glass. Sabil folded a worn jute sack and placed it on top of a pile by his roaster. A dusting of bean husks swirled in the air, pushed around by the dusk air.

Sabil swept the floor in wide, concentric arcs. He scooped a small pile of husks into a dustpan and then to a waiting bin. Flicking off the lights in his roastery, he went out on the cobbled street and rolled up the intricate rug drooped over the entrance and heaved it on a table by the door.

Locking up, he latched the heavy wooden shutters, gave them a nudge and walked off down the narrow streets of Old Dvor.

As the light began to wane, so too did the sounds of the ancient town.

Most sellers had already closed up shop, leaving behind a medley of storefronts, some dark, some lit.

"Care to take the last of my plums, Sabil?" The old lady turned and gestured to a small pile of ink-purple fruit, as she packed the rest of her produce.

"Why not, but only a few for the road, thank you." He picked out a fistful of plums. Not the hardest. Not the softest. He stuffed them in his pocket and tapped a token on the side of her stand.

Making his way to the Lacka, he picked them out, one by one. Removing the stone, he squeezed it between his fingers, waiting for a dustbin. As he approached each can, he'd take a shot. It's a good thing the light was fading.

Soon Sabil reached the banks of the Lacka. The lights of Dvor Castle reflected in the river's glassy waters. The speed of the current was only given away as the rapid flow hit the pointed stone pillars of the Hara Bridge.

He made his way over the bridge, stopping right before the opposite side. Sabil rested his broad palms on the soft stone parapet and looked across the city.

Dvor was transitioning from the bustle of day to the hubbub of evening. He turned towards the castle but the water lapping the bridge drew his attention to the small square cut into the stone walkway below. Sabil thought about all of the games played, won and lost. Mostly won.

His moment of meditation was cut short by synchronised sharp sounds of metal hitting stone. They came from the top of the hill. An evening salute from the guards, perhaps.

Sabil sluggishly clambered up the hill with all the grace of an intoxicated duck. Flanked by an aura of soft light, an elegant figure fanned down in the opposite direction.

Irnes wore her floor-length wool cloak, its graceful crimson outline illuminated by the lights of Dvor Castle. As they neared, Sabil smiled and dusted himself off.

"A pleasure." At that moment he realised he'd forgotten to leave his dirty work apron in the roaster.

"Always." She stopped and raised her cloak's thick collar around her ears.

Sabil went in for a hug.

Irnes took a short step back, eking forward her hand, instead.

"Rare to see you out on the streets alone?"

"I have a lot on my mind, Sabil. An evening walk helps to tidy one's thoughts."

"Care to share? Perhaps I can help."

"I doubt it. Politics, power. A world you left some time ago." She tucked her hands into her deep pockets.

"Of course. Well, in that case, I leave you with the city to listen to your thoughts." He took a step to the side.

"Very kind of you." She mirrored his step, blocking the way. "The city is very much mine, there isn't a lot to leave."

"Only a turn of phrase." Sabil took another step to the side and started to walk on "Nothing meant by it."

"Although." He stopped and turned around. "Do keep in mind that Dvor is no more yours than it is mine. Or any other citizen of the city."

"Can't say I agree." The straight edge of her cloak swirled around. "I made this city what it is. And I'll be sure to secure its future as the centre of this Core."

She turned sharply and clacked down the hill.

"Don't mistake respect for ownership, Irnes." Sabil straightened his pose, climbing the hill with a firm gate.

****

The Morel Temple sat twenty miles out of Nussa, on a peninsula jutting into Lake Naya. The immense body of water stretched out over the horizon in three directions.

Centuries ago, the narrow strip of land around the temple was a bustling town with its own streets, shops and low, compact houses.

After the Temple waned in influence, the town slowly emptied as life withdrew back to Nussa. Shops closed, houses deserted, crumbled and decayed. Soon nature took back the peninsula, leaving only the sharp clinical lines of Morel's many astronomical structures. The whole site resembled a surreal geometric masterpiece.

When Kala became head of the Nussa Core, he set out to find a location for a new institute dedicated to the sciences. Fascinated by Morel, he chose to bring life back to the temple area.

Almost straddling the equator, The Institute of Applied Science was a vast research, manufacturing and testing complex. The facilities were used to take new technologies from idea to reality.

Indeed, the IAS had been first to create a working prototype for pulsed AB. It was only afterwards that BISE and Flavia managed to stabilise the technology for use in Gliders and, eventually, Orus.

Adopting its ancient foundations, the low buildings of the IAS encircled the Morel Temple like a saucer protecting a fine porcelain cup. A broad break in the buildings jutted out at the tip of the peninsula. The flat, open launch site melted into Lake Naya's calm waters.

A team of engineers hurried around a stubbly matt cylinder at the centre of the launch site. They checked over parameters, set power curves and confirmed other science stuff.

"Run the initial sequence."

The chief engineer entered a series of commands and the huddle stepped back. The cylinder stood alone in the middle of a smooth concrete platform.

The device itself was rather indistinct, a hockey puck the size of a boulder. Its surface was smooth but dull. It had no distinguishing features aside from a fine lip, a gentle groove running around its base as if someone pushed their finger into clay as the potter's wheel spun.

At a safe distance, the chief engineer waved a command to start. The others gave a brief thumbs up and looked on. A hum rose out through the puck. Imperceptible, vibrations could be felt through the firm concrete ground.

"Power at point zero five."

The puck briefly resonated as it gradually separated off of the ground. Fine dust shot out from underneath. Caught by the fine rim, it whirled into a ring before dissipating out.

Seven feet off of the ground, the engineer waved again. The puck vectored about its centre and stood upright in mid-air. The group exchanged a smile.

"Bring it down."

Rotating through the remaining 270 degrees, the puck levelled off with its lip at the base. It lowered and kissed the ground with a high pitch hum.

The group left the puck and headed a few hundred feet to an igloo-shaped bunker at one end of the launch site. It sat like a pimple on an otherwise smooth field.

Inside, Frey sat with his elbows resting on a desk, surrounded by a bank of monitors.

"We're ready, sir."

"Run the test." He barely looked away.

The engineers filed in, taking their places around the monitors. They had a surround view of the puck, sitting on the launch site as the sun shone down through a crystal-clear sky.

"Cycle launch to twenty miles."

"Airspace clear."

"Go."

Half a moment after giving the command, the puck was gone, disappeared. It had disappeared, without sound or spectacle. The only sign of change was a hairline ring around the place where it stood.

"Stationary at twenty miles."

A monitor zoomed in on the clear sky. The puck came in to focus. It was there, calmly rotating around its axis like a token flipped in mid-air.

"Bring it back. Rendezvous, rescue and return curve."

Monitors showed the puck flattening out. No motion could be discerned as it travelled down. An altitude counter began ticking down, fast.

"It's too fast, reduce the pulse."

"We're at minimum descent."

Frey slammed on the table. "Slow it down!"

The counter rushed faster and faster; its last three digits imperceptible. Tracking the puck, it seemed stationary until the last moment. A flash of green and blue flickered on the monitors before a heavy rumble rippled through the bunker. The lights flickered and the monitors were white, their view obstructed by a fine mist.

Frey leapt towards the door.

"Sir, it's not safe, stay inside."

Belligerent, he slammed open the heavy concrete door. A rush of mist flooded the igloo. The engineers coughed as fans turned on to clear the air.

Frey looked out over the launch site as the dust cleared.

The puck sat motionless, right where it had left the site... Same place, only burrowed, two feet into the ground. It had excavated a razor-sharp hole only a few inches wider than the cylinder itself. The puck neatly sat in its self-made hole like a toddler's shape sorter.

Frey rushed back into the bunker. "What was the maximum load?" He shouted.

"Six g average with two peaks at fifteen. It was stable for over 99% of the return."

"So, you only 1% killed them." Frey threw a glass across the bunker. It smashed it against the opposite wall bouncing shards in all directions. "They'd die."

"Sir, we're still tweaking the power. It is hard to control the pulses when they resonate with each other. We need..."

"You need what? More time?! We don't have more time!"

"We will send an update to BISE and try to work out a fall-back."

Frey leapt across the room, thrusting two men out of the way. He grabbed the chief engineer by his collar, clenching his fists through his cotton shirt. "You'll do no such thing."

"But Sir."

He pushed him against a wall, “You’ll do no such thing, do you understand? From this point on, you will tell BISE that everything is running to plan. You will stay here until the pulse is stable.” Frey clenched harder. “Do you understand?”

“Yes, sir.”

He let go, turned and stormed out of the bunker. The team barely looked at each other in silence.

* * ●

TWENTY

The afternoon sun cast a zig-zag shadow from the handrail and on to the stairs leading up to The Residence. Warm to the touch, Adroa ran her hand over the smooth limestone.

"Last time you met, you were both teenagers."

"I remember."

"Me too, can't have made the best of impressions." Noake stopped his ascent up the stairs, catching his breath.

"You were just as speechless." Sirem shouted from a landing some way up.

The broad stone staircase made a beeline through Mount Rhoda, up to the residence. Three terraces cut the line every couple of hundred feet like angled beads on an itchy necklace.

"I'm sure he doesn't remember us."

"Oh, he does." Adroa reached the final landing and stood by Sirem. "I've been sure to remind him now and again."

"And what exactly do you expect from us?"

“Nothing much. We’re here to say hi. I’ve wanted to come over to Flavia for a while, thought it might be nice if you joined.”

“Seems rather convenient.” A call boomed out from above.

“I’d say the sun is blocking my view.” Adroa shouted up towards the end of the stairs. “But it’d be futile to pretend.”

Ashok bounced down from the top stair. The fading sun shone through his linen trousers, faintly glinting off of their electrum piping.

“What a rare honour, you dressed up.” She reached him and they embraced. The two youths filed in behind.

“Well, we have guests, don’t we? Should always aim to make at least a good first impression.” Ashok smiled and shook Sirem and Noake’s hands.

“We’ve met before, sir.” Sirem near-curtseyed.

“Hmm. I think it’s best for all of us if we make a fresh start. It’s Ashok and we’ll have none of that.”

“In that case.” Noake arched his back, sticking a hand out. “It’s a pleasure to meet.”

“Very good. Are we done with these delightful pleasantries? Can we make our way inside?” Ashok led the way.

He slowed his pace as they walked through The Gate of Nations.

“Amazing.” Sirem gawped at the giant scenes carved across the gate.

The group entered the hypostyle hall. The route was, as always, deliberate.

“Why don’t you both explore the hall while I catch up with Adroa.” Ashok waved towards the imposing courtyard. “In a few minutes, the shadows will converge.”

“I’ve heard about that.” Sirem grabbed Noake by the hand and pulled him towards the centre of the hall. As dusk fell, the surrounding columns’ shadows broadened and bent. Soon they would weave into a perfect circle in the middle of the open space.

“This is your idea of a romantic evening together is it?”

“Well, you know it doesn’t hurt to mix things up now and again.” Adroa smiled.

“I’m pretty sure that would be rather frowned upon at the Kap.”

Noake and Sirem explored the intricately carved columns around the hall.

“Fine. I want you to spend some time with the two of them. They’re ready. They have a lot of potential.”

Ashok looked out as they scurried from pillar to pillar. “No doubt they do, but they’re so young.”

“We were rather young too, don’t you think?” Adroa leaned on an epic carving of Orus and Hela. “Ayla is coming home tomorrow. We need to start thinking about the future.”

“I can’t wait to have her back.”

“Me too, but don’t change the subject.”

"Dogged, nice." Ashok held her by the waist. "They're perfectly polite youngsters and it will be a pleasure to host them here."

"But?" Adroa mirrored his grip.

"But I'm not ready. I've decided to keep my position. In Flavia and in The Council. Just for another four, five years max."

Adroa reeled. "It will always be 'just another...'"

He pulled her back. "No. I need to finish what I started. When Ayla gets back, we will both help her develop BISE. I promise I will work with Sirem and Noake to prepare them and, when the time is right, they can go up for the vote." They kissed and walked towards the centre of the hall.

He paused part-way. "You've told them about your plans for them, right?"

"Does it matter?"

He stared into her eyes.

"Not verbatim, no."

Ashok raised his eyebrows.

"But it's more than obvious. What's the point, if it will never happen anyway? You're going to cling on forever."

"To you, at least."

Lake Jona would soon be a memory. Skipping stones off of the surface never grew old. The reduced gravity meant that a carefully angled pebble would easily skim over towards the horizon in grand arches.

Ayla paused by the lakeshore after polishing off a carefully chosen pile of stones.

She knelt down and stroked the mirror-still waters. In the distance, she could see their basecamp by the water. The bulbous tree was still indented, its crown like the split cap of a mushroom where it had propped up Orus 6.

Taking a deep breath, she turned and walked into the forest towards Tomias Knob.

"Final preparations done on our side."

"Thank you, Petra. The boys are running the last checks on Orus 5 too."

"We're going live in half an hour. Hope you don't mind but one of the camera pods got a great sequence from your stone skipping."

"Mind?" Ayla made her way through the thick forest. Their many walks had largely cleared a path, but it was still broken by countless roots and fallen trees. "Why would I mind the world seeing such a masterful display?"

"Good, good. Once you're en route to Earth we will begin a series of tests on Orus, as rehearsed. The IAS are standing by with their rendezvous craft, should the need arise."

The ground gradually rose to form the base of Tomias Knob.

"Good. And we're still planning to rehearse the rendezvous procedure during the journey?"

"Yes, it is scheduled in there."

"Thank you, Petra. I can't describe how reassuring it has been to have you on the other end of the line these past days."

"It's been a pleasure to stand by your side, Ayla, make sure you come back safe."

"Couple of days and I'll be back in my chair." She made her way towards the top of the mound. At its crest, Ayla looked back at the open vista. Rhodonia's forest stretched out ahead of her.

"Well, a couple of days and two weeks of quarantine. But we can always toss it in the chamber for you."

"Boo, I keep forgetting. Forget the chair, make sure there's a case of wine in there. Get in touch with Hallough and ask for a case of Verbesh. Make sure he can't refuse!"

"I doubt he'd put up a fight. I'm sure you know how many regulations that would break."

"And I'm sure you know how little I'm joking." Ayla made her way down to the clearing.

Orus 5 stood primed and ready for launch. Orus 6, his damaged sibling, lay on its side at the edge of the space.

"We go live in three. Get ready for the world. Operations out."

Shuffles echoed through the ship's open port.

Jonah sat, strapped into the Captain's chair, running a series of checks. "For a morning as serious as this, you'd think you'd want to be ready and strapped in more than ten minutes before launch."

"Priorities." Tomias kissed Ayla by the side of Orus. He climbed a stepladder to the port. Ayla grabbed on and leapfrogged over him, reaching the port first.

Ayla strapped in next to Jonah as Tomias remained at the base of the craft. His improvised seat was surrounded by cases filled with rock, soil, water and fauna samples gathered over the curtailed mission.

"Operations to Orus. Systems stable."

"All clear on our end, Operations." Jonah signalled the others. "Helmets on, port sealed."

"Launch sequence start in eight minutes."

"Our visit to Hela has been far from straightforward." Ayla spoke to the monitors. "When we set out, what seems like an age ago, little could we have expected to have Jonah as our Captain on our return."

"While the nature of this operation had to change." Jonah added. "These first steps will pave the way for a series of missions in the near future."

"While our technology hasn't been perfect, it has proved fit for purpose." Tomias didn't want to be left out of the limelight.

"Green across the board. Launch in four minutes."

"The reduced gravity on Hela means that, at full power, Orus 5 can vector straight to our desired escape velocity of 3 miles per second."

"Two minutes to launch."

"In less than a minute we should be clear of Hela's gravity well at three hundred thousand feet." Ayla turned, resting on Jonah's shoulder and gave a thumbs up to Tomias.

"One Minute."

"Cells on, engine on. Breaking ground contact." Jonah slowly raised the ship off of the moon's surface. Not a sound or a tug hinted that they were now a foot off of the ground.

With Orus standing on its tip, the cockpit stared straight up towards Hela's teal sky. They hovered motionless.

"Twenty."

"Raising restive power." Jonah toggled a switch. A vibration ran up the ship from toe to tip.

"Resonance?" Ayla looked over.

"Sure."

"Ten. Safe launch, Orus. We're waiting for you."

Petra sat at her desk in the control room. She positioned the two camera pods in the air around the ship. One stayed stationary while the other panned from a few hundred feet away.

It was a beautiful, cloudless day. Orus stood at the centre of the clearing atop Tomias Knob like a dart moments before it hits the bullseye.

The forest fanned out around the hill. A corner of Lake Jona could be seen at the very edge of the frame.

"Three."

"Two."

"One."

Jonah initiated launch. A sudden force thrust them into their seats. Unyielding, it pushed further and further as little changed in their forward view.

"Thousand Feet. Stable."

Petra watched the monitors as Orus fired off of Hela's surface. The wide camera showed the craft shoot straight into the sky.

"Twenty thousand."

The teal sky darkened.

A loud shudder resonated through the monitors.

"Report?"

"Stable. Minor resonance."

"Eighty thou..."

Another shudder cracked across the monitors.

"Orus, you're red. Base is red."

"Cells overheating. Aborting launch." Jonah killed power to the engine. The shaking grew, "Instruments out."

"Hundred thousand feet. Still climbing. Apex, hundred and twenty."

Petra struggled to get a lock on Orus.

"Ayla, Tomias." Jonah turned. "Two power bursts. One at apex for ten seconds to move us into a glide. Final thrust above the surface until cell redline. Ayla, I need to you time the apex burn."

Orus slowed its ascent. The force thrusting them backwards evaporated.

She had strapped her father's chrono over her sleeve. "Confirmed." Ayla raised her hand.

"Apex."

The view ahead was black.

"Go." Jonah thrust the engine to full power. He tilted the craft on its side. A blue-green crescent came into view. Orus fell back towards Hela in a shallow arc.

"Mark." Ayla signalled to stop the engine.

The camera pods raced through the sky, trying to get a lock on the plummeting ship.

"Descent fast but stable."

The Tethys Ocean loomed below.

"We need to avoid a water landing." Ayla tried to look back but couldn't turn her head.

A camera pod briefly locked onto Orus as it shot by. The rear still glowed a menacing orange.

"We're coming in, twenty thousand, final thrust. Reversing AB"

"You're too hot."

"We have no choice."

The ocean swelled below. Clusters of waves scratched along the surface.

"Hull holding. Speed slowing. Five thousand."

"Get ready for a hard landing."

Less than a thousand feet from the ground one of the camera pods managed to catch up with the falling ship. Drawing alongside, it focused on the glowing tip.

An explosion ripped through Orus.

The camera showed flashes of burning metal hull drizzling down towards Tethys.

"Tommy!" Petra heard Alya scream before communications were lost.

Less than a hundred feet from destruction, Orus cleared the ocean. The hull started to catch on branches and crowns lighting a fiery trail.

The ground ahead rose up, swallowing Orus whole. Still moving at speed, the ship disappeared into the dark forest. A choppy pulse of purple light briefly flickered in the gloom.

A bed of smoke permeated through the trees. A blood-red glow seeped through the thick branches.

Flames licked through a pile of dry branches. The wood splintered and cracked. A warm glow lit the soil raised around the hole.

Hire perched, hunched over the fire with a knobbly stick. He poked and prodded the embers with little apparent aim.

Opposite, Tisa reclined on a thick rug draped over a log. She stretched out her hands, rubbing and warming them by the glow.

It was a cold, clear night in Nyore. A heavy sprinkle of stars surrounded Hela. The full moon weighed down above them. Her turquoise glimmer cast a stony blanket over the Earth.

"It's been three hours. Three hours without news. How is that possible? The cameras can't even get a view from all of the smoke." Tisa threw a pebble on the fire. It collapsed a pile of twigs sending a cloud of sparks into the air.

"We're yet to see, let's give them time." Hire methodically arranged a fresh pyramid of kindling at the centre of the hearth.

"They're lost. I can feel it. The mission was doomed from the beginning. They should have stopped after Jonah crashed. We're not ready."

"You're young, still impatient, still at time's mercy."

"What does that mean? Should I be offended?" Tisa pulled a woven blanket over her knees. It was covered in a thick diamond weave, mirroring the night's sky.

"They were always going to go up. They already had gone up before you and I were born. In the same way, they're already back. On their way here, down the Great Trade Road."

"Did the smoke get to you, Hire? Some funky tree sap in there?"

"It's so hard for us to see. Time creates a fog. A fog we're forced to walk through, seeing no more than the tip of our nose ahead." Hire stared up at Hela. "If we could take a step to the side, step out of the fog, we would see a very different universe."

Tisa tried to follow his gaze. "I don't understand. At least it's nice to listen."

"Did you know that they took a secret experiment with them? It will change the way we see."

"How do you know?"

Hire gazed at her across the fire. "In the years to come, the worlds of science and belief will become one. We are about to enter a whole new period."

"You're doing a good job of ignoring my questions."

"You'll get answers to most soon enough."

"I find it difficult to see how, Hire. Whatever they carried with them is lost, a smouldering pile deep in some Helletic forest." Tisa slipped down the rug, lying flat on her back next to the fire.

A warm breeze came up from the valley. It blew through the fire, disturbing the flames.

Right as it abated, a ruckus erupted in the village, some way behind Tisa. She turned but couldn't see over the thick log. Hire looked past her, towards the clamour, and smiled.No more than a minute later the patter of feet crunched through the grass. One of the villagers ran towards their fire. Waving with one hand, a monitor in the other.

Ashok swirled the lacquered crema of his espresso with the back of a thin electrum spoon. Leaning back, he placed his arm around Ardoa and held her tight.

They sat in silence looking out as the Andes rushed below them. The Glider ran high, a thousand feet over the jagged surface. Still, the mountain's sharp peaks rose close to the craft.

As they looked on, the landscape began to transition. Rocky, desolate ridges began to blend into softer valleys, sprinkled with shrubs and cut by the occasional turquoise stream.

"A few minutes and we'll be coming in to Pacha."

"Thank you, Mito."

Adroa stood and leaned on the panoramic monitor. Ashok pushed off of his chair and joined her. A solitary peak rose out at the boundary between the mountains and the emerald fields ahead. Like a sentinel, it kept silent guard over the lands.

A silvery glimmer lit the Glider as they passed by. Looking back, Ashok saw the Lighthouse of Pacha, hewn deep into the peak. Its polished surface, worn down over the centuries, still reflected the sun's rays. The lighthouse loomed over Pacha, staring past the sprawling city out into the Southern Ocean.

The Glider swept over Pacha's web of tree-lined boulevards. The city was based on a nestled grid pattern. Broad city blocks narrowed towards the coast. A strip of green marked the boundary between city and ocean. The city park ran a full six miles along the coast. On one side, Pacha unfurled towards the Andes. On the other, a sheer drop to the Ocean. A low wisp of clouds traced the park, flicked up by the humid winds.

A solitary building sat within the park. The Patagonia Core Residence was perched precariously over the cliff. It consisted of a series of sharp, angular stone blocks stacked on top of each other. The extensive compound resembled the work of a particularly talented toddler.

The Glider came to land within the Residence gardens. Adroa and Ashok emerged out of the chrome craft and onto soft, manicured turf. The air was warm and moist. They wore almost matching ivory linen chitons. Adroa's had a thick electrum rim, tied by a lapis blue belt while Ashok's was plain and undecorated.

They were greeted by Maritza, Chief of Staff to Matias.

"Welcome." She spoke quietly, averting her gaze out above the waves and toward the horizon, "The others have gathered in the garden, come with me."

Adroa reached out and hugged her.

A line of palm trees flanked a path leading to the house. Small beds of tropical flowers were arranged like pebbles nestled in the grass.

The path ended at a wide terrace flanking the house. The ground was made from rays of fired bricks, all converging on a central circle. There, The Council leaders spoke around an elegant tigerwood table. Senior advisers were seated along an outer circle of chairs. The whole formation was flanked by a ring of freestanding awnings providing much needed shade from the morning sun.

As they saw the couple approach, all discussion died down and the guests stood. The rhythmic pounding of waves rang up the cliffs.

"Hello, everyone."

"Welcome, Ashok, Adroa." Matias came to shake their hands.

"Thank you for coordinating this at such short notice."

"Of course."

Ashok greeted everyone individually and took his seat at the table next to Adroa.

"I took the liberty of preparing an agenda as we have a lot to discuss." Matias flicked through a stack of documents.

"If it's alright with you." Ashok spoke quietly. "I'd like to start by saying a few words. They may have an impact on the proceedings."

"Of course, go ahead."

"The mission to Hela was always meant to push the limits of our capabilities. To show our potential and define our future after a turbulent time. In some ways, I believe we did that. Despite our different visions…" He looked across the table to Kala who sat with his hands clasped, resting on the table. Frey perched behind him, leaning closer to the leaders.

"Despite our different visions, we managed to come together…"

Frey let out a shallow huff. Kala turned, scowling over his shoulder.

"When we faced a setback, we rallied once more and reached Hela. All of the promise, the potential, realised in one landing.

Unfortunately, we were unable to complete the mission." Ashok paused. "Our children are lost. That responsibility ultimately falls on my shoulders."

"That failure." Frey murmured.

"That's enough!"

"No, Kala, he's right. I pushed for this mission; I oversaw the development. It is my failure of planning and execution."

"And leadership!" Frey sat back.

"Yes, of leadership."

"It is high time you admitted it."

"Enough!"

"No, we can't continue like this!" Frey stood and walked up to the table. "We put far too much trust in you and look where it got us. It's time for you to go."

Kala stood, looming over Frey and grabbed him by the shoulders. "You're out of line. Ashok has transformed our world."

"And we're very grateful. But it's clear he's passed his peak. He needs to step out of the way."

"Make way for what? For you? I've tolerated your conniving for too long." Kala pushed him back. "It's time for you to go. Do you think I don't know about your schemes? Your backdoor discussions with Core leaders around the world? What were you hoping to achieve? Go. Leave now." He turned his back and sat down at the table.

"Who do you think I did it for, Kala? For you!"

"Leave, that's not how we work. That's not the world we agreed to rebuild."

A guard in ceremonial garb emerged out from the Residence. Bouncer duties were rather unexpected at such gatherings. He stood by Frey, pointing towards the house. Frey paused, motionless, scanning the gathered leaders. He pushed the guard aside and walked off.

"I apologise, Ashok, he doesn't reflect my opinion."

"He's right, Kala. He's annoying and a massive twat, but he's right. It is time for a change."

"What do you mean?"

"As of the end of this meeting, I will be stepping down from The Council. In the coming weeks, I will also step down from Flavia."

"But Ashok."

"It is hard to reconcile the pain I feel. Impossible to place it to one side and continue." He took Adroa's hand.

"Kala. It is my strong desire that you head The Council. We might disagree now and then."

"Slight understatement."

"But your heart is in the right place. Neatly exemplified by what happened just now."

"It will be down to the other members of The Council to vote on your desire."

"Adroa has two students who she has been pushing me to consider for some time. I'm considering one of them for Flavia."

"Gently nudging." Adroa kept hold of his hand.

"Sabil has had a change of heart and is now planning to take on Irnes for Dvor. If the people support him, I would like him to look over and support Adroa's favourite as she takes on Flavia."

"Sirem is lovely, yes. With a little guidance she will be a phenomenal leader."

"Finally, if you have an opening for your Chief of Staff, Kala, perhaps you would like to meet her other pick. He's as bright and focused as a young Frey... but far less of a douche."

The others laughed.

"With such a recommendation, how could I resist? And you, Ashok?"

"I will take a step back and spend some time in Dharma..."

Maritza shuffled and nervously tapped Matias on the shoulder. She whispered into his ear. Noticing, Ashok paused.

"Another coup, perhaps?" He smiled.

"Ashok, everyone. Follow me into the house immediately." Matias shot bolt upright and headed for his office, barely waiting for the others to stand.

A ray of sunlight pierced the darkness, resting on her eyes. Its golden glow was traced by clouds of dust and smoke.

She tried to swat the light away like a pesky fly. An intense pain ran through her body as she tried to move her arm. Screaming out, she choked on the acrid air.

"Ayla." A weak voice broke through the void. "Are you alive?"

"I guess so, death hopefully wouldn't hurt this much." The creaking of bent metal, the whir of generators and the harsh smell of burnt coolant overwhelmed her senses.

"Tommy, are you there?"

"Yes." His voice was muffled, hidden away from sight.

"We need to get out of here. Can you both move?"

"I think so." Ayla found herself tilted to one side, hanging by her seat harness. A cross-strap had lodged itself deep into her right shoulder. She undid the strap with her left hand and slipped out onto the ship's wall.

Jonah released his straps and fell forward onto the smashed panoramic monitor. Ayla rolled over and they lay side-by-side. Looking up through Orus, they could see Hela's teal sky framed by jagged edges of the torn hull.

"Tommy!" She reached out to Tomias. He was pinned against several equipment boxes which had broken loose. One lay across his lower body while two small cases covered his head. A streak of blood ran along the polished aluminium, dipping down towards Ayla.

"O-us 5 –epo-t –"

Broken audio crackled through a speaker.

"Orus re-ort."

Still gathering strength, Ayla and Jonah slowly stood. With his feet on the monitor, Jonah crawled up and sat on the back of his seat. He reached down and pulled Ayla up. Orus had crashed tip-first, at an angle.

"This is m-s-n con-ol –port Orus."

Pulling themselves up by the ship's notched side-panels, they reached Tomias. Removing the boxes from his head, Ayla revealed his face. She kissed him as Jonah lifted the larger case from his legs. Tomias shouted in pain, starting Ayla.

Once the case was removed, a break below the knee was clearly visible. Blood had soaked through his ripped trousers.

"It might be ironic, but this is actually full of our medical supplies." Jonah rummaged around the case. Before Tomias had a chance to scream again, Jonah tore off his trouser leg, sprayed the wound and bandaged it. Finding a splint, he secured it around the leg.

Meanwhile, Ayla had found two backpacks. She filled them with all the medical and survival equipment she could find amongst the mess. "Come on Tommy." She pulled on one of the backpacks and gave the other to Jonah.

"Let's go." She grabbed a monitor.

The exit port was directly opposite. Jonah jumped up and held one of its protruding handles. He managed to twist and force the port open, pulling himself out and onto the edge. Ayla dragged Tomias up, letting him rest on her shoulder.

She raised and pushed him over to Jonah, who pulled him out of the craft. With Ayla out, they sat on the port's rim and scanned around.

Orus had burrowed deep into something resembling a dry field. The gravelly ground was pierced by a thick carpet of grey-brown pine needles. The ship was cracked in two. There was no sign of its pointed tail.

In one direction, the field continued off into the distance. In the other, a mossy hill rose out of the surface. Earth teased beyond the field, above the horizon.

Ayla slipped off of the craft and onto Hela's surface. The needles crunched under her boots. Jonah followed and they reached out to catch Tomias.

"Operations, can you hear us?" Ayla tried to activate the monitor. "It has power but no connection."

"Perhaps if we get to higher ground. Is it giving a location?"

"It's showing us on an island off South coast of Rhodinia - not far away from the Irephus volcano"

"That's at least a hundred miles from our camps."

"Tommy, we can head up that hill to try and connect with Operations. We'll come back to get you."

Tomias threw a hand around Jonah. "No chance, let's go."

They made their way to the edge of the field. The dry needles abruptly stopped giving way to a carefully manicured lawn of thick moss.

"Operations come in." The moss was sodden with water. Their feet sank up to their ankles. Each step was a chore. Suddenly, the ground stiffened. A step to the right sank into the sponge once more. A step forward and loam stayed firm.

Ayla scratched away the surface with her boot. A thin layer of moss crumbled away to reveal a row of stone slabs tracing a path straight up the hill.

"Operations to Orus. Report."

"Operations! Can you hear us?"

"Ayla? You're alive. Are you alone?"

"Petra, it's good to hear your voice. We're alive and well. Tomias has a broken leg and we're all rather beaten up but we're fine."

"Incredible news. And Orus?"

"The ship didn't fare as well. It has broken up. We are on an island, around a hundred miles away from our camps." Ayla looked back towards the wreckage. "If Orus doesn't catch fire tonight, we have several weeks' worth of supplies on the ship and very rudimentary shelter."

Their connection cut.

"Let's keep going, it should be more stable at the top. Tommy, how are you holding up?"

"All good. Like a walk in the park... After falling out of a Glider."

"That's the spirit." Jonah pat him on the shoulder as they hobbled up.

"I realised what a scam this mission has been." Ayla climbed ahead.

"Because of the two near-fatal crashes?"

"No. That's fine. You got a massive lake, Tommy got a scraggly knob... what did I get!?"

"How about that escarpment by Tethys with the water flowing out. Ayla Rock. Fancy a nice escarpment?" Jonah laughed.

"No, that's terrible. How about this whole area? The monitor says we're a thousand feet above Tethys here. I say we call it the Aylonian Highlands."

"Delightful." Tomias groaned.

Eventually, the hill began to level off. They reached a rounded stone lip jutting through the moss. It marked the edge of a broad crater. The round hole sliced into the hill's peak.

Ayla placed her backpack on the ground and sat on the crater's lip, surveying the view.

Earth dominated the horizon. A low, dense forest drew ahead of them. It ended abruptly at a toothed stone coastline. Stretching out to the horizon, Tethys laid an uneasy bed for Earth. Amongst the violent waves, a wisp of creamy grey smoke rose out of a broad conical island – at the centre, Irephus stood firm. Ayla could just make out a rim of green circling the base of the island.

"Operations to Orus. Can you hear us?"

"The link should be clear now, Petra."

"I am going to bridge a connection through to Pacha."

"Pacha?"

"Ayla, can you hear us?" Adroa trembled. "I'm here with your father."

"Mum!" Ayla teared up.

"How are you? We thought we'd lost you." Ashok nudged into the frame.

"We're fine, scratched, bruised and a little hungry, but the three of us are fine."

"Do you have any supplies?"

"Yes, there are several cases of ration in the ship. Might be a little smoked but I'm sure they'll be fine."

"Ayla, Tomias, Jonah." Ashok held Adroa's hand. "I'm leaving for BISE. Stay safe. We're going to get you back."

The connection cut once more.

"It's getting a little chilly."

Jonah sat Tomias next to Ayla and removed his rucksack. He took out three squares of silver cloth and handed them out.

The squares unfurled into large insulating ponchos.

"These would have been perfect for a party in our Kap days." Ayla smiled.

"Now what are we going to do?" Jonah threw on his poncho and sat down.

"We're alive and we're together. We'll be fine." Ayla glanced down towards the smouldering heap. "Perhaps we should go back to the ship and take some supplies. If Orus hasn't exploded by now, it should be fine."

"Look!" Tomias pointed towards the Earth.

A shadowy pimple crawled along her surface.

The eclipse first covered Flavia then Nussa, scrawling all the way to Saphan. As it passed, tiny dots of sapphire light pierced the darkness - Hela mirrors, scattered across the land.

Ayla leaned into Tomias who rested his arm on Jonah. They gazed down to Earth in silence. Hela wasn't quite ready to say goodbye.